HOT WOMEN'S EROTICA

HOT WOMEN'S EROTICA

EDITED BY

MARILYN JAYE LEWIS

Hot Women's Erotica
Compilation and Introduction copyright © 2003, 2005 Marilyn Jaye Lewis
All individual stories in this collection are © 2003 by their respective authors.

Published by
Blue Moon Books
An Imprint of Avalon Publishing Group Incorporated
245 West 17th Street, 11th floor
New York, NY 10011-5300

First Blue Moon Books Edition 2005

First published in 2003 by Venus Book Club, 401 Franklin Avenue, Garden City, New York, 11530

ISBN 1-56201-476-5

9 8 7 6 5 4 3 2 1

Printed in Canada
Distributed by Publishers Group West

TABLE OF CONTENTS

INTRODUCTION

by Marilyn Jaye Lewis

Most of the many writers writing erotica today are usually unaware of the rich place literary erotica holds in the history of fiction, and perhaps are even less aware of how short-lived that history has been in the United States, or of what a small role female-scripted erotica played in the early days of "legalized" erotica publishing in America.

It doesn't actually matter, since the essence of well-written erotica doesn't rely on what has come before it; human nature appears to be human nature regardless of the sexual era it comes to us entrenched in. Only the courage to get those stories *published* relies on history; that thanks to the idealistic and tenacious efforts of publisher Barney Rosset, infamous former owner of Grove Press, the publishing of erotica has been legal in this country since the early 1960s. And in addition, thanks to audacious pioneering lesbian magazines in the '80s, such as the original *On Our Backs* or *Bad Attitude* (where I cut my erotica-writing teeth), women writers of all sexual persuasions have come to the forefront of today's literary erotic fiction with little to fear about expressing their sexual preferences but fear itself.

In this collection of contemporary women's erotica, I've tapped the talents of both newcomers and established voices. I've called together award-winning fiction authors, like O. Henry Prize-winner Janice Eidus with her humorous erotic tale of the ping-pong vampire; SM favorites like Claire Thompson writing about the thrill of sexual degradation alongside self-confessed computer geeks, like Catherine Lundoff, writing exquisitely about the undead; sex advocates along with housing advocates. I've even brought in the talents of that small but celebrated breed, the women who actually *earn their living* from writing and publishing erotica full-time, like Cecilia Tan and Alison Tyler. I conscientiously sought out the current female voices that would give you, the reader, the best sampling of the literary heights women's erotica has reached in the early years of this new century.

Contrary to once-popular opinion, women readers of erotica are into the details. They like the sexual exploits of a story spelled out in no uncertain terms. Yet, they also like the *stories*; they like the erotic details unveiled in terms of the relationships involved, or the emotional terrains examined. While "jerk-off" stories hold a time-honored place in everyone's erotica, women's erotic stories tend to be most successful when exploring psychological or emotional relationships at the same time.

This collection kicks off with a stellar example of how hot eroticism can weave seamlessly through a well-told story. In *Albert's Lunch*, Lisa Wolfe tells a tale of obsession so simple and ordinary in its poignancy that any reader can recognize the familiar soul within it. And later on in this collection, *The Orange Grove* by Kiini Ibura Salaam tells a lush and sensual tale of sexual awakening under an orange tree made all the more touching by its unexpected ending. Iris N. Schwartz's *The Dairy Kings* delights the senses with its delicious images of very masculine men in clean white uniforms and the sumptuous dairy products they bring into one woman's ordinary Brooklyn world.

This is not to say that men can't tell erotic tales that thrill women, because throughout time they certainly have. But women authors have come into erotic storytelling the hardest way—often by having to challenge *each other's* fanatical political or religious beliefs; and by overcoming that culturally ingrained "need to please" and "unwillingness to offend." Most of the women included in this volume use their real names, while a select few have chosen to write under pen names for their own personal reasons. Like it or not, erotica, more than any other genre outside of romance, still pressures men and women alike to explore human sexuality behind the safety of pseudonyms.

While I hope you delight in reading this wonderful collection of erotic stories as much as I've enjoyed bringing it to you, I also ask you to spare a moment of thought for the cultural challenges each writer has faced in an effort to bring her story to the page. I think it'll help you feel that much more enchanted by the stories these women were inspired to tell.

ALBERT'S LUNCH

by Lisa Wolfe

He couldn't get her out of his mind. He checked his work one last time, found a stopping place, locked the screen, got up, and stretched. Even though he'd been staring at the screen, absorbed in his work for the last few hours, as soon as he stopped for a second—boom—she popped in. He went into the kitchen.

He didn't want to call it an obsession. He wasn't *obsessed* with Alix. He didn't even want to be with her anyway. Anymore. Not if she didn't want to be with him. It just isn't logical to want to be with someone who doesn't want to be with you. Is it.

And he had been over all this before, anyway. Hadn't he.

But the images kept floating up with such regularity. Alix naked in the kitchen, pouring water from the kettle into the teapot, the way her shoulder blades moved so easily in her back. And stretched out on her back on the bed, the sunlight coming in the window, her arm flung up behind her head. His eyes moved from the soft round of her belly to the hollow of her hip, to the muscular groin and thigh, and then inward to the soft flesh of her inner thigh. Everything with her was either soft or hard. That way she had of looking right through you, her blue eyes reflecting the light.

Enchanted. I am enchanted by her, he thought, as he got the bread out. Tuna, probably. Tuna sandwich is the easiest. How fortuitous that they ever met, riding the train that day, when it turns out that she rarely rides the train. How fortuitous, *ha!* He shook his head as he mashed up the tuna with the mayonnaise. Yeah, right. Now he can't get her out of his mind and she is far away. *In a land far, far away*, like a fucking fairy tale. Not far away geographically, no, she only lives across town, it takes five minutes to get to her house, he could be there in a heartbeat. No, she is just— look, face it, Albert, you know she doesn't want you. And time goes on. Doesn't it.

He put the other piece of bread on top. Forget lettuce and tomato, it's too hard. He grabbed a paper towel to use as a plate, and went into the living room. He sat on the sofa, chewing.

When she wore her hair up, there were these renegade brown curls, shot through with gray and golden threads that inevitably escaped from the clasp and fell lightly along the length of her neck. He wanted to be one of those curls.

And when she was thinking about something, there was that slight creasing in her brow, then her gaze would slide off to one side and she'd get that expression, and you'd know she was someplace faraway, unreachable, in a special world all her own. And her mind! God. The way it dove down, staying under for a long time, swimming this way and that, and then she'd come back to the surface, laughing, shake out her wet hair, and present him with what she'd found, a question or glinting piece of insight that pierced his sensibilities with curiosity. And the curiosity would harden to desire. He wanted to dive in with his dick and hands and mouth, deep into the core of her, so their insides could meet, just like their minds.

The way she smelled, kind of a woody, sweet smell, and when he put his face between her legs it was like entering the wet trunk of a tree after a rainstorm, the bark peeling off all around him, and the deep, mulchy smell driving him out of his mind.

"What if," she had said, "what if the dream world is more real than this one?"

"Than the real world?"

"Well—is this actually *real*—let's call it the waking world."

"Well, okay. The waking world. What if."

"If that were so," she said, "it wouldn't matter if we saw each other here or not, because you could see me there, in the real world. The real dream world." She looked straight at him, her piercing eyes green today above her emerald sweater.

"How can you be so—so facile about it," he said. "I mean here we are. We're living in *this* world. This one." And he placed his hands around her waist and pulled her toward him and they touched lips, just barely, the edges of their lips touched. He could hear her breathing change. She pulled away.

"I'm not *facile*," she said.

"It's not an insult."

"Oh yes it is," she said, and she picked up her sketch pad and began drawing, moving the pencil quickly and single-mindedly. Blocking him out. She was blocking him out.

She had gone from wanting to see him a few times a week, to once a week, to the final pronouncement, when she had said she "really didn't need to see him at all."

Didn't *need* to see him? Shit. He picked up *The New Yorker* from the coffee table and thumbed through it. They came every fucking week, you barely glanced at the cartoons in one and then the next one arrived. He read a blurb about how ice-cream sellers have a bad time when the summer weather is cool. People don't eat as much ice cream, and business suffers. So they have special weather insurance, but they don't call it that, they call it a "weather derivative." Albert dropped the magazine on the floor. He wondered if he could get some kind of derivative for just—life, for all the unexpected shit of life.

The phone rang. Maybe it was her. No. Of course it wasn't. She wasn't going to call him, after all this time. That was absurd. He looked at his watch. 1:15. He finished his sandwich while he waited for the answering machine to kick in.

The machine beeped. "Albert, man, where are you? It's Tim. You're working, I know you are. Pick up. Pick up the phone. Look, there's this beautiful woman I want you to meet. Remember we talked about this, about you getting out more. She's a mathe-matician, okay? Very smart. And she has a killer ass. I'm not kid-ding. Call me back. I'm at the lab." Click.

Alix's ass loomed into his vision as clearly as if the director were right there, yelling "Close-up! We want a close-up on her ass!" Her ass was wide and soft and silky. It was like a milky white heart, smooth and plump but firm underneath. He was stroking the small of her back, then moving his hand down her sacrum and along her crack, to the fleshy place at the bottom of her buttocks. She was humming softly. Then he put one finger gently inside her opening. She let her breath out "aah," and then another sharp intake of breath. He moved his finger farther in. He licked her ass cheeks and moved his other hand between her legs. He put one finger up inside her and stroked her clit with the other one. She was writhing and gasping, making a nonverbal sound like "Nnn-eh," kind of a combination of no and yes. Then she started thrust-ing more rhythmically, and suddenly she flipped him off her and onto his back, straddled him, and with that woman-on-a-mission look on her face, grabbed the condom packet off the bedside table, ripped it open with her teeth, slid it on him in one movement, and climbed on. He could feel the hot wetness of her through the condom and she yelled "Uh-huh!" like she was a witness at a revival church meeting. He felt like saying *I See the Light!* because he did, everything was getting very bright inside his head, and his dick was hard as a rock, with her pounding on top and him com-ing up to meet her, his breath coming harder, the sweat pouring down his back and his stomach, and both of them sliding around in his sweat.

He sat on the sofa in his living room, his hand moving rhyth-mically. The image of her, so clear, her face flushed, her cunt suck-ing him in and out, and he was thrusting up into her, her hard, pink nipples between his thumb and forefinger. He was twisting and pinching them, just the way she liked it, she was wild with it and ramming herself on him like he might be snatched away from her at any moment and she had to make sure she took in every second of this. He could feel her juices even through the condom. He dipped a finger inside her alongside his dick, put it in his mouth, and licked it off. He could feel himself almost coming and took some deep breaths to head it off while he watched her close her eyes and bite her bottom lip. Now she was moaning so loudly it almost sounded like she was coming, but she wasn't there, not yet, he knew her, and as he stroked and pulled and squeezed himself, on his sofa in his living room, he felt his come building up and ready to burst and he fast-forwarded to her coming, screaming and grabbing him and then he came just after so they were rocking together in his release and her after-waves.

He groaned. His pants and boxers were halfway down his legs. His hand and belly were wet. The VCR light was blinking at him. Oh shut up, he said, to the light. Alix was fading. It was all fading. He used the paper towel from lunch to wipe up. More or less. He went back to the kitchen and threw the paper towel in the trash.

He looked out the window at the sprawling oak tree and the dying grass. The way time passes. It seemed like only yesterday that she was right here in this kitchen, looking out the window.

Maybe Tim was right. He could hear yesterday's conversation in his head. "Get over it, man, it's been six years. This is insane."

"Five years and seven months," Albert said.

"Whatever," Tim said. "Too fucking long. The thing is, if you want to be single, fine, be single. But don't keep telling me about this woman who dumped you ten or nine-something years ago. When there're all these fine, super-smart women coming in and out of the lab on a regular basis. Falling on your lap—in your lap, you know what I mean."

Albert went back to his desk and sat down. He stared at the screen. Tim was right. He wasn't going to think about her anymore. From this moment forward.

To unlock your screen, enter your password.

He typed in his password, *a-l-i-x.*

And went back to work.

BOOBS

by Kate Dominic

I was going to smack the next person who commented on my beautiful "implants." Every inch of 42DD cup perched on my comfortably padded brunette frame was all my own. The areolas outlined ever so faintly when I wore tight or sheer tops were there because of good genes helped by a goodly number of boyfriends who realized that the key to getting me hot enough to fuck was to suck me off, really, really hard.

I was already tender from a hot session with an old college buddy I'd run into on a business trip. We'd fucked our brains out. He got me so sensitive that I'd been masturbating at least twice a day since I got home. I held my nipple to my mouth, licking the tip while I held a vibrator to my clit.

Friday night, though, I was lassoed into attending another boring industry awards event. Same old, same old—mundane speakers, lousy hors d'oeuvres, dull conversation. As I turned from a rousing discussion on shipping rates with a half-drunk VP who was almost falling into my chest, I once more felt eyes on me. This time, it was a reasonably attractive forty-something man encased in a very expensive dark blue linen suit that showed off his assets to his advantage. He was three or four inches shorter than I was, but I'm tall for a woman. As usual, it was several moments before his eyes made the trip up from my chest to my face. Unlike the other gentlemen who'd spent their evening's "networking" ogling my breasts, though, this one had the good grace to blush. And surprisingly, he didn't back down from my stare. Instead, he snagged two glasses of zinfandel from a passing waiter and walked over to offer me one.

Since the evening was such a wash professionally, I told myself I should start thinking in more social terms. This one wasn't bad, and my vibrator needed a rest. As he got closer, I saw that while his face was average looking, he had a nice mouth with full pouty lips and the intelligent blue eyes I'm so fond of. His tight blond curls were liberally streaked with gray, but neatly styled. However, he was still the fourth man this evening who'd started a conversation by staring at my breasts. I accepted the wine without a great deal of overt enthusiasm.

"Sorry," he said, smiling as he offered me the glass. "You're very pretty, but I shouldn't have stared." He blushed again, this time grinning unrepentantly. "Well, at least not so blatantly. If I promise to behave, can we start over again?"

For just a second, I wondered what the wine would look like all over that expensive navy linen. But, well, his smile was somewhat endearing, and I'd had my fill of both quasi-polite innuendo and work for the day. I sighed dramatically and rolled my eyes.

"Okay, bud. Let's see. Pleased to meet you. Lovely weather. Great implants. That about cover it?" I emptied my glass in one swallow.

He choked. I mean, down the wrong pipe, sound like he's never going to breathe again, choked. I pounded his back until he gasped out a strangled "thank you," then I held his glass as he wiped the tears from his eyes. He was still wheezing when he turned and stared at my breasts again.

"They're implants? No shit?"

Days like this made me wish I traveled 24/7 for the company. "No, buck-o, they're not implants. I've just had enough idiotic 'compliments' for one day. I figured you were about to make another."

The relief that washed over his face caught me totally off guard. He'd finally regained his breath, though. I waited until he'd finished his wine to give him my most scathing look.

"No implants comments, huh?"

He put his glass down, shaking his head vigorously. "All the women in my family are really well-endowed, and they all nurse their kids. I've seen natural breasts all my life, so I'm kind of partial to them. Around here, almost everybody with big boobs has implants. I appreciate the rare occasions when I can see the real thing." He stopped, horrified. The flush raced all the way to his ears. "I mean, breasts. Breasts! Not boobs. That's what my sisters call them. Damn!"

His cheeks were the color of my lipstick. I'd never seen anybody blush that much before. And his eyes were once more locked onto my boobs. His face really was pretty sweet, though, and the bulge in the front of his pants was intriguing. At that point, I decided that networking the event was a lost cause. I held my empty glass out to him and hid my smile when he sighed in relief.

"It's okay. I call them boobs, too." I scanned his fingers—no sign of a wedding ring. "So, you're here alone?"

He nodded, motioning a waiter over for another glass. Then his sparkling baby blues looked directly into my eyes and he formally extended his hand. "I'm Daryl Woodson, Accounting Director for Jenson Plastics."

"Ellie Jones," I said, pleasantly surprised at how firm and warm his grip was. I like a man with good hands, especially one who understands the value of eye contact. "I'm Client Services Manager for your arch competitor."

Several hours later, and long after we'd switched to sparkling water, we caught a cab to my place. Although my initial intent had been an early evening capped by a fast fuck, I'd been surprised to discover that I really liked ol' Daryl. He made me laugh. And his interest was obvious. He couldn't take his eyes off my breasts. I'd dripped soup on my blouse at dinner, and he'd kept his napkin firmly in his lap long after I'd finished wiping the spot clean.

When we walked in the door of my apartment, I expected the usual grope and grab routine. I was once more pleasantly surprised when he took my head gently in his hands and touched his lips to mine. That man kissed me until I thought I'd pass out. Damn, the things he did with his mouth! He licked and probed and sucked on my lips and tongue—and gave me his. Eventually, my legs turned to water. When I tried to lead him to the bedroom, though, he shook his head and whispered, "Living room, please. And leave the lights low." So, I let him kiss me all the way to the couch. We sat down, kicked our shoes off next to the faux bearskin rug, and necked until my lips tingled.

"Wow." I gasped when we came up for air. "You are one hel-luva kisser."

"Thanks," he grinned. His lips were red and wet and, damn, they were sexy. "I've always been a pretty oral person."

"Oh, indeed!" I stretched, rubbing my hands down over my breasts. "Maybe we should confirm that assertion."

I was really turned-on from all the kissing, so I shivered when my palms slid over my nipples. Daryl rubbed his knuckles over my neck.

"I could show you oral, Ellie. If you're up for it." He reached down and resituated himself, not even trying to hide what he was doing. I looked at his distended crotch, looked back into his sparkling eyes, and smiled.

"You're on, hot stuff."

Daryl planted a quick kiss on the end of my nose. Then he told me to scoot to the far end of the couch. He handed me the TV remote. When I my raised eyebrows, he shook his head.

"The 11:00 news is about to start. Turn it on."

I did, laughing as he shrugged out of his jacket and pulled off his tie. The next thing I knew, he was lying with his head pillowed on my lap, unbuttoning my blouse.

"Watch the news," he said firmly. I looked up, the blur of motion on the TV barely registering as Daryl's hand trailed over the side of my breast. His touch was slow and sensuous. He stroked over the upper curves, caressing every inch. Then he deft-ly unhooked the latch of my bra, catching my breasts as they fell out into his hands. I sighed in relief, enjoying the usual end-of-day freedom from confinement and the pure pleasure of his hands touching me. He lifted my breasts, one at a time, and fondled them. Eventually, he let the one closest to his face rest against his lips, and eased the other down onto my chest.

"Wow," he said, softly kissing the sensitive tip. "Somebody really sucked you off." He licked gently. "You're still red."

"Well, yeah." I was stunned to feel my own face blushing. "I like a lot of breast stimulation . . ." I let my voice trail off, truly shocked that I was embarrassed. I'd never had any trouble asking for what I wanted. But Daryl was admiring my nipples in a way that had me totally off balance. He smiled against my still-sensitive skin and turned my head gently toward the TV.

"Watch the news," he said, quietly stroking his fingertips down the valley between my breasts. "Don't pay attention to me. Pretend we're an old married couple. We've just come home from a party and we have all the time in the world for some good lovin'."

His light kisses were making my pussy hum. I dutifully turned my eyes to the glowing box and "watched" the news. I have no idea what the newscasters were talking about. Daryl licked and laved through the whole first story. My nipple was so sensitive I wanted to scream. As the next spot came on, I barely heard him whisper.

"Your nipples look so hot." He flattened his tongue and licked once more over the tip. "Watch the news."

He wrapped his lips around my whole areola, resting for a moment while I shivered at the heat and moisture of his mouth. Then he started to suck. Softly at first, very lightly, then gradually harder and stronger. He had my entire nipple in his mouth, his strong warm hands wrapped around my breast and cupping it, holding it in place for his mouth to take. He barely came up for air, the entire ten long minutes of the national news.

Eventually, I was shivering hard, little moans escaping from my lips as his fingers stroked intimately over the sides and top and bottom of my flesh. It felt like he was drawing the sensation forward to where his lips kept up a deep steady rhythm. And the bruising heat emanating from my nipple let me know Daryl was giving me one helluva hickey. The pulses echoed deep into my belly, almost to the point of mini orgasms. I clenched my pussy, wiggling my damp panties against my skirt.

"Daryl," I whispered, "I really want you to fuck me." I groaned as he took the tip between his teeth and gently shook his head. With a quick, final nip, he released his grip. I looked down, clenching my pussy muscles hard as he touched his finger to the well-sucked peak. It stretched out, shimmering dark red, even in the dimmed lights. Daryl's eyes sparkled, his lips slightly puffy. His cock looked like it was ready to split the front of his pants.

"You're going to be so sensitive Ellie." He rolled the tender tip between his fingers. I gasped, arching up as my pussy twinged in response. "Move to the other end of the couch, hon. Local news is about to start."

I did, wordlessly, afraid that this was too good to be true, and almost afraid of what was coming next. Daryl situated himself again, and took my other breast between his hands. He licked slowly and sensuously over the nipple. "Watch the local news, Ellie."

I was almost insane by the time it was over. My nipple was so sore and sensitized that even the tiniest licks made me shudder, and my pussy was begging for attention. A large spot of precome wet the front of Daryl's pants. As I sat there panting, Daryl stood up and started unbuttoning his shirt.

"Get undressed quickly. We have to be naked by the time the weather starts."

By that time, my pussy needed satisfaction so badly I'd have done anything he said. I was stepping out of my sopping panties when he grabbed a condom from his jacket pocket, and rolled it on. Then he laid down on the rug and shoved a pillow under his head. His dick wasn't terribly long, but I'd never imagined a cock could be that thick. It stuck up like a short, fat flagpole. He wrapped his hands around it, holding it pointing stiffly up.

"The commercial's almost over, Ellie. Straddle me."

I planted my knees on either side of his hips and slowly lowered myself onto him. My cunt was sopping. I groaned in relief as the heat of his latex-covered cock slid up into me, groaned again at the pure satisfaction of his shaft stretching my pussy walls unbelievably wide. When I was seated to the hilt, Daryl cupped my breasts and rubbed his thumbs over my nipples. Even in the dimmed lights, they had taken on a deep, reddish purple cast. I hissed, squirming on him, shivering as my cunt quivered over his cock. I was so sensitive that every brush of his thumb echoed all the way down to my trembling pussy.

"You are so beautiful," Daryl whispered, leaning up and licking my areola. "I love knowing those are my bruises on your nipples now." When the commercial ended, he wrapped his hands around my left breast again, pulling me inexorably down to his mouth. "Watch the weather."

I didn't know if I could stand much more. I leaned forward and took my weight onto my arms, my fingers curling into the soft warmth of the rug. His mouth lined up perfectly with my breasts. I whimpered when his lips closed around my nipple. I was sore and sensitive, and so fucking horny I could hardly stand it. Then Daryl was sucking again. Softly. Insistently. Rhythmically. Very gently, very slowly, he increased the pressure and pace. The tremors vibrated all the way down to my belly, into the deepest part of my pussy. I ground against him, panting.

"Don't move," he growled, nipping lightly at the tip. I gasped at the pain, my whole body stiffening as my cunt walls gripped around him. "Oh, yes, Ellie. Like that. Milk my cock with your pussy. Just your wonderful hot pussy."

I couldn't have stopped the tremors if I'd wanted to, and I didn't want to. I couldn't take much on one side anymore, not all at once. Daryl alternated; smiling at my whimpers each time he moved his lips from one peak to the other. He worshiped my breasts with his mouth, slowly working up to where his tongue again rasped over the excruciatingly sensitive nipples. They were even darker now, elongated and glistening with saliva, and so tender I cried out each time he closed his lips over an areola and sucked it gently into his mouth. My pussy spasmed with each rhythmic tug. An incredible orgasm was building inside me.

"Sports," he whispered. "Watch the sports. Oh, Ellie, I want to suck your nipples while you come."

"Fuck sports," I gasped, clamping down hard around him. I hadn't noticed the TV for a long time now. His dick twitched inside of me.

"Yes!" he growled. "Like that!" He held my breast in his strong, warm hands, licking determinedly over my throbbing nipple. "Oh, yes, honey. Let your pussy climax around me. I want to shoot up your cunt while I'm sucking you off."

Daryl drew me deep into his mouth. Sensation shot through me. I screamed as the orgasm washed up from my belly. Waves of pleasure shuddered through my pussy walls, echoing the heavenly, torturous pulls of his rhythmic sucking. He gasped and bucked up, turning his head to my other nipple. He sucked so hard I thought I'd faint. His hips surged up into me and my cunt spasmed once more as his climax shuddered through him.

I hung there over him, my pussy still squeezing his cock, my nipples so tender I could barely stand for him to even kiss them now. He grinned, his lips red and swollen as he cupped my breasts and stroked the sides.

"The news is on in the morning, too, Ellie. Is it okay if I spend the night?"

"You can stay," I said, yawning and wincing at the same time. I lifted my sated pussy lips over his still half-hard shaft and snuggled down next to him, carefully turning so my breasts weren't touching him at all. A reprise would be nice—later. And I could purely get attached to fucking a cock like his on a regular basis. "Tomorrow, we'll be sticking to headline news only, though, sport."

"We'll see," he whispered. With no warning, Daryl gathered me into his arms and deliberately rubbed his chest hair over my nipples. I jumped and gasped, and he laughed softly. "Then again, we may want to watch the week in review."

TEN MINUTES IN THE EIGHTIES

by Alison Tyler

For ten minutes in the eighties, I was beautiful.

I've been beautiful since, but never like that.

Never again.

Before those magical ten minutes took place, I not only *wasn't* beautiful, I was hardly noticeable. Simply put, I was just another lowly freshman at UCLA, one of 40,000 others who called the campus home. Shy, insecure, terrified—those three adjectives fit me perfectly. In a land of voluptuous vixens and bottle blondes, I had no idea that with my sleek build and darkly mysterious features, I was far more than pretty. It never occurred to me that men would—and did—find me attractive or that all of the things girls lay awake at night and hope will happen to them would eventually happen for me.

Rather than put myself in a position to be rejected, I didn't give the guys a chance to approach. I kept my peers at a safe distance by creating a mood of constant motion. I hurried to class, spent hours studying in various libraries around campus, and used my free time cultivating miscellaneous interests as a deejay at the college station and a flunky on the student paper. I was a good girl all year long, until the end of spring finals, when I finally let down my guard and got drunk with the rest of the students on my dorm floor. With no prior drinking experience, I downed five beers in one hour, and wound up to the great surprise of my dorm mates making snow angels on the cool turquoise-and-white tiles of the bathroom floor. Five beers will knock out any lightweight. And at 5′3″ and 105 pounds, I was a lightweight.

In the morning, I experienced my first-ever hangover. For hours, I lay on the slim twin bed and stared at the ceiling, willing the rushing sound in my head to subside. When I eventually took a chance at walking upright, I realized that I'd missed the cafeteria's sole Saturday daytime meal. If I wanted to eat, I'd have to wait until six P.M., or fend for myself. Miserable, but yearning for sustenance, I took a taxi a mile off campus to the nearest grocery store. For a long time, I wandered aimlessly up and down the aisles, filled with an overpowering craving for something, *anything*, but not knowing precisely what. After choosing two items with the care that some women use when buying expensive jewelry, I took my place in line at the checkout. My self-prescribed day-after cure was a bottle of tomato juice and a can of Pringles (the only things in the whole store that seemed even mildly appealing).

It was while I was standing there with my red plastic basket in hand that I started to become beautiful.

I didn't know the transformation was happening right away. All I knew was that the handsome, dark-haired, forty-something man next to me in line was staring at me, his head angled so that he could look at me over his shades. I felt myself flush, pale skin turning scarlet, embarrassed because I had on the clothes I'd worn during the festivities the evening before, the clothes I'd ultimately slept all night in: faded blue jeans, a rah-rah-style University T-shirt in Bruin colors, and a thin navy blue hoodie. My turbulent raven curls had escaped from their standard ponytail style, falling well past my shoulders to reach the middle of my shoulder blades. Purple smudges of fatigue made my brown eyes look even darker than usual. I hadn't bothered with makeup of any kind.

Nervousness made me bite into my bottom lip. I felt overexposed beneath the fluorescent lighting and underprepared for a confrontation with a stranger. I tried to look extremely interested in the multitude of processed foods filling the fat woman's cart in front of me, but I felt the man staring relentlessly, and so I slowly turned to face him. As if encouraged by my action, he took a step closer to me, and in a low, soft voice, he whispered, "You have a look."

The way he said the words gave me an unexpected wave of confidence. Or maybe it was the lack of sleep talking. I don't know precisely why, but I met him head-on and said, "The drunken, slept in my clothes, barely post-hangover look?"

He shook his head. "That's not it. Something else. Something special."

I bit my lip again, harder this time. Here was a true Hollywood-style line, but I was no Hollywood starlet. Flustered and confused, I looked down at my white Keds, looked out the window at the half-filled parking lot, looked up at the bars of ugly lighting. Suddenly, it was my turn to pay for my groceries, and I fumbled in my pocket for my folded bills, then grabbed the change and my small paper bag of supplies and started to leave the store. The man abandoned his own few items on the gray conveyer belt and hurried after me.

"Where are you going?" he asked, his hand on my shoulder. I didn't flinch away from him, but I pulled back, surprised by the power in his touch.

"Back to campus. I have a cab over there—" I gestured to the far corner of the parking lot. The blacktop glittered where shards of broken glass had melted into the oily asphalt.

"Tell him to go. I'll take you." He hesitated, as if he could sense the insecurity that had cloaked me for so many years, as if he could actually feel it. "Anywhere," he promised, "I'll take you. Wherever you need. Wherever you want to go."

I looked at him carefully. Here was the exact situation my parents had spent my entire teenage life worrying about and doing their best to protect me from. I was going to take a ride with a man I didn't know. And all their warding off of evil spirits did nothing to stop me. For some reason, I obeyed his command, paying off the cab and following him to the expensive, shiny silver sports car parked nearby. The car gleamed like foil in the bright sunlight.

"You should never accept a ride with a stranger," he told me severely as he opened the passenger door. "Especially a stranger in Los Angeles."

"I know."

"Then why are you choosing to ride with me?"

I smiled. I had been given the perfect answer. "You have a look," I said, and he laughed as he got into the driver's side and then slid an unmarked cassette into the tape deck. "I'm a music producer," he told me. "I just heard this tape for the first time. The boy's going to be huge."

It was Terence Trent D'Arby's *Introducing the Hardline According to . . .* and that music is embedded in my mind as a soundtrack to what happened next. The man drove me to his house high up in the Hollywood Hills where the movie stars live. He led me through the huge, well-decorated rooms, all the way to the mammoth patio in back. There, he gently took my clothes off my body and had me touch myself while he watched. And I was beautiful. For ten minutes in the eighties, I was so beautiful it was hard to handle.

I'd never done something like this before. Technically, I was a virgin. I'd had some kissing experience in high school, some back-seat petting at a local drive-in theater, but shyness had kept me pure. Now, in the heat of the day, I touched myself while a stranger watched. I ran my hands over my body. I let my fingertips graze my nipples until they stood up hard and erect. I kept my eyes on the man as I let one hand wander lower, reaching to touch my pussy while he watched. The pool behind him was a true, aqua blue. The sky above matched that Technicolor brightness. Standing there on the tiled deck, looking out at his multimillion-dollar view, I put on a show with my nakedness and my roving touch.

"That's right," he said, nodding, his voice hoarse as if he were as surprised by my actions as I was. "Do that."

He was seated on a deck chair, with his hands on his thighs, his sunglasses low down on his nose so he could look at me over the rim. I felt power in being naked. Felt a power in the way he drank in every touch of my fingertips on my stripped-bare skin. It was as if he were touching me, as well. When my fingers found the wetness coating my lips, he sighed before I did. I closed my eyes and leaned my head back, arching my slim hips forward, running my hands over my hipbones. The tiles were hot under my bare feet. The air was still and clear. My hair tickled against my naked back. My eyelashes fluttered against my cheeks.

I knew that he wouldn't touch me. Not unless I invited him to. Not unless I asked. But I didn't. I didn't need anything from him except his gaze. Because the way he stared at me—that's what did it. That was the magic that made me beautiful. I used my fingers to spread my nether lips wide apart. I ran my thumbs up and down over the ridge of my clit, first my right thumb, then my left, then both together, vying for control, until I knew that I was seconds away from coming. I touched myself harder; my eyes closed tighter, my whole body flexed as I waited for the change to take me away.

My mind was filled to bursting with images. I saw myself relaxing with a beer the night before, letting my guard down for the first time ever. I saw myself the way this man must have seen me, unwound, let loose from the tight confines I'd kept myself in all my life. I saw myself opening up, from the split of my body, from the cages within. This picture of freedom brought me to the brink. For me, there was nothing more freeing than standing naked in front of a total stranger—a man whose name I didn't even know—and letting him see everything.

He said, "Oh, God," when I came. He said the words for me, so that I didn't have to, and then, as if my pleasure had released him, he took off his sunglasses and came closer, on his knees on the patio, so very close to me, but he still didn't touch me. "Oh, Jesus," he said, as I brought my fingertips to my lips and slowly licked my own juices away.

"Don't stop," he said, and I knew from the sound of his voice that if I chose to, I could ask him for things. That he'd give me whatever I wanted. But all I wanted from him was his gaze. "Do it again," he said, "please make yourself come again."

With my fingers wet from my mouth, I parted my pussy lips for him, but this time, I slid two fingers deep inside myself. He was close now, his breath on my skin, and I pushed forward with my hips again, feeling his hair softly tickling against my naked thighs. I let him watch me from inches away as I fucked myself. I let him see everything, the way my clit grew so engorged with the heat from within. The way I worked myself hard with my fingers, thrusting my wrist upward against my body, slamming my hand inside me when the need grew stronger and then stronger still. I used only my right hand this time, my thumb rubbing back and forth over my clit, and when I felt the climax building, I put my left hand on his head and twined my fingers through his thick, dark hair, grabbing onto him, anchoring him as I came a second time.

"So beautiful," he said in that same low, steady voice. "You have this look, this goddamn beautiful quality. I knew when I first saw you—"

I picked up my clothes from around me on the tiles, and I dressed carefully, not hurrying. I felt as if I'd never hurry again, never be nervous again. When I was ready, he drove me back to my dorm, as he'd promised he would. Delivered me back in perfect condition, unmarred and unhurt, although I wasn't the same person. Not at all. I'd transformed under his gaze. I'd changed.

I guess, sometimes that's all it takes, one person's gaze, one person's opinion, to make all the difference. Like the way he'd said that D'Arby would be big—a single person's opinion, summing up a powerful truth. It happens all the time in the media, the way it happened for me that time in L.A. In fact, just this weekend, I read a five-star review of D'Arby's latest CD, and the reviewer wrote: "For ten minutes in the '80s, D'Arby was on top of the world."

And for almost those same exact ten minutes, I was beautiful. For the first time in my life, I was so fucking beautiful it was hard to handle. Yeah, I've been beautiful since. But never like that.

Never again.

THE PERMANENT

by Catherine Lundoff

Run, my mind sings. *Run.* And I do. I am almost flying now, my heart thudding against my ribs like a rabbit pursued by hounds. My bare feet pound against the dirt as I do my best to outstrip whatever it is that hunts me. *Bare?* I glance down at a frothy lace confection of a nightgown, at my pale naked feet twinkling below me in the darkness. *Why am I wearing this . . . thing?* The thought jars me awake just ahead of the phantom grasp of my pursuer.

Just ahead of the alarm as well. I sit up, heart still pounding as I turn off the clock radio. When I look down, my nipples are gradually relaxing and I can smell the dampness like rust between my legs. I scramble for a tampon, coffee, and clothes, then drag my carcass out to catch the bus. It stops in front of a big red brick building with high arched windows. Two large stone pots filled with scraggly brown leaves and twisted stems stand on either side of the doorway. I wonder what it was before it died.

I'd also wonder why they don't shell out for landscaping, but I've been inside. I know the answer to that already. Genteel decay doesn't begin to cover it. Once through the doors, I have to stop and blink for a while to adjust to the dimness and the dust. There are ancient red velvet curtains and musty old Persian carpets and dark, dark wood everywhere. I don't see Terese until I almost bump into her. Not that I mind that part. She and her brother Gerard are the best part about working here, besides the pay, of course.

"Hello, Magda," Terese purrs down at me, not bothering to step back. She's about five inches taller than me and round and curvy in all the right places. Her big black eyes come into focus as my eyes adjust and she flashes a bright white grin at me.

I love hearing her say my name. In her deep voice with its indefinable accent, "Magda" becomes an exotic Eastern European beauty with cheekbones to die for and yards of black hair. Of course, I do look just like that, except for the cheekbones. And the hair. Well, all right, and I'm not particularly exotic; can we drop it already?

Terese moves slowly away from me as Gerard comes into the hallway. "Hello Magda. We've got some fun stuff for you tonight." He smiles reassuringly, teeth dazzling in the gloom. He is long and lean in contrast to Terese's abundant curves. They both have the same melting eyes though, and black hair that looks more like ravens' wings than ravens' wings if you know what I mean. Their hands are pretty similar too, all long fingers and slightly tapered nails. Just the right size to fit into all kinds of inappropriate-for-the-workplace things.

On the other hand, Samuels, the other employee, is more than a little creepy. He has eyes that kind of slide away before they really catch yours. I follow Gerard into the next room where Samuels wanders up to us. When I glance up it looks like he's trying to smell my hair or something.

I back up until Gerard speaks. "Didn't you say that you wanted to get started on the billing, Dick? I'll be in to talk to you about it in a few minutes." Gerard's voice has just the right authoritative ring to it and Samuels dutifully trots off without a backward glance. I hope the office lights are too dim for Gerard to notice my small sigh of relief. I wouldn't want him thinking that I don't play well with others.

He keeps the lights low and they work mostly at night because he and Terese are both light sensitive. I'm finally getting used to it; soon, like their general gorgeousness, I'll just take it in stride. I tell myself that when he leads me over to his computer. His hand rests lightly on my shoulder. All of a sudden, I want that frothy lace horror I was wearing in my dream. I wonder if he'd like taking it off. Then he breaks the mood by taking his hand away and standing tantalizingly out of reach as he tells me what he wants me to do.

But I'm having trouble concentrating. The room is getting warmer. Maybe it's just the dark red velvet of the curtains drowning out the setting sun's watery light. Maybe it's the rise and fall of Gerard's voice as he speaks to me. I reach up and unbutton the top two buttons of my blouse but he doesn't seem to notice and it doesn't cool me off at all. The room spins slowly around me and instead of listening to the wonder of invoices, I find myself imagining the touch of his lips, the feel of those long fingers on my skin.

"You're confusing her, brother dear." Terese slinks in to sit on the edge of the desk, as close to me as she can get. I turn my chair a little so my leg touches hers ever so slightly, just enough to send shivers up my spine. I am getting wet listening to them banter back and forth above me, soaking my tampon until I wonder if my blood will pool beneath me in a small sea. I contemplate throwing myself at both of them. But what if they say no? How humiliating would that be? *Coward* says the little voice inside my head.

Terese leans forward to point out something on the screen and I can see down the front of her dress. Round breasts glow like alabaster against the soft dark blue of the cloth and I long to bury myself in them. She reaches out and I feel her white fingers caress my face. I turn to kiss them. *Wait, that's not it all. She's reaching out to get a paper from Gerard. Damn, Magda, get a grip.* I drown in her eyes anyway and come up gasping.

My fingers play with the next button on my blouse. "Are you too warm?" Gerard purrs solicitously and from somewhere a cold breeze startles my flesh from its daydreams. Goosebumps run down my arms and my nipples leap erect and I gasp aloud at the sudden chill.

"Too much, I think." Terese stands up, her fingers now gently stroking the goose bumps from my bare arm. I chew my lip in a frenzied effort at self-control. I should go get a glass of water, take a break, do something, anything, so I don't make a fool of myself. Not here, not in front of them.

With a huge effort, I make myself say, "I'm fine, really. Well, I should get started on this stuff." They both smile down at me and for an instant, I remember my dream and my body braces for flight. Then the moment's passed, leaving nothing but my pounding heart behind as they glide like panthers from the room. Terese gives me what I interpret as a smoldering gaze over one shoulder and my lips part in a soft pant.

The door shuts behind them and I am left alone in Gerard's office with its ancient wood furniture and red velvet curtains and a giant stack of invoices. When I look down I can see the rivulets of sweat run down between my breasts. *Are you showing enough cleavage there, Magda?* the voice of my common sense demands shrilly but I ignore it in favor of wishing that I had worn my good lace bra today instead of my sad nylon one.

I don't rebutton the shirt, but I do make myself work for a while, make myself pretend that the growing wetness between my legs isn't there. I try to squelch my new fantasy of being chased through the woods by both of them. And better yet, being caught. It works for a while. Then I give up and begin typing with one hand as I unzip my boring khaki skirt with the other. I stick that hand inside the waistbands of both skirt and underpants.

My fingers swim upstream to my clit and I imagine they're Terese's tongue, circling, stroking, then darting inside me. Heat washes up my thighs and I quiver against their touch. I abandon the keyboard to stroke my nipples through my shirt and bra, first one then the other, pinched into points with my, no her, free hand. My clit hardens beneath my fingers, her tongue, skin slick with my own juices, with her imagined softness. Her phantom fingers slip inside me and I ride the wave, cresting it with a soft moan, legs shaking against Gerard's chair.

I hear the click of the door before I open my eyes. In an instant, I am looking doggedly at the screen, both hands resting on the keyboard. Casually, I reach back and zip up my skirt. But when I look up there's no one there.

Dinnertime rolls around eventually and I go and eat my sandwich in the backyard. It's about the size of a postage stamp and overgrown with old rose bushes and morning glories. I can pretend that I'm Sleeping Beauty while I sit on the old iron bench and remember what summer looks like. Samuels glances out the door at me, faded eyes sliding all around me, but he doesn't come outside.

I'm overjoyed when he disappears back inside. There's something creepy about that wrinkled face with its weird eyes shifting and wandering but never quite coming to rest. If it weren't for the pay and the chance to lust after hotties like Terese and Gerard, I'd ask to be pulled from this job. Not that I think that way once I'm back inside.

I close the door behind me and notice Terese through the open door of her office. She's meeting with someone, perhaps an actual client. They don't seem to have all that many of those, possibly because of the evening hours. Or maybe it's that silly slogan: Forever Insurance Insures You Forever. I mean, who needs insurance *forever*? Lifetime total is usually enough for most people.

Terese leans forward, talking with her hands all the while and looking earnest. Definitely a client. I wander back to Gerard's office in time to find him sitting at his desk. He gives me a sleepy grin and ushers me back to his chair. The way he hangs over me when I sit down almost makes me wonder if he can smell my wet warmth and I squirm against the upholstery at the thought.

I wonder what would happen if I turned around and unzipped his fly and took his dick in my mouth. In my mind, it's just the right size and he groans at the touch of my tongue. I rock my head back and forth, then pull away to lick my way slowly down to his balls. His breath quickens into short gasps as I embrace him with my mouth once more. He clutches my shoulders in an effort not to ram himself down my throat. I can feel him shake with desire and I smile a little. I just love polite boys.

He reaches down to grab one of my hands and pulls it up to his mouth. I can feel his mouth on my fingers, then his tongue on my wrist: distracting, but not unpleasantly so. I work harder until I can taste his salty tang and as he comes in my mouth, I feel his teeth sinking into my wrist. I groan in surprise and desire, panting as I watch him drink from me. His tongue pulls at my wrist like a tongue on my clit and I spread my legs, straining against the chair. My fingers stroke my clit until I forget where I am and come in waves.

When I'm ready to start paying attention again, he's gone and I've got nothing better to look at than the computer screen. I remind myself sternly that there was no way Gerard was going to be doing the temp at work, not with the door open, anyway. The voice of my common sense takes over despite the imagined slight ache of jaw and wrist.

I type listlessly until it's time to go home. Terese's client is gone and she and Gerard are talking softly to each other when I say good night. They stop talking to smile at me as Samuels holds the door open for me. I wonder if he lives upstairs. He's always there when I get there and still there when I leave. I look up at the curtained windows of the second floor where I have yet to venture. They look deserted but my flesh crawls a little as my eyes meet their glassy blank stares.

The dreams are more intense tonight. This time, I worry that something serious will happen if I get caught and I run faster than ever. Still, something grabs me and I fall, tumbling not to the ground but into the afternoon and safety. The last thing I remember seeing in my dream are the curtained windows of the second floor of Forever Insurance as I run past them, pursued by whatever it is. Terrific. I hate it when my subconscious works overtime.

I decide to take the proverbial bull by the horns, or any other available body part, and check out the second floor. Once I knew there were no dead bodies or whatever up there, I'd get over this whole thing. Or so I tell myself.

The groovy ghoul is the only one at the office when I show up. "Terese and Gerard are meeting with clients downtown," Samuels informs me in a voice like a damp fog. His bulbous, colorless eyes gaze just past me until I get impatient and slightly queasy. I flee to Gerard's office and my very safe invoices. Joy.

But at least I'm not working with him. He has his own office down the hall. As long as he's busy, this is probably my best chance for checking out the dreaded upstairs. I just need to know that I'm overreacting, then I can make it all go away. Tomorrow I'll go have lunch with some friends, maybe catch a matinee. Get back to normal, whatever that is.

I do remember being normal. That was the time when I wasn't having weird dreams about things chasing me and could enter invoices for hours at a time without even once thinking of fucking my bosses. Back then, I wasn't looking at little cuts on my wrist and wondering where they came from. It's not like anything actually happened yesterday so I really don't have a clue. I rub them a little and they fade under the pressure, disappearing into my skin like they were never there. Bizarre.

I wait a reasonable amount of time before I head out into the hall. I poke my nose around the door of Samuels' office and wave the universal signal for "see you later." He bares his teeth at me, whoops, no, that was a smile. Sort of. He goes on talking on the phone, so I move as quietly as I can to the big staircase, just out of sight of the door. It has dark wood banisters that curl at the ends and it's very dark up at the top. *All right, just go up, look around, then back down* I tell myself.

I'm shivering a little on the first step and more on the third. By the time I get to the seventh I know this isn't a good idea. But on step ten I know I might as well go all the way up. Five steps more and I'm on the landing. There's a little light coming in from somewhere, but not much.

The air is really still up here, like it's anticipating something, and it's a lot cooler than downstairs. There's a short hallway to my right and I walk down it, swearing to myself that I'll just peek into that open door on my left. Then I'll go back downstairs. Just one little look . . . the room is almost empty, except for the two long boxes on the floor and the hurricane lamp on the table above them.

I make myself open the boxes. I just have to know. They aren't sealed or anything but the dirt inside doesn't tell me much. Maybe they're into gardening. Or maybe, they're . . . *What?* My little inner voice demands. *Bloodsucking fiends from Transylvania?* Outside in daylight, I would have laughed. Up here in the dark, crouched over two big boxes of dirt, I start shivering.

I close the boxes as quietly as I can and stand up very slowly. Just a few steps and I'll be down the stairs and out the front door. Then all I have to do is call the agency tomorrow and tell them things haven't worked out. I don't see Terese in the doorway until I bump into her. "Hello, Magda. I see that I don't need to chase you this time." Her eyes are black pools and I fall in, drowning until I would crawl over broken glass to get to her. Or let her chase me through my dreams until she catches me.

Then she kisses me, with lips so cold they burn mine and a tongue that freezes the inside of my mouth. I kiss her back, trying to warm her with my breath, my desire. We move slowly down the hallway to another room, her hands busily unbuttoning my shirt. Tonight, I wore my good bra, the red lace one with the snap in front. She has both shirt and bra off in moments. Her cold lips pull away from mine and drop to my breast. She takes my nipple in her mouth and it hardens until it's almost numb.

I don't feel her teeth sink in, just the sense that she is drinking, draining me of something I didn't know I had. Something I hope I don't want. She unbuttons my skirt and it falls to the floor. My underpants follow after an expert tug. I am pushed backward onto a bed, an antique four poster with curtains. *Black velvet, natch,* the analytical portion of my brain notes, as my eyes adjust slightly to the glow of the single candle.

Terese releases my breast and looks up to meet my eyes at the thought. I whimper as I watch her lick my blood from her lips and she smiles knowingly and slides down between my legs. Her icy caress finds my clit and strokes it, first with fingers, then tongue and I shiver and shake with longing and desire. She tugs the tampon from me and I close my eyes as she slides her tongue over it.

Then I come, bucking wildly against the glacier of her mouth, and she drinks from me like a goblet.

One moment, it's just us on the bed, with me writhing against the persistent pressure of Terese's fingers and teeth, then Gerard's there. His pale skin glows against the velvet of the curtains as he climbs in next to us. Terese lifts her face and bares her fangs at him, my blood staining the pale glow of her chin. "Share and share alike, sister dear," he responds as he kisses me and I know they've done this before. For an instant, I wonder what happened to the others: are they dead or what?

Then I find myself on all fours, my face buried between Terese's suddenly very naked thighs. I lick fiercely because I want to be the one they keep, the one they share between them and tell all their secrets to. I want them to want me like I want them: desperately, all barriers gone. Terese is very dry against my tongue, but I hear her breath hiss against her fangs, feel her body stiffen slightly.

Gerard slides up behind me, his fingers guiding himself inside me until he fills me with his biting cold. Terese pulls my hand up to her mouth and sucks fiercely on my wrist as he rides me, my groans muffled in her flesh. I try not to get too distracted, my tongue still coaxing her clit, begging her to lose herself in me. Gerard sinks his teeth into my shoulder and I whimper at the momentary pain. I want to surrender but my instinct for survival is too strong and I struggle, fighting against losing myself utterly.

Terese releases my wrist and slides down between my arms to kiss me. "Gently, little one. We will not hurt you. Much." Her voice purrs on the word and I relax into her arms as Gerard shifts position so his fingers can stoke their way up between my thighs. He is still inside me when I come again, howling against Terese's neck. As one, they drop their mouths onto both sides of my neck and begin to feed. My body shivers in arousal, in terror until I pass out.

When I come back around, I'm at Gerard's computer, fully dressed and very tired. It's the end of my shift. I notice that the stack of invoices is gone from the basket and I feel as empty as it is at the sight. Are they out of work for me? What if they don't want me back? The place is very quiet as I log out and get my jacket and there's no one around to ask if they have work for me to do next week. I crawl home, depressed at the loss.

I don't remember why I'm so tired or sore, at least not at first. But I don't have any dreams that night. Then Bob from the agency calls in the morning and says that Forever Insurance loves my work, but they don't have anything for me just now. He tells me about some other gig and I answer like a robot until I can get off the phone. Then I curl up and cry around the big empty space inside me. I wonder what used to fill it. My fingers find my wrist and I massage a sore spot, dully surprised that it hurts at all.

I get up to look at myself in the mirror and I look like I haven't slept for days. Bats could nest in the dark caves of my eye sockets. I wonder what Terese and Gerard would have seen in me, if they could see anything in me at all. The imagined touch of their hands thrills me for a moment, and I close my eyes, then open them and make myself head for the fridge. It wasn't real, none of it. I just have to get over them.

I'm insanely hungry this morning, for whatever reason. It's only after I rummage around for a while and the cold freezes my fingers that I realize that I'm supposed to remember last night as an elaborate fantasy. But what if it wasn't? Then I got used: a little blood, a little sex, and then put away like yesterday's news. The words hang there in my mind until I get good and pissed. *Who the hell do they think they are?* I wanted them to keep me, maybe even make me one of them, but what do they do instead but try to glamour it all right out of my head.

That night I will myself to sleep, thinking of nothing but my dream until I am back on the road. Nothing pursues me yet because no one knows I'm here. I lean against a tree in the dark, waiting, my own blood running freely down my legs. They will come, called to me by its rusty scent. My fingers toy with a small crucifix, then stroke the rough wood of the stake that I dream into being. They need a new employee at Forever Insurance. I just hope they can see that before I have to hurt them. Much.

PENCIL TRICK

by Tara Alton

I noticed my roommate, Madeline, and her girlfriend, Sean, were in the bathroom together.

Sean hadn't gone home the night before. They were topless in front of the sink, their breasts pressed together as they whispered in each other's ears. I felt a twinge between my legs. Hurrying back to my bedroom, I pulled out one of my ex-husband's magazines that I'd stolen from his drawer.

I had taken only a few things from him during the three brief years we were married. Mostly it was the porn and then it was the pencils. He was an architect and I always seemed to be borrowing his special pencils from his drafting board and not replacing them. I didn't do it intentionally. I needed something to write with and it was the most convenient place to find it. Then I would forget to replace it. So he bought me a fistful of pencils of my own to deter me from taking his. They were kid's pencils, printed with Hello Kitty and Barbie Pink. I was shocked. Not at the pencils themselves, but how he saw me as a child to be dealt with. After that, I still took some of his pencils occasionally, but I never used them. I hid them in my bottom drawer.

I know you must be thinking this doesn't sound like a healthy relationship, but in the beginning I liked to think it was. Everyone said we were mismatched. I even heard his mother saying once that I was more like a pet than a wife, and he would lose interest in me like he had lost interest in his golden retriever puppy who had lasted less than three months. I didn't believe her. We were in love.

I met him at the local IGA grocery store. I was a cashier and he was a professional businessman, slumming at a grimy little grocery store, looking for his childhood favorite banana flips, his one indulgence in his highly regimented lifestyle.

The first thing he asked me when I told him I wanted a divorce was if he could still come to the grocery store and get his flips.

That was where I had met Madeline—at the IGA. Before her Internet site took off she was working as a stock clerk. Now she painted pin-up girls, cigar-smoking bunnies, and sacred hearts on unconventional items like bowling pins and toilet seat covers and she sold them online.

Even at the store when she wore her smock, I had thought she looked gorgeous with her jet-black hair and blue eyes. She had an infectious smile and a twinkle in her eyes, and she came across as very wholesome and sweet. No one had any idea she liked girls, in a biblical manner, except for me. She had told me her last roommate had left because the bitch didn't like the sounds coming from her bedroom, and if I ever knew anyone who wouldn't be offended and needed a room to let her know.

After I broke up with my husband, I called Madeline. The room was still available.

Giggles came down the hall from the bathroom. I yearned to join the girls. Not wanting to look too obvious, I pulled on a fabulous skirt and a pair of high-heeled shoes, as if I were getting dressed and something had occurred to me. It wouldn't matter that I was naked from the waist up, my nipples exposed; we were all girls after all.

Digging out the handful of his architectural pencils from my bottom drawer, I paused in the doorway. I'd tried this trick once before and it had failed miserably. In an effort to get my husband's attention, I'd strolled naked into his office and did the pencil trick with one of his pencils. He didn't respond.

And yet he has all this porn, I thought later. His dick can't be dead.

His porn was mostly girls with girls. So I figured if he thought this was so wonderful, then maybe it was. I started checking out women in the grocery store, and I found this new world I'd never seen before, cleavage, camel toes, and tight-ass jeans. I started masturbating to his magazines when he wasn't home, leaving the pages sticky with my fingerprints. When we went out, I began to check out women right in front of him. He didn't notice.

Madeline and Sean noticed me right away in the bathroom doorway though. They broke apart from their nuzzling. Sean gave me a sly, wicked smile. She was a tall, leggy ash blond with a narrow rib cage and full breasts. Perpetually late for everything, she had been fired from her last three jobs. Madeline loved to brag how Sean used to be a lingerie model. Sean had even posed for a national biker magazine in a bikini on a Harley, but she had lost her career to her legendary temper, after having been jailed for road rage and missing a photo shoot for the final time.

Suddenly, I felt shy in front of her. She seemed so worldly, and I seemed so IGA.

"I was trying to decide what to wear with my skirt," I stammered. "And there's this top I like, but it looks better without a bra, but I'm not sure if I can get away with not wearing one."

I held up the pencils. "Have you heard that if you place a pencil beneath your naked breast and if it stays put, you're too large to forget the bra?" I asked.

I lifted my breast, stuck the pencil beneath it and let go. Their twin gazes on my breasts were lovely. My pencil hung precariously for a moment then fell to the floor.

"I've never done that," Madeline said. "Let me try it."

I was frozen in admiration as she lined up three pencils beneath her ample breasts.

With a wide smile she looked at Sean, who removed the pencils with an especially soft touch. Very sexy. I was getting moist. Then Madeline slid two pencils under each of Sean's breasts.

All this breast touching between them was creating some seriously aroused looks between them. Wonderful, I thought glumly.

They were getting all turned-on by each other. I was ready to go back to my bedroom when Madeline grabbed me by the elbow.

"I've got a thought," she said.

She lifted each of my breasts and Sean wedged the pencils in against my rib cage. Then Madeline gently pressed my breasts down. A thumb touched my nipple. I held my breath. Was it hot in here?

The single pencils stayed put until they slid the pencils out. I felt like a very sexy pencil holder at a girls' boarding school. I wanted to touch these girls, explore all their girlish curves and find out what made them moist, but nothing happened. There was an awkward silence. I had interrupted them after all.

"Well, I should finish getting dressed," I said. What I really meant was that I should go to my bedroom and masturbate.

"Wait a minute," Madeline said, glancing down at my feet. "I just love your shoes."

Both of them admired them.

"I have a lot more in the bedroom," I said.

We all traipsed into my room like it was a sleep-over, a bare-breasted sleep-over, but what was the point of putting on something now. When I had been married, I had been encouraged to buy a lot of shoes. Every time my husband did something wrong, I got a new pair. Every time I did something right, I got a new pair as well. Sometimes, it seemed like he was using the shoes like treats for a misbehaving puppy.

Madeline and Sean sat on the bed while I modeled several different pairs of shoes. I spun around. Hey, they weren't just looking at the shoes, I realized. I blushed.

"I know," Madeline said. "Why don't you take off your skirt, so we can see your legs better?"

"Okay," I said.

I took off the skirt. Thank God, I'd pulled on panties. Goose bumps raged across my skin. Could they see how wet I was?

"What about the underwear?" Sean asked, her eyebrow raised.

Here it was. The moment of truth. This had nothing to do

with the shoes. They wanted to look at me naked. I could do one of two things, tell them it was a big mistake or drop my drawers.

I pulled down my panties and stepped out of them.

Madeline clapped her hands.

"See I told you she was cool," she said to Sean.

Standing there naked, I felt a little like a nude Skipper doll waiting to see what the big girls were going to do to me.

"Now what?" I asked.

"Why don't you touch yourself?" Sean asked.

Feeling self-conscious, I slid my hand between my legs. My thumb grazed my erect clit, sending an electric charge across my thighs.

"Have you ever done this for a man?" Madeline asked.

I shook my head.

"I used to love playing with myself in front of guys," she said. "Now, it's even better with girls."

She beckoned me to join them on the bed. I sat between them. Madeline held my hand while Sean brushed my hair off my shoulder. My skin tickled with gooseflesh. Suddenly, I was very aware of how nude I was. They still had on their pajama bottoms. All I had on were the shoes. Feeling self-conscious again, I crossed my legs. It was one thing to stand naked in front of them, but sitting right next to them was totally different.

Lightly, Sean kissed my shoulder, her mouth leaving my skin hot.

"Come here," she said.

She patted her lap. Nervously, I straddled her, wondering if Madeline minded.

Apparently, she didn't. She was smiling. I looked down, realizing how exposed my crotch was. Sean started stroking my ass with soft fingers. I couldn't resist squirming under her touch. I wanted to grind myself against her stomach.

Her hands traveled up to my breasts where she took them in her hands and gave them a hard squeeze. I gasped.

"Put your arms in the air and stretch," she said.

Wondering why she would want me to do this, I did it anyway. My back arched. My breasts came forward, rising up in the air. She pinched my nipples hard, pulling on them until I cried out.

A slow, sly smile spread across her mouth as she let go.

Sliding back on the bed, she reclined like a goddess who knew exactly what she was doing. With a shake of her hair, she laid down and patted her sternum. Her breasts spread out, her long torso a smooth plain of sexy skin.

I was confused. I didn't know what she wanted. Was I supposed to kiss her there? I looked at Madeline for guidance.

"Scoot up," Madeline coached me.

Inching up, my pussy bumped her mound, then traveled along her stomach, her ribs. She had to know how wet I was at this point. I reached her sternum. Grabbing my ass, the soft fingers gone, she urged me forward to where I would be riding her face.

If I felt self-conscious before, now I felt totally exposed. She could see all my private business.

"I feel like a girl in a dirty magazine," I said.

"You're our porn star," Madeline said.

Suddenly, a wave of panic came over me.

"This is too quick," I said.

I was so nervous I was trembling. Sean's steel grip was barely keeping me steady.

"We'll go slower," Madeline offered.

She knelt in front of me. We kissed. I was amazed at what a good kisser she was. This was what her lovers had felt when they kissed her. No wonder they were crazy about her. Playful. Sexy. A cat lapping her tongue into my mouth.

As she touched my breasts, I got a chill. She kissed them, starting around the outside and moving inward with slow circles. Wetting the tip of her finger, she slowly touched the top of my nipple. Then, very lightly, she took her fingertips and squeezed my nipple between them. I gasped. Slowly, she brought her mouth down on my nipple. She sucked it in her mouth, flicking it with her amazing tongue.

Sean was fingering the crack of my ass. Everything was starting to feel like warm maple syrup. With soft kisses from her slightly parted lips, Sean approached my inner crease. She teased me,
licking all around it, never touching my pearl, sliding her tongue
upward, beside it, up over my clit hood, and down the opposite
side. I was in such sweet agony I could barely concentrate on what
Madeline was doing to my nipples.

Then using a wide, flat tongue, Sean slid it from my opening
to my clit, giving me a sensation that stole my breath away. I
gasped. Suddenly, she lightly nipped my hood and my clit, no
teeth, and sucked me into her mouth. I cried out. She let go.

Madeline brought her mouth back to mine, clenching my
breasts almost so hard they hurt. Sean buried her mouth between
my legs and began not just eating me out, but kissing me there like
she was kissing my mouth. I could feel myself swelling. I lifted my
hips to meet her next kiss. She lingered over a longer kiss and I
stuck to her like glue, pressing down on her mouth to keep the
contact.

Sean's tongue slid inside me while Madeline's tongue was back
in my mouth. It was overwhelming. Both of them were inside me
with their tongues. I felt Sean's hands relax on my hips. She
wasn't reaching for me anymore. She was letting me move on her.
She wasn't fucking me with her tongue. Rather, she was letting me
fuck her tongue with my pussy. I was doing it all, giving myself
pleasure by using her mouth.

I lifted my pelvis into the air with the tension of my rising
orgasm. My body grew rigid, my breath short. This wasn't my ex-
husband—even on his best night when we were first in love. This
wasn't anything near what I felt with those magazines where I got
myself really worked up. This wasn't my childhood bedpost. It felt
as if my heart was about to stop. Every muscle in my body tensed,
and the only thing I could focus on was the overwhelming pleasure that seemed to spread up from my toes to the rest of my body
as I cried out.

Shaken, I climbed off Sean. Giggling, the girls got up and

sauntered into Madeline's bedroom where they shut the door. I stretched out on my bed, more at peace and satisfied than I had ever been before. Finally, I had found myself.

If and when I managed to get up, I was going to go back into the bathroom and pick up the pencils from the floor. I was going to mail them to my ex-husband with a little note of thanks. Even if he didn't know what it meant, I would.

FREE FALL

by Holly Farris

Let's bungee naked."

Is Tom serious? Rebecca imagines which parts of her athletic body would torque (either uncomfortably or dangerously), then decides he will have more to fear.

"Your cock," she says, patting the swell in his khaki shorts like his club is hers to brandish. A maple-hard beauty, especially when they lie in their secret creek-side bed, Tom's cock has aimed toward wild grasses cradling the small of Rebecca's back more times than she can count. She never shies from outdoor adventure.

It was not always so. Midwinter, invited by her indifferent apartment-mates (girls who had lived off-campus several semesters), Rebecca was flattered to join them for happy hour. She should have been suspicious. Eighteen, and drunk from both alcohol and the rush that she hadn't been carded, Rebecca leaned against the wall in the dingy hallway outside the club's unisex bathroom. Pretending to read graffiti, she tried to recover her balance. She should have gotten drunker, instead of filling up on mozzarella sticks a skinny waitress had carried to the table. Tom was yanking his fly, arranging his balls inside tight jeans, when he came out the bathroom door.

"Next," he said. Tom's next.

Without saying a word, he brushed his hard chest over Rebecca's unfocused eyes and flushed cheeks, snarling her hair on his white shirt's middle button. When she didn't move, and with his big hands curled into fists at his sides, he lifted his right leg slightly and rocked his pelvis slam-bam to the music. A male dog lifting his leg, marking territory.

"You're nasty," Rebecca had said.

"And you're fat," he said. "Which is worse?"

A thinner girl would have left Tom, blue balls, and risk, right there. A fatter girl wouldn't have had the pleasure of walking away.

Rebecca lay on his smelly sheets, washed in the bathtub without soap powder, shedding virginity an hour after she saw him. Up until summer, she ate and was eaten—who knew the term meant sex?—even after her friends revealed they had set up the encounter, made a wager with him to deflower her. Unknown to Rebecca, Tom was a virgin with women. He preferred men whose sexual appetites were unformed, the quick impersonal contact.

Rebecca was embarrassed to have her physical self known by her roommates and him, but it was a body unease she'd always felt. She was used to keeping corporal secrets, especially from herself. Scratchy pills on Tom's cheap cotton bedding became a comfort, and she fretted about whether he would answer the door when she knocked. One afternoon, Tom was restless. Rebecca had sucked him off twice.

They wandered in a Kmart, where the women, all fatter than Rebecca, shopped for halter-tops and sandals. Tom cut through this section, veering past children's toys, avoiding office supplies. He walked ahead to a destination. Where departments intersected, Tom handled plastic off the shelf.

"I want this," he said.

It was an eyeball. A liquid center floated a blue iris inside the case, plastic that locked a gaze on Rebecca. Its precisely drawn black pupil was permanently dilated, and the package sloshed when Tom tore off the wrapping. He forced her fingers around it, and it was surprisingly heavy, like his erections. Clear letters at the globe's equator said MADE IN TAIWAN, very blocky and formal, and INSPECTOR 69. Tom pointed and whooped too loudly in the store, laughing after she got the 69 joke.

"I want this," he said again.

"Need money?" she had said, unimpressed with the thing, wanting to leave.

Tom turned sideways to Rebecca, appearing to lose interest. "Take it," he said, hissing while she hid their damage behind other still-boxed eyes on the shelf. "I'm gone."

Rebecca didn't remember whether the eye went into her bra, down her panties, or up her cunt. Breathing fast in the parking lot, with the smooth egg glued to skin covered by clothes, she offered it to Tom like a trophy. "Throw it away," he said. She left it on top of the microwave at her apartment. Her roommates, sympathetic to Tom's need to drive this woman away, had thought up the challenge.

Rebecca melted forty pounds, carving room between her body's perimeter and her clothing, the better to hide Tom's stolen trinkets. As she toned, she craved exercise outdoors, away from his bed and merchandise. It was she who had tempted him into public sex along the trails. He urged her to try jumping.

"Afraid I'll break my cock?" he taunts after suggesting today's naked jump. He fingers the chinstrap on her helmet, which he holds. "I want this." He means adrenaline, from an escapade Rebecca is sure to dread.

Thinking how the wind will part for them on the catwalk of the old water tower, he is hard. Cool air—light like the back of her hand, caressing his wiry crotch, his flat belly—is the least he's due.

Tom can be cruel, though never uninspired. He often makes Rebecca wait, and beg, for him when juice slicks her suntanned thighs. Often, he pushes into her before she's ready, and before he licks her, liking how she chafes. Rebecca, he decides, should suffer: ass gooseflesh and cold-puckered nipples on the tower, before he rewards her up there.

He parts weeds at the bottom of rusty steps notching the tower. Pulling her down over his prone middle, he unzips. He yanks her nylon shorts' leg opening wider, then angles his cock into her slit. The new Rebecca never wears panties.

This late September afternoon, she's a wet tunnel of flesh, slippery against his. Her pubic hair tangles him before he moves. She is bark surrounding a sensitive core. He squints past Rebecca's rocking shoulder, trying to count ladder rungs, delay the spurt that fills her.

She's not disappointed he can't last. They roll apart, avoiding a flowering thistle they hadn't noticed. Its purple phallus hums with bees.

"Tired?" he asks, and she listens for a contest.

"More hiking?" she proposes, a challenge of her own, hoping they'll stop at another secluded spot. Tom is already standing, brushing leaves stuck to his elbows. He turns his back to her so she can dust off his T-shirt shoulders. She's surprised when he puts on his helmet.

"Enough hiking," he says. "Ready to climb?" He ruffles her short hair in a way she resents. Just when she thinks she'll move out of his reach, he hands her the other helmet. When she puts it on, he snaps her chinstrap gently. He kisses her cheek. She wishes she smelled herself on his lips, a lingering sign he hadn't fucked so hastily.

"I'll go ahead," he says gallantly, pointing at the first rung up from the ground. Studying from her angle, Rebecca notices the dented metal tower flares at the top. In fact, the tiny deck connecting shaft and bulb reminds her of Tom's circumcised ridge.

Tom has climbed several steps when Rebecca is glad he has gone ahead. She had not wanted to climb naked, though jumping will be all right. She would be happier had they hooked themselves to the ladder with harnesses, but she sees all the safety equipment they need snaked over Tom's strong arms, crisscrossing his chest. Rebecca begins to climb, ignoring small clods of dirt Tom's hiking-boot treads kick into her hair.

Whether it's nerves or the fact that the sky has clouded, Rebecca, who should be sweating, is suddenly cold. She tells him, wondering if he will send her down. "We're close," he says about the deck, and she has her answer.

The platform feels like solid land after what they've done to reach it; she's confident it is sturdy. When they sit in their tiny, high camp to rest, Tom offers his sweatshirt. They laugh together, now that they are to get naked.

"What I'd do for a beer!" Tom says, wiping sweat from his grime-streaked forearms.

Rebecca shivers; the sun is drastically lower. She wonders at the hour, thinks they should have planned more carefully. She knows they must strip before attaching the thick ropes and guides, and she's reluctant to be so exposed. Trying to keep up with Tom's plan, she shucks off her shorts, and slingshots her sports bra off a rotted section of railing. These are Rebecca's only other clothes, because she peeled her hot boots and socks off to celebrate reaching the top. Tom turns his naked back to her, denying her a frontal view. His cock dangles, dark and shriveled by the cold. She sees this in the split his ass makes when he crouches. His boots and socks are still on, for he will climb up when they're done and detach their last rope moorings, then climb back to her. She'll watch from the ground.

After fastening the hitch, Tom rocks on his heels, arranging rope on the wooden platform. He stands, then steps into the sling he's fashioned, intending the complicated net to absorb the shock at the most downward point of their jump. They never use ankle cuffs. Rebecca does the same with a second set he's made, hating that she must give up his sweatshirt tied around her tits. Her leg muscles quiver, probably from the climb.

Rebecca feels Tom spoon against her back. His chinstrap scratches her neck, and their helmets clack when he tries to chew her ear. One of his hands holds all their ropes, and Rebecca thinks of a bride with an attendant lifting her train. She feels his free hand, rolling his limp cock against her ass. She fears losing her balance, until he quits touching himself and holds her roughly around the waist. He cranks her forward, intending to enter her right on the ledge. She wonders if she can distract him enough to forget the jump, but he is miserably soft.

"Fucking," he says, his voice behind her a strangle. "I want to jump fucking."

Rebecca needs to get wet for him. His guiding arm leaves her waist, but she cannot know why. From the ropes he's managing, Tom slips a noose he's fashioned over his head, tightens it against his jaw. She assumes he tries to arouse himself, and it works, for he is suddenly huge. He drives between her upper thighs, teasing her cunt. Glad-cum trails over her ass cheeks; he pokes a liquid tip at the hole. His club bobs, the most polished, inanimate, it has ever been. When he slams so much inside her, she gasps.

Two strokes later, Rebecca and Tom, still joined, maneuver her delicate toes over the edge. He ruts and bellows, stretching her as he continues to grow.

"Now," Rebecca rasps, the cue they employ. He hurls them away from the tower. They're flying, and Tom approaches the perfect thrill.

AWKWARD CONFESSIONS

by Debra Hyde

When you wake to a hand clutching your breast and a morning erection pressing into your backside, the last thing you notice is dappled sunlight, birdsong, and a dog's barking. This morning, like countless mornings before it, I rolled over to meet him, meeting his broad, unmistakable smile with my blurred, sleepy sight.

"Know what was best about last night?" His voice sounded naughty and conspiratorial.

"What?" I croaked, morning hoarseness. I stretched and tried to put my leg over him. I couldn't; I was still chained to the end of the bed.

"Throwing the blanket over you and just leaving you there when I finished with you."

Finished with you. I shivered at the sound of those words. Martin had, after all, used me, deliciously and selfishly, and when he finished pumping every last drop of his desire into me, he had tossed the blanket over my bound, spread-eagle form and simply left me there.

A pulse of arousal shot from between my legs at the memory of it.

"That worked for me too," I admitted sheepishly.

Martin kissed me, softly, gently. Last night, his kisses had been rough and determined, brutish even.

"So what did you think when I did that?" he asked.

Did that—my body bound and immovable, nipples burning, newly freed from those biting nipple clamps he likes, him dripping from me, and all of it rendered anonymous by a blanket.

Describing it to Martin, though, was another matter. I stumbled for the right words.

"Hot. Objectified. Kind of *I've been used.*"

"You were used."

Used. As simple as that. Martin's hand was matter-of-fact as he slipped it between my legs and squeezed me there as casually as he might plant a peck on my cheek.

"I daydreamed for awhile and then I napped, I think."

"Ah, so you did nap. Good! Maybe now you'll shake that jet lag."

"Maybe."

But I wouldn't shake something else off quite so easily. My daydream had taken me places that I loathed acknowledging, and I didn't like the lingering humiliation it had left me with.

Martin released me from his clutch and began playing with me. He teased my labia apart and wiggled a finger into me, into my last-night slickness. He brushed other fingers over my clit, lightly, just enough to get my attention, just enough to arouse me. He dipped down to my breasts and sucked a nipple into his mouth.

I moaned; I couldn't help it. Something about the tug on my nipples made me instantly ready.

Martin noticed, let go, and laughed.

"So what did you daydream about?"

Damn! He had me! A subtler form of interrogation the CIA couldn't have invented if it tried.

As good as it felt, did I really want Martin's touch this morning? Did I really want his attentions if they meant revealing my thoughts to him?

Would it make any difference anyway? He could, if he wanted to, tease it out of me and I knew that fighting him would only make matters worse. The last time I resisted, Martin wore me down by making me come so many times, my clit hurt.

True to form, Martin put a finger to my clit and caressed me. "Tell me," his whisper invited. Timidly, I attempted to refuse him through my only recourse, whining. "You'll laugh when I tell you."

He shrugged, uncaring, and returned to my breast. More arousal. Jet-lagged still, I surrendered without a fuss, reasoning that I had to save what little energy I had for something other than an early-morning erotic smack-down.

"Well, it was years ago. It happened years ago. My parents had made plans to visit some friends at the lake, and I asked if my boyfriend and I could follow them in his car. They said sure. I guess they were surprised that I wanted to go on a family outing for a change, even if it was with the boyfriend in tow."

Martin's finger pursued me at a steady pace but I could, for the moment, talk over it.

"Anyway, we went, we swam, we visited—and the whole time, my boyfriend and I leered at each other. We got all hot and bothered, and it got so intense that we just had to escape the parental units and go fuck somewhere. We 'decided' to take a walk but what we really did was hustle off into the woods, strip down just enough to do it, and fuck like bunnies."

My clit was starting its own dialogue with Martin at this point and I had to keep it to "just the facts, ma'am" to fight its growing distraction. I remembered the boyfriend fucking me.

"He had a skinny cock. Matched his toothpick body. But, boy he could jackhammer me, and doing it in the woods really made it raunchy. We left condom litter behind."

I remembered the boyfriend squeezing the come from the reservoir of the condom so it went up his dick before he pulled it off. I remembered kneeling before his glistening, drooping dick and putting my tongue to it and then my mouth around it.

The memory made me moan and arch towards Martin. I wanted to fuck, not talk. Martin, however, had other plans. He stopped sucking and probed me with something akin to Twenty Questions.

"How old were you?"

His question leered at me every bit as much as his eyes. Both were so indelicate, they embarrassed me.

"Were you . . . barely legal?"

"I wasn't jailbait!"

I spat the word and then resorted to name-calling. "Pervert! Reprobate! Sleaze!" I sputtered into silence, too soon out of options.

"You forgot chauvinist. So, that's it? You fucked like bunnies?"

I whimpered timidly again. What came next was what I couldn't bear to reveal.

"Tell me."

This time, Martin wasn't whispering. He pressed his hand flat against my cunt, palm to clit, fingers about my labia and slit. His grope was encompassing and controlling, and I knew he could do any number of things with it: grab and squeeze me, pinch my lips between his fingers until I screamed and squirmed, or swiftly work me to climax.

I was lucky. He chose Option Three and I chose to conclude my story. Better to confess, even if it made me feel like a dry-humping slut all over again.

"We left before my parents did and, on the way home, we started talking about how hot fucking in the woods was. I got horny all over again. My boyfriend started jerking me off in the car."

Just like you're doing now, I pouted silently. My cunt throbbed in agreement, thrilled and exuberant even as it colluded against me.

"We were really going at it. It was wild—we were driving along, me riding his hand, all hot and bothered and about to come. Then, I looked into the rearview mirror."

I paused and tried to lose myself in Martin's hand. I didn't want to go on, at least not verbally.

"Go on."

I moaned and humped his hand harder.

"No. With your story."

"No," I pleaded.

"Yes," he demanded. He pinched my labia between his fingers. "Yes," he reiterated.

My labia burned in his grip, and the words I didn't want to share knotted in my throat.

"Go on."

Burned, they burned, my labia, my throat.

"I saw . . ."

"Yes?"

Inside, I screamed, "Let go!" Outwardly I babbled, "I saw . . . I saw . . ."

Martin pinched even harder and my resolve broke. The lump in my throat burst like a dam and the pinnacle of my confession spilled out.

"I saw my parents pull up behind us in their car! They were waving at us!"

Martin released me and burst out laughing.

Who wouldn't? I mean, my parents had pulled a fast one on us: They'd taken a shortcut and headed us off at the proverbial pass. Came up on us just as I was ready to hit the ceiling!

"They caught you jerking off! Oh, for Pete's sake!"

I groaned in embarrassment and tried to push myself hard into Martin's hand, wanting to forget.

"Not yet," he said, and he actually took his hand away. "Did they realize what you were up to?"

"Amazingly, no. My older sister did though."

"Ms. Femme Dyke herself? She was with them?"

"Yeah and, boy, was she furious. She was so offended to catch me jerking off with a boy that she glowered at me for a week. I died a million times over."

"I'm sure."

Martin's empathy was, at best, limited. After all, he liked my embarrassment; that's why he diddled with my mind. Still, it didn't seem like too much to ask for absolution, so I spread my legs and begged, "Fuck me?"

It was an invitation ripe for an RSVP. Martin rolled over onto me and slipped in. He grabbed one of my tits, then took me with the same frenzy that my boyfriend had displayed those many years ago.

His pounding was just what I needed. I needed him to over-whelm me, to take me with such force that I could clench and come and then go mindless. I wanted mad, ravenous sex to ravage and soil me and make me sore.

Oblivion . . . I wanted it so badly. And I got it so good that I barely knew when Martin came.

Sadly, though, oblivion between the sheets is fleeting. Always, it passes too soon, fading when afterglow sets in or when one of you gets up to take a piss. Martin was already on his feet.

"Let me up?" I ventured.

"Think again."

He threw the blanket over me.

At first, I lay there stunned, senseless, but then, the double entendre of his words hit me. Did I really have to endure this maddening exercise yet again? Couldn't he hike the blanket high enough to fuck me now, again, before my thoughts set in? After all, access to my cunt is so much more enjoyable than access to my mind. At least for me, it is.

But not for Martin, apparently. He wanted more memories, more embarrassing confessions to tease his dick. And when the image of two dykes in the alley behind a pizza parlor where I once worked came to me, I knew he wouldn't be disappointed.

A priceless incident, I had spotted them kissing and groping each other and I froze on the spot, bug-eyed and clutching a bag of garbage. I didn't even have the common decency to drop the trash in shock.

"Watcha staring at, bitch?" the bull dyke had demanded.

"Maybe she likes to watch," her partner observed.

Butch snorted and raised Femme's skirt, exposing ass, pussy, and no panties. She brought the girl off right there in front of me. As the girl bleated through a noisy, wet orgasm, I fled, trying to escape that which I was drawn to.

"What, you don't want a turn?" Butch yelled after me. "Ungrateful bitch!"

"Coward!"

Only later, when that word echoed in beat with my pounding heart, did I realize that I had hurled that last insult at myself.

Oh yes, Martin's going to love this one, no doubt about it. But I won't. I'll have to confess to yet another lurid incident, and I'll have to squirm and suffer all over again. And when the ache of embarrassment grows too strong, I'll pray for oblivion.

Dykes. Pussy. *Coward!*

Oblivion, senseless oblivion. I'm going to need it.

THE PING-PONG VAMPIRE

by Janice Eidus

Unless you travel in certain circles, I'm sure you've never heard of me. But not too long ago, I did have a pretty big reputation in my field. In those days, I wrote treatises on sports and games. My best-known book was *The Semiotics of Softball*. Whenever I was asked why, as a female, I'd been drawn to the world of sports, I answered that there was a hidden language in sports just ripe for decoding. I compared myself to an Egyptologist, obsessively deciphering ancient drawings. I spoke of a love of language, of a burning desire to unearth the hidden meanings of symbols, the buried subtexts of texts.

But that was all a big fat lie. The truth, which I never told anyone, was that I had a thing about jocks. I just loved their sweaty, mesomorphic, hunky bodies—their tight butts, thick necks, and muscular thighs. This is one of the dreams I used to have back then: I'm standing in the middle of the male locker room after a game. The smell of victory is in the air. The guys are all naked, swinging their towels around, smacking each other jubilantly on their buns. I'm wearing only a black, lacy garter belt, black stockings, and black high heels. I'm delirious from the odor of soiled jockstraps, wet towels, and sweaty flesh. Then, jock after jock flings me down on the locker-room bench and makes love to me. They all follow exactly the same athletic rhythm, as though there's been a huddle beforehand. They're gentle, they're rough, and then they're gentle again. And, together, we score a mutual touchdown.

Believe me, I knew that these dreams really were all about my submitting to a bunch of insensitive brutes. But I felt entitled to whatever fantasy life I wanted. Since sexual fantasies, like myths and fairy tales, were a part of the collective unconscious, why should I be held singularly accountable for dreams shared by so many women?

In real life, though, I had nothing in common with the jocks. In high school, I once overheard Davey Smith, the captain of the football team, say to Petey Grofer, the quarterback, "Rowena Ardsley? She's got no tits, no legs. She's a walking encyclopedia, that one." Petey Grofer laughed, and the nickname took. I became known as The Walking Encyclopedia, a nickname I rather liked. Mostly, I stayed home alone, worrying about what I would do for a living when I got out of school, how I would reconcile my braininess with my fantasies of jocks.

❧   ❧   ❧

In college, though, things fell into place: I began writing term papers in which I deconstructed the games that the jocks played. My professors were impressed, not having any idea that for me, writing those papers was like writing erotic prose, that it was a sensual experience. At night, before I fell asleep, I read my own papers aloud to myself, and then I dreamed my locker-room dreams all night long.

I wasn't unattractive. I had nice features, and thick red hair that I kept pinned-up in a bun. I wore classic, tortoise-shell eyeglasses. I had a quiet beauty, like the prim, bespectacled nurse in that old movie *The Interns*. The one who, during the hospital's Christmas party, removes her eyeglasses, lets down her hair, and reveals herself as a wild sexpot. Really, though, I didn't have any desire to do the same. Except in my dreams, of course, which I took no responsibility for.

After graduate school, I became a college teacher. A few years later, I was awarded tenure. Then, out of the blue, I was invited to take a year off from teaching to become a member of The Sports, Games, and Toys Institute, a brand-new think tank located somewhere in the mountains of North Carolina. The Institute was a purely commercial venture. A group of scientists, scholars, doctors, artists, and journalists would all live together for a year in a large house. A staff would serve us our meals and clean our rooms. We would be paid a large stipend. All we were being asked to do was to invent as many new games, toys, and sports-related items as we could, all of which were intended to become huge money-makers for Game-i-Con, the conglomerate that was sponsoring the Institute. Game-i-Con was desperate to compete with the Japanese, who, rumor had it, were about to enter the sports, games, and toys industry with the same fervor with which they'd previously entered the electronics industry.

I hesitated to accept the offer. I was used to my quiet life: teaching, writing books, dreaming about jocks. I didn't even attend sports events in person. I watched them on TV instead, because I was too afraid of losing my self-control. I certainly didn't have the slightest desire to go off and live with a bunch of strangers. But my department chairman loved the idea. He thought it would be prestigious, and he pressured me to accept. So, reluctantly, I packed my bags, and I flew down south. I fell asleep on the plane, and the entire way there I dreamed of garter belts and jockstraps.

❧   ❧   ❧

To my surprise, though, I settled in quickly to life at the Institute. There were fifteen of us altogether: eight men and seven women, all unmarried and childless, each of us a specialist, each obsessed with our own particular specialty. I hadn't been the only one in that group who'd been known as The Walking Encyclopedia back in high school.

Days at the Institute were easy and routine. We spent the

mornings brainstorming around the long marble table in the conference room on the main floor. Then, after lunch, we'd break up into committees. I was on The Language Committee. Our goal was to come up with new, catchy names for old games, in order to convince people that the old games were brand-new.

After dinner, we'd break up into various groups and entertain ourselves for the rest of the evening. I joined the ping-pong group. We would head downstairs to the musty basement where there was a wobbly ping-pong table. None of us knew how to slam the ball, or even how to put spin on it, and so we'd play a few non-competitive, unathletic games.

Finally, after ping-pong, I'd climb up those steep stairs to my bedroom. I'd change into my flimsy white nightgown, and I'd lie in bed and read aloud excerpts from my own books, until, in a kind of erotic reverie, I'd fall asleep, and I'd dream my dreams of submission and domination in the locker room.

ᕦ   ᕦ   ᕦ

After about three months of this routine, Game-i-Con's CEO—who dropped by periodically for progress reports—announced that a new member was coming to the Institute. None of us were thrilled by his news. We were a pretty stodgy bunch, not the sort who welcomed change.

The new member's name, we were told by the CEO, was Byron Ravage. He was a ping-pong champion. He was also a poet, and he had written a book called *The Ping-Pong Poems*. "Byron Ravage is a true Renaissance man," the CEO said, passing around a glossy headshot of a brooding man with shiny black hair to his shoulders. He wore mirrored, aviator-shaped sunglasses with metal frames. His lips were thin, angry lines. He looked skinny and tense, wired to explode.

I took an instant dislike to the face in that photo. He didn't look like the rest of us. He looked too cool, or too hip, or whatever. His ping-pong poems were probably sloppy little verses, not at all rigorous. This was not the face of a man who could compose a sonnet or a sestina. I wasn't impressed.

Lucas Smith, who was known for his invention of a Frankenstein doll that made terrifying guttural sounds, also seemed to take an instant dislike to Byron Ravage's photo. Lucas, who was religious, began fingering the cross around his neck, and muttering something that sounded like, "And so, the beast returns," but I couldn't be sure.

All I knew for sure was that I wasn't looking forward to Byron Ravage's arrival. I hoped that he wasn't going to volunteer to be on The Language Committee. I also hoped that he wouldn't join our tepid little ping-pong group. Maybe, instead, he would join the group that watched the evening news on TV. Or the group—which included Lucas Smith—that watched films every night on the VCR. Or the group that drank themselves into a stupor, night after night, in front of the fireplace in the living room. Or, perhaps, best of all, he'd keep to himself.

❧   ❧   ❧

Just as I feared, after Byron Ravage's arrival, the atmosphere changed. First of all, his physical presence was unnerving: he always wore those off-putting, nasty-looking mirrored sunglasses, and he always dressed in black. What had been such a pleasant atmosphere became an unpleasant, sexually charged one. Helenska, for example, a fortyish blonde who was an illustrator of sports figures, began dressing in low-cut sequined gowns. Quite frankly, I'd never thought that Helenska was really brainy enough for the Institute, and now I was certain of it. And Gertrude, a retired German scientist, began telling bawdy jokes in a loud voice at mealtimes.

Helenska and Gertrude, and all of the other women as well, wanted to go to bed with Byron Ravage. Their lust for him embarrassed me. I never fantasized about him. He was no jock. Ping-pong was just too namby-pamby a game for my taste. A little green table, a little white ball, a little low net. Why, anyone could play ping-pong! Even *I* could get the ball over the net now and then. I didn't believe that Byron Ravage would have had the strength to throw me down on a locker-room bench if he *wanted* to.

The men at the Institute, unlike the women, all seemed to hate him. On sight and instinctively. As though he were some sort of threat to them. Lucas Smith, for instance, always gnashed his teeth, muttered under his breath, and fingered his cross whenever Byron walked by.

I assured myself, though, that neither the women's lust, nor the men's hatred, had anything to do with me. I didn't like the man, sure, but what was the big deal? I would just keep on thinking up new names for old games. I hadn't had much success, though. All I'd come up with were Pockethole Ball for Nok Hockey, and Netracket for Tennis.

One night before dinner, a couple of weeks after he'd arrived, Byron Ravage announced that he would give a poetry reading that evening. I'd pretty much avoided him up until that point. I never sat at his table at mealtimes. And, luckily, he hadn't joined The Language Committee. In fact, he'd told everyone he wanted to wait a bit before he decided upon a committee. Which, I think, relieved all the men, and disappointed all the other women. Also, he'd proved to be a loner, which meant that I could stick to my nightly routine of a few tepid games of ping-pong. I really didn't want to break up my routine to attend his little performance. But finally I decided it would be too rude not to.

After dinner, Byron, wearing his mirrored sunglasses, a pair of tight black jeans, and a black sweater, pulled up a chair for himself in front of the fire. The men gathered in a group, pulling their chairs close together, way in the back, as far from Byron as possible. They gnashed their teeth, muttered, and frowned a lot. Lucas Smith chomped ferociously on a cigar, although I'd never seen him smoke before.

All of the women, except for me, gathered together in a cluster on the rug. They sat as close as possible to Byron, without actually climbing into his lap. They preened, sighed, rolled their eyes, licked their lips, and smiled seductively at him. Helenska wore her lowest-cut gown yet, a pink, frothy, floor-length affair. Gertrude had put a blue rinse in her hair, and was wearing pearls around her neck.

I sat in the middle, between the two groups, on the rug, resting my head on my knees. I felt apart and separate from both groups, almost as though, at that moment, I was neither male nor female. Nor human at all. As though I belonged to some whole other species. And, just when I had that thought, I looked up and saw Byron Ravage staring right at me, with such an intense look that I had the strange sensation that he was reading my mind. And that he approved of what he read.

"I'm not going to read from *The Ping-Pong Poems*," Byron spoke in a smooth, velvety voice, turning his attention away from me. He skillfully managed to make eye contact with each and every one of us while he spoke, working the room like an old Las Vegas pro. "Since I think you all need a break from sports metaphors," he grinned, "I'm going to read a poem of mine that has no need for metaphors at all." He began to recite an old-fashioned ballad about a woman with blue eyes, dark hair, and bright red lips, and how this woman meets a mysterious stranger who dresses all in black and has glimmering white teeth, which he eventually sinks into the skin of her long neck, and how both of them are then transformed into eternal, vampire lovers. There was one catchy stanza that he kept reciting throughout: *Vampire/Do It/Bite Me/Delight Me/Vampire/Do It/Bite Me/Excite Me.*

When he finished, Helenska and Gertrude were both weeping. Their faces and collarbones were bright red and flushed, and their eyes were glassy. The men were all staring down at their feet and muttering and frowning. Lucas Smith looked as though he were going to choke on his cigar.

I stood up and clapped politely, surprised by what an old-fashioned poet Byron Ravage had turned out to be. Then, without looking at anyone, including Byron Ravage, I climbed those steep stairs to my bedroom. I got into my white nightgown, I lay in bed, and I began reading my own work aloud. But for the first time ever, I felt restless, as though I needed more than the sound of my own voice to turn me on. I didn't fall asleep until well past midnight. And instead of dreaming about jocks in the locker room, I dreamed about vampire lovers in long black capes who made wild love to me on the tops of ping-pong tables.

In the morning, I was amazed at the effect that Byron Ravage's poem had had on me. I grew more determined than ever to avoid him, and to concentrate exclusively on my work for The Language Committee. In fact, I decided what I would do next would be to invent a new name for Ping-Pong. A name that Byron Ravage wouldn't like.

❧   ❧   ❧

A few weeks later, at breakfast, Byron Ravage made two more announcements. First, he said, looking right at me, he'd decided that he wanted to join The Language Committee. And, second, he said, still looking right at me, he wanted to play ping-pong in the evenings.

Well, I thought, I would simply resign from The Language Committee. No, that would be too obvious. Besides, I'd grown obsessed with trying to come up with a new name for Ping-Pong, a name that would change the meaning of the game forever. None of the names I'd come up with fit. Not Back 'n' Forth Ball, not Slam-Spin Ball, and certainly not Little White Ball.

But, as it turned out, Byron Ravage was so silent during The Language Committee meetings that I really had no need to quit. He sat apart from the rest of us, his legs stretched out in front of him. He didn't seem to care a twit about inventing new toys, games, and sports-related items for Game-i-Con. Still, sometimes I had the uneasy sensation that he was watching me.

I did, however, stop playing ping-pong. Soon after, I began hearing rumors that the games had changed, that Byron encour-

aged people to play for money, and that one night he even insti-
gated a "strip" ping-pong game.

So I joined the VCR crowd instead. Lucas Smith was more or
less in charge of the movie selection. He was a horror-movie buff,
with a lifelong fascination for vampire movies. Among the films
we watched were Bela Lugosi's scary *Dracula*, Andy Warhol's
tongue-in-cheek *Dracula*, and Frank Langella's moody *Dracula*.
Although I liked Bela's version best, Lucas seemed to prefer Frank
Langella's version. He took copious notes while he watched it.
But it was much too dreamy and romantic for my taste. Also, I
didn't like the fact that Miss Lucy was still madly in love with
Dracula at the end. That just didn't seem right. Naturally, whenever I watched those blood-sucking Count Draculas on the VCR
screen, I couldn't help but think of Byron Ravage, and of the
poem he'd read to us, and of the way he'd looked at me that night
by the fireplace. Not that I believed that Byron Ravage was a
vampire. What I believed was this: just as the collective unconscious was filled with our sexual fantasies, it was filled, too, with
our fantasies about monsters and demons. I simply wondered
what it was in Byron Ravage's particular psychological make-up
that had inspired him to write a poem about two vampire lovers.
That was all.

Then, one night, Helenska and Gertrude, who had both
joined the ping-pong crowd after Byron began playing, appeared
in the doorway of the VCR room. They stood there silently for a
moment, staring right at me. We were watching a humorous film
that night, about a bunch of rich, snotty teenagers in L.A. who
became vampires. I was in a pretty good mood, because just that
morning, I'd come up with what I thought was a halfway decent
name for Volleyball: Smash.

"Rowena, come downstairs and play ping-pong with us,"
Gertrude said imperiously, touching the shimmering pearls
around her neck.

"Byron wants to play with you, Rowena," Helenska added in

a shaky voice. I remembered hearing some rumors that she'd recently been ill.

"Yes, he requested *you*, Rowena, specifically." Gertrude's voice was unfriendly.

Lucas Smith was staring intensely at me, as though the decision I was about to make—whether or not to play ping-pong with Byron Ravage—was the most momentous decision I would ever make in my entire life. Although I didn't want to play, I also didn't think there was any reason for Lucas to stare at me like that. He was annoying me so much that I said, "Sure, I'll play." Lucas fingered his cross and turned away from me. But before he turned away, I saw both sorrow and anger in his eyes.

I closed the door to the VCR room behind me, and I followed Helenska and Gertrude down the stairs to the basement. Helenska, who was wearing a garish green gown and golden pumps on her feet, really did look ill. She was pale, and her hands shook. I remembered more details from the recent rumors about her: She'd been playing much too much ping-pong with Byron Ravage; she'd been running a fever; she had no appetite; she experienced mysterious, asthma-like attacks during which she gasped desperately for air.

When I got downstairs, Byron was standing in an arrogant pose, leaning his bony hip against the corner of the ping-pong table. He smiled at me with those thin, mean-looking lips.

"I want you to know, Mr. Ravage," I said, "that I'm not interested in playing for money, or in stripping."

"Ah, Rowena Ardsley," he said, in a humble voice, "how you misread my intentions. I simply want to play a good game of ping-pong with you."

Helenska and Gertrude stood together at the side of the table, watching us. They looked at Byron with adoration. They looked at me with distrust. Helenska appeared to be growing weaker and weaker.

The game began. Immediately, it became apparent that not only would I lose, but that I would lose without scoring a single point. Byron was the King of Ping-Pong. He was merciless. He played like a savage, like a man possessed. His mirrored sunglasses glittered. He was everywhere. He was a wall, returning my every shot. He was a military strategist, playing to all my weaknesses, forcing me to run around the table in a way I'd never run before. He smashed the ball so hard it ricocheted around the room. When he put spin on the ball, it spun so fast it became nearly invisible. He smiled cruelly each time he scored a point. He insisted on playing game after game with me. And I had no will to resist him.

At around eleven o'clock, Helenska felt too ill to remain downstairs in the musty ping-pong room. She asked Gertrude to help her climb those steep stairs to the second floor. Although Gertrude gave Byron one final glance of regret, she agreed to help Helenska. They'd developed some sort of sisterly bond, it seemed, in their shared lust for Byron Ravage.

And then I was alone with him, with no audience. And no protection, either, I realized. I was sweating and flushed.

Slowly, with great deliberation, he walked toward me, holding his paddle in his hand. I wondered if he were going to hit me with it. Instead, he laid it down very gently on the tabletop, and he placed his hands on my shoulders. His sunglasses were glowing. I wanted to look away from him, to break free of what I knew was the riveting gaze behind those glasses. But I couldn't. "I've been waiting for you for a long, long time, Rowena Ardsley," he said. "Longer than you can imagine. You are special. You are the one I've wanted. Helenska," he spat out the name, "is nothing to me. I will suck her dry of her essence and then simply turn her into one of the ordinary Undead. Women like Helenska are a dime a dozen, easily seduced, easily bitten, easily discarded. And when I'm through with Helenska, perhaps I'll move on to Gertrude. And then to the others." He smiled. "It's true, I'm a bit of a compulsive biter, but I've really had no choice. It's been all about survival. Nevertheless," he said, seductively, eyeing first my breasts, and then my neck, "I know that you, Rowena Ardsley—dreamer of jockstraps and garter belts, semiotician of the locker room—are unique. And so you shall be my equal, my match. I shall not dominate you, except when we both *want* me to, of course. And you shall not dominate me, except when we both want *you* to. In other words, as a species apart, we are free to defy all the old, standard, boring formulas for love and romance. Do you understand?" He waited for my response.

Well, I ask you, what's a girl to do at a moment like that? Because suddenly I believed both in vampires and true love. I nodded my head.

"Then it's settled," he said. "I claim you, Rowena Ardsley. You and I shall play ping-pong together for all the centuries to come."

And, before I could do or say a thing, he leaned forward and sank his sharp teeth into my neck. And I would be lying to you if I said that, even for one second, I tried to resist.

❧　❧　❧

I don't remember much about the few days after that. I spent them in a delirious, feverish haze. I do remember, though, that I lay drenched in sweat on my bed, wearing only my flimsy white nightgown, and that I kept dreaming about making love to Byron Ravage on top of the Institute's ping-pong table. In my dreams I wore nothing but a black garter belt, and he wore nothing but a long black cape.

I also remember that, at one point, Helenska entered my room and stood over me, her face a ghastly white, her teeth sharpened to fanglike points, with fresh, thick blood dripping from her mouth. And I remember her saying, "Why did he choose you, Rowena Ardsley, to be his vampire lover, to play eternal ping-pong with, while I've been condemned to the endless life of the mainstream, the banal Undead? I hate you, Rowena Ardsley!" And then she was gone—poor, pathetic creature of the night that she'd become—and I fell back to sleep.

I also remember, at some point, all of the men at the Institute, including the CEO of Game-i-Con, standing over my bedside, too, all muttering something about saving me, and vengeance, and male bonding, and how it was their duty to rid the world once and for all of the inhuman beast in human form. Their voices were loud and angry, and it seemed to me, in my feverish haze, that not only Lucas Smith, but all of them were wearing crosses around their necks, and that they had strung wreaths of garlic around their waists. The smell of all that garlic made me feel even sicker.

Finally, after I don't know how many hours or days or weeks, the fever passed. I felt fine. I felt, in fact, like a brand-new woman, as though I had been reborn. I was no longer the same Rowena Ardsley. And what I wanted at that moment, more than anything in the world, was to be with Byron Ravage, to be in his arms, to make fierce love to him.

I rose, turned on the light, and looked at myself in the small, oval mirror over my bureau. What I saw was this: red eyes, pointy teeth, chalk-white skin. I looked absolutely ravishing! But the light hurt my eyes, so I shut it off. I wasn't even slightly surprised that I could see clearly in the dark.

Still wearing my flimsy nightgown, I slipped out of my bedroom. I headed directly down the long dark corridor that led to Byron's bedroom. I opened his door. Although his room was dark, I saw him clearly, and I know he saw me clearly, too, as I stood there in his doorway. He lay in his bed, on top of the covers, with his head propped up against the wooden headboard. He wasn't wearing his mirrored sunglasses. For the very first time I saw his eyes. Like mine, they were red. And, like mine, they burned with passion.

I entered his room, closing the door behind me. I walked to his bed. I stood over him.

"Ah, Rowena Ardsley," he said, "now you are almost ready. I need to bite you just one more time. For you are halfway there, halfway transformed. You are half woman, and half creature of the night. Which means that you are only half mine. But if you will just lie here beside me, my darling, I shall fully transform you, to turn you into my Queen of the Night, into my Queen of Ping-

Pong. You shall be my eternal, garter-belt-wearing, ping-pong-playing bride!"

Obediently, I sank down beside him, ready to join him for all eternity. It was the most erotic—the most sensual—moment of my life. He reached out for me, and I offered him my neck. But just then, the door to his room was flung open, and all of the men of the Institute burst in, shouting wild obscenities. The nauseating smell of garlic accompanied them. They carried flaming torches, and weapons of all sorts: knives, pistols, machetes, rifles, and silver daggers. The men of the Institute had become a lynch mob.

I screamed, but my screams were useless. They grabbed Byron, and they threw a green ping-pong net around his neck, pulling it so tightly he couldn't breathe. They stood over him, twisting the net tighter and tighter, and then they took the ends of it, and they pinned down his arms. Lucas Smith was clearly the head of the group, the ringleader. At last I understood why he'd taken such copious notes during Frank Langella's *Dracula*. He'd been noting how, in the movie, the vampire hunters had captured Dracula in a big fishing net. And, Byron, like Frank Langella, writhed and struggled, trying to break free. Then he moaned aloud. It was a heartbreaking moan, filled with agony and bewilderment and rage. But there was absolutely nothing that I, who loved him so, could do to help him.

Byron, caught in that net, began to turn ancient before my eyes. He was transformed into the oldest creature on this planet. He grew hideous and mottled and grotesque. And, as he grew old and frail, as his life ebbed, I could feel myself growing wholly human again. I could feel the blush returning to my cheeks, and the points vanishing from my teeth. The red glow of the world—my new fiery vision—was fading. I was miserable. I didn't want to go back to being Rowena Ardsley, semiotician of the locker room, dreamer of sexual submission to brawny jocks. I wanted, more than anything in the world, to be a vampire. I wanted to play ping-pong with Byron Ravage for all the centuries to come. I wept and wept.

"Hoorah!" I heard Lucas Smith shout. "We may have lost Helenska, but we've saved Rowena!" Perhaps he thought my tears were tears of gratitude. "Hoorah!" all of the other men shouted, and then, congratulating each other, they slapped one another on the back. They had the same kind of excited camaraderie among themselves that the jocks in my dreams always had. Turning their backs on Byron, they all stared at me. And I saw pure savagery on their faces, and I knew what was going through their minds. They wanted to take me at that very moment, to have their brutal way with me, just like the jocks in my dreams. I felt unable to breathe. I felt claustrophobic. At that moment, there were just too many damned sexual fantasies crowding that one small, dark bedroom. Too much damned collective unconscious all around. And I didn't want those men to rape me. But then I saw Lucas Smith fingering the cross on his neck, and I knew that he would resist the temptation, and that all the other men would follow his lead. I was saved. I could breathe again.

And that was the very same moment, when their backs were turned to Byron and they were wrestling with temptation, that I saw it, what none of the rest of them saw: the sleek black bat that freed itself effortlessly from the ping-pong net and flew gracefully and swiftly out the window.

      ❧   ❧   ❧

Five years have passed since that night. I have no doubt, no doubt at all, that Byron Ravage is very much alive. Somewhere, he gains strength for his triumphant return. The King of the Vampires, the King of the Ping-Pong table, has not been vanquished. All other men pale in comparison to him. And I don't feel at all like a victim, you must understand. I've *chosen* this fantasy, after all. I've chosen to love a vampire.

Meanwhile, I've returned to the university. Game-i-Con went out of business, and the Institute was destroyed a few months later in a mysterious fire. I do hear bits of news now and then about the other members of the Institute, though. I heard, for instance, that Lucas Smith drove his car off a cliff one day, and that he didn't even leave a suicide note behind. And that the CEO, who'd become destitute, had taken a deliberate overdose of drugs. And I know, of course, without being told, what Helenska is doing. She's out haunting a graveyard somewhere under cover of the night.

And, although I continue to teach and to write books, my scholarly reputation is waning. Instead of being considered a writer of brilliant, if rather obscure, tracts about sports, I'm now thought of as a wild-eyed eccentric because now I write exclusively about Ping-Pong. Eventually, I suspect, I'll have drawers full of unpublished manuscripts. But I don't really mind. I've dedicated myself, body and soul, to decoding the hidden language of the game's slams, spins, and strategies. Because it *is* Ping-Pong, I've come to see, that is the chosen game, the game that glows with the eternal fire, the game that, ultimately, will entice Byron Ravage to rise up from his long sleep beneath the earth, to walk once more among human beings. It's simply more subtle than other games. A brainy game, not a brawny game. Sure, it's not for everyone. But I refuse to apologize if Ping-Pong is only understood by the select few who can discern its erotic nature.

So I keep myself busy while I wait for Byron to return to me. In addition to my writing, I collect sexy black garter belts, which I keep in a trunk beneath my bed. Oh, and by the way, I've finally come up with a new name for the old game of Ping-Pong. A name that I think will please even Byron, whom, of course, I no longer wish to offend. The name that fits the game like a sleek black glove is Vampire Ball. I'm sure you agree.

THE ORANGE GROVE

by Kiini Ibura Salaam

Ophelia places her wet hands on her young hips and pauses a moment. The whites are hanging on the clotheslines; the darks are soaking in the washtub. The midday sun is high. She turns and looks up the hill at the big house. Cecelia is there, waving from the kitchen door. Ophelia waves back. She covers the washtub and climbs the hill for lunch. The food disappears from her plate quickly. She doesn't make conversation and she doesn't look up until the plate is empty. Within minutes, she's back on her feet. She mumbles a "thank you" in Cecelia's direction, drops her plate on the pile of dirty dishes, and shoots out the door. Cecelia watches as Ophelia clatters down the wooden steps and runs, wildly, back down the hill.

Ophelia runs past the washtub of soaking darks, past the freshly washed whites, past the water pump, into the grove of orange trees. With her heart pounding in her chest, she picks a tree. She touches it lightly, then lays down beneath its branches. Her fingers find the hem of her skirt and she folds and unfolds and folds and unfolds the cloth. Her teeth find her forearm and she nervously latches on, nervously gnawing at her skin. Her eyes shut, then open again, shut and open again. The wildness is tearing through her insides. She wills herself to keep her eyes closed.

Not five minutes pass before she hears the weight of his walk. She imagines the grass bending beneath the arch of his foot. She aches to turn over and watch him draw nearer, but that is not the game. The game is for her to pretend to sleep as Paul creeps up and lays fruit at her feet. This is how they played it yesterday, and the day before, and the day before that. It was here in the orange grove that the game began. The orange grove, Ophelia's secret sleeping place. The orange grove that no one entered during the lunch hour. The orange grove that Paul discovered two weeks ago. He discovered a sleeping Ophelia too. He placed three sugar apples by her side. He planned to leave them there and sneak off, but he found himself wondering. Is she ticklish? What does her laughter sound like? How much sweetness do those hips hold? Could her lips make me forget the hard hours of the day? He walked five paces away and sat down. He rested his arms on his knees and waited.

Two weeks ago, when Ophelia opened her eyes to find Paul there, she lowered her eyes immediately. She accepted the fruit with a hesitant hand, but refused to return his gaze. They sat in silence until Paul had to return to the fields and Ophelia had to go back to the wash. The next day Ophelia rushed back to the orange grove hoping Paul would be there. He wasn't. She wrapped her arms around her body and waited. He came five minutes later, carrying a small bunch of sweet bananas. On the third day Paul introduced himself. Ophelia let her name slide from her lips in a whisper. She could barely breathe under the weight of her shyness. By the fifth day, she could respond to his gentle questions. After seven daily gifts of tenderness and fruit, a fragile friendship was born.

Today Ophelia doesn't feel shy at all. Her skin tingles under a million pinpricks of anticipation. When she is sure Paul is settled, she turns over and opens her eyes. Paul is there, sitting across from her, grinning. At her feet is the largest, reddest mango she has ever seen. She sits up and lifts it from the earth. Its heft presses against her palm. With downcast eyes, she bites into the skin. Juice leaps to the mango's broken surface. She licks her lips, then clamps a piece of skin between her teeth. As she pulls the skin away from the fruit, her eyes rise to meet Paul's. She is terrified by the intensity burning there. She drops her gaze and fixes it on the soft rounded mango mound. A small wave of pleasure ripples across her face as she opens her mouth and tastes sweetness. The mango surrenders to her and Paul witnesses every maneuver. His eyes are on her mouth, her lips, her teeth. He sees the juice streaming down her chin, crawling over her wrists, leaking from her elbows. In the warmth of Paul's presence, she devours the fruit, bit by bit.

Ophelia holds the mango seed between wet fingers and sucks each end. As she is lost in this task, Paul inches closer and closer. Slowly, he reaches out for her right hand. She looks up when she feels his touch. With his eyes on hers, he pulls her hand to his mouth. Ophelia drops the seed. As it nestles into the grass, Paul presses his lips against her wrist. Her eyes shut instantly. She inhales deeply. With his mouth still pressed to her flesh, he breaks into a slight smile. He turns her hand over until her palm faces heavenward. His tongue darts out as he licks the tangle of sweetness clinging to her palm. The mango juice disappears from her skin, one slow tongue lick at a time. She lets out one big shivering breath as Paul slips from her palm to her fingers. He sucks each trembling finger, one by one, until the only fragrance left on them is his.

Everything inside Ophelia is alive. Desire zings through her like a prophecy fulfilling its promise, sudden and strong. Chaos spreads through her cells, pulling sound from her ears. Everything in her, on her, around her is tingling. Heat swells inside her urgently, warming her, wooing her. Without warning it drops, humming first in her uterus, then expanding down down down. In the space where her legs meet, in that tightly packed flower of folds and valleys, her future is singing to her. Her eyes fly open as she draws a deep greedy gulp of air.

The only landscape in Ophelia's sights is Paul's. There are miles of him. Miles of cheek and jaw, neck and throat. Miles of shoulder and arms and fingers. Mimicking Paul's motions, she pushes her mouth against his neck. Her tongue absorbs his heat;

it burns like a fever she wants to catch. She doesn't mind the dirt that must be there, covering every hardworking muscle of him. The salty sweat coating her taste buds is an intoxicant. With tongue and teeth, she begins an exploration of licks and sucks and bites. Paul groans beneath her mouth. He wordlessly winds his arms around her and drags her to him. Ophelia catches her breath in fear. His motions are too erratic, too driven. Panic overwhelms her and she pushes him away. Paul loosens his grip on her, but does not let go. His embrace is solid, fierce, certain. He hums softly until her eyes find his. There, in the almost-black brownness of his eyes, she is embraced again. Fearlessness slowly invades her hesitation. Her tension unwinds. He raises an eyebrow in question. She offers a slight smile in answer. He presses a quick kiss on her temple. A tiny sigh-moan-groan escapes her lungs. She trusts this man.

Paul draws his hands up her back. She wraps her arms around his neck, then pauses. She feels his hands rubbing her shoulders, caressing her arms. A breeze sweeps past her ears. She throws her head back and laughs. The orange grove is a blur. Paul's thumb finds the hollow of her neck. Her breath catches in her throat, then hurls itself out into the orange grove. Ophelia feels she is drowning in inexperience; shouldn't she *do* something? She decides she should follow Paul's lead. That means caressing the mound of muscle that is his back. That means pushing through fabric, pressing against skin, feeling all of him as deeply as she can. She is sure Paul can feel her heart's desperate beat beat beating. His fingertips are right over it, and heading downward. His fingertips spiral around and around and a twin energy spirals down and down Ophelia's center. He dips down between her breasts then circles them, one at a time. Ophelia watches as his fingers circle closer and closer to the tip of her breasts. Before he even touches them, her nipples are hard and ready for his touch.

Ophelia feels as if all air has left her body. Paul looks up at her deviously, then lets his fingers wander down her belly. He massages the length of her legs, which are wrapped around his waist.

At her ankle, he slips his fingers beneath her skirts and inches them up her legs. When he reaches her knee, she tugs his shirt from his pants. Her arms beneath his shirt, she pulls herself closer to him. When he reaches her upper thigh, she is pinching his skin in a vigorous massage. Ophelia is no longer conscious of the sounds flying from her mouth as Paul's fingers meet her inner flesh. They begin a soft exploration that has Ophelia's eyes blinking rapidly. Her lips draw back from her teeth. Paul's fingers thump around her inner walls and she begins to pant. They dip into her wetness and she begins to whine. She pushes her pelvis against his hand. His fingers dance with her hips. Paul strokes his thumb against Ophelia's clitoris, and she reaches a frenzied rhythm, lifting and twisting and thrusting.

It is suddenly very hot in the orange grove. The air beats and pulses against Ophelia's flushed skin. It is too hot. Too hot for words, too hot for clothes. She unties the front of her dress and pulls at his shirt. In a rush of cloth and elbows, Paul's shirt is discarded. He forces her dress down around her shoulders and kisses the newly revealed flesh. Ophelia pushes him away and attacks his chest. Each kiss is bolder than the last. She loses her shyness in his skin and sinks her teeth into his flesh. With one strong arm beneath her back and another behind her shoulders, Paul tilts Ophelia back to the earth. He places a kiss on the top of her head, then pulls her away from his chest. He looks her straight in the eye, Ophelia holds his gaze. The two lay, bare-chested and quiet; two children of god, fed on mango, sheltered by orange, nourished by love. Ophelia smiles. She brushes her fingers across Paul's cheek and kisses him. He opens his mouth and deepens the kiss. They draw breath from each other like it's food, like it's fuel, like it's life.

Behind tightly clenched eyes, Ophelia sees the two of them thrusting and gyrating in the orange grove. She rolls over and bangs her elbow and hip on the hard wooden floor. Her eyes fly open and she breaks into laughter. There is no orange grove, no mango seed, no Paul. She is alone, in her dimly lit quarters, sprawled on the cold floor. She drags herself back onto her pallet and covers herself with a patchwork quilt. "So dis is dyin'," she mutters to herself, "relivin' all me memories." She wishes she were back in that orange grove, back in Paul's arms. "Sixteen years old" she thinks shaking her head softly. "Sex fo' de firs' time." Her chest begins to heave as her breathing sputters into heavy coughing. Feet shuffle toward the door. Ophelia shuts her eyes and holds her breath as the door creaks open. Without looking, she knows it's her oldest daughter Iona, the one conceived that day in the orange grove. Iona stands hesitantly in the doorway looking at her mother's withered old body. Ophelia lies still, feigning sleep. After some seconds of silence, Iona sighs, shuts the door, and creeps away. Ophelia giggles softly like a child. She glances at the closed door, then closes her eyes. She raises her knees and slips her hand under her nightgown. With dancing fingers and sweet memories, she eases herself back to the orange grove.

THE DAIRY KINGS

by Iris N. Schwartz

Maurice King was the last man left delivering fresh milk on Manhattan's Upper West Side. The last man, to Yvette Stein's knowledge, to bring to your door glass-bottled, direct-from-his-Queens-dairy, Guernsey-fresh whole milk, low-fat milk, whole and low-fat chocolate milk, and, upon special request, whipped and sour cream. Plus, since last month, Maury's Extra-Thick New York Original Chocolate Syrup, fast becoming a cult item among the sucrose cognoscenti and soon to be, Maury had confided to Yvette, *the* product to raise the King Dairy family's semiflaccid sales.

Yvette was happy to hear that. She didn't want his family's farm to go out of business. She reveled in the taste of their milk, the convenience of home delivery, and the sight of Maury's creamy olive skin, glossy black hair, and bovine-brown eyes set against his crisp King Dairy whites.

Yvette, thirty-two years old and newly single, lived in a butter-hued, one-bedroom apartment on the far West Side, with fringed-velvet pillows tossed atop a pale leather couch, honey-toned parquet floors, and gold-, pumpkin-, and crème fraiche-colored Oriental rugs, all of which conspired to complement the milkiest complexion this side of West End Avenue or Wisconsin.

After her divorce was finalized, Yvette began surrounding herself with things denied to her in her marriage: objects of beauty, a multitude of aromas, varieties of textures and tastes. And she gave herself the time and the right to enjoy them. Her apartment was the new lover whose arms of Egyptian cotton and silk cradled her every night. The lover who tickled her nose with bayberry pot-pourri, who caressed her tired shoulders and lonesome breasts with King Dairy milk baths. The lover who kneaded her worried thighs with aloe squeezed from his gently scissored plant.

The first luxury Yvette allowed herself after moving into divor-cée digs was home delivery of her favorite beverage, the cool, pale liquid that brought warm memories of its fresh taste and the even fresher milkman who had delivered to her own family in Brooklyn.

On Avenue U, in a neighborhood as far away from Manhattan as Brooklyn's Sheepshead Bay but offering none of the Bay's salty water and circling gulls, and nearly as distant as Coney Island but devoid of Coney's gut-churning rides and dilapidated, funky charm, the smoothest, richest, whitest milk had been delivered to Yvette and the rest of the Stein clan by Vincent DelGreco.

Every weekday Vinny trucked through the outer boroughs delivering cream-on-the-top milk from DelGreco Farms on Long Island. By the time he got to the Steins' walk-up apartment he was hungry and thirsty for more than could be obtained by throwing his dark head back and closing parched lips around a bottleneck of clear, thick glass.

Yvette remembered Vinny treating her differently—sneaking sidelong glances or exaggeratedly averting his eyes—starting from the time she was twelve. It was the summer of her first period, and Yvette had started to fill out rather nicely, with pallid, full breasts offsetting what her mother called "my little girl's childbearing hips." This is not to say that Yvette's hips were overly large or cow-like: They were, rather, womanly and welcoming, as alluring as her waist-length, light auburn hair, sun-catching waves always soft and slightly tousled, as if Yvette had started to brush and then left due to tasks of a higher priority.

What these tasks might be no one could say, as Yvette was a very private young woman. She'd escape to her room as soon as she felt a need to be alone, which was often, and often for reasons her family could not fathom. Yvette felt that Vinny, however, was somehow privy to her yearnings, or perhaps she simply wanted him to be.

Alone in her room on weekends, after Mr. and Mrs. Stein had driven to one of their many unnamed destinations, young Yvette would turn the pages of her parents' moldering sex manual, one that dated from the 1930s, if not earlier. She'd caress the pages while imagining herself in the quaintly drawn female's place.

The pages were tan, like the Turkish halvah all of the Steins loved to consume, tongues in mouths flicking at rectangular sweetness. The pages' ends were brittle, and some were dog-eared, too, leaving Yvette to wonder if certain positions were more satisfactory than others and, if so, to whom.

Yvette didn't want to think of her parents coupling. As she'd turn the pages and slowly touch herself, the face of Vinny DelGreco would come to mind, followed by the bulging-veined forearms and sweaty, dark-haired chest of the Stein family milkman, and soon twelve-year-old Yvette would imagine herself fiercely kissing nineteen-year-old Vinny, even as she was puffing up her pillow and pushing her lips against its case.

On the Friday before her thirteenth birthday, while Yvette was on line beside a Cabana Joe's ice cream truck, ready to close her mouth around a chocolate-coated, fudge-centered ice cream bar, she spied Vinny DelGreco tooling down the street in his milk truck. She thought it odd that he'd be here: The timing didn't coincide with his usual Avenue U drop-offs. Nonetheless, Yvette turned toward him and waved, a gesture he returned.

She restored her gaze to the outside of the freezer truck, biting her bottom lip as she studied the brown and white dots of the painted toasted almond bar. Next she rediscovered the Creamsicles, so otherworldly, neon orange, ready to drop off their sticks and plop onto her tongue. Or onto *Vinny's* tongue. And he could pass it with care to hers. Yvette quickly looked at the ground. Someone on the block might glance at her face and see clear through to these torrid thoughts.

Yvette was one eager customer away from first in line when she felt a sweaty hand brush her own. She closed her eyes, feeling heady from the rough-skinned but tender touch, a pungent, masculine aroma, and the enveloping warmth of the sun. She would be thrilled if that hand belonged to Vinny, and terrified, as well.

When she opened her eyes, Yvette knew the hand had been Cabana Joe's, the fortyish owner of his business and sole driver of his truck. He must have reached across her to give somebody change. What, exactly, had her reaction meant? That she wished for more than lonely weekends exploring herself? That a Vinny *or* a Joe could give her what she desired? That she was disloyal to Vinny? That she was a slut? Cabana Joe was asking her what she wanted. Yvette stared into his face, turned, and ran away.

The adult Yvette smiled, remembering disappointment at the lost fudge and creamy vanilla, guilt over the polymorphous nature of her lust, and shock at finding Vinny in front of her apartment building upon her return: his tall, hard body leaning against brick, big grin on his face, twin bottles of DelGreco chocolate milk perspiring in his grip.

Yvette must have worn that shock like a milk mustache, for the dairyman started laughing as soon as she approached.

"So, I hear it's your birthday," he half spoke, half sang. Vinny moved closer. He was now so near their faces almost touched. He placed the chilled bottle against her cheek. She sprang back, as much from cold as from propriety. Vinny opened his milk and had himself a swig. "Happy birthday to you, Yvette."

Yvette clutched her bottle, skipped her fingers over the glass, touched her face.

"I know your parents brought you up better than that. Aren't you going to thank me?" The outside of the bottle was streaming from the heat of his grip.

"How did you know? I mean, thank you." Surely he'd leave if she kept this up.

"Mrs. Stein said this is a very special weekend for you."

The adult Yvette shook her head at this. To this day she

believed Vinny had lied about his source, as both Steins had gone away that Saturday as usual, delaying their weekend jaunt for ten minutes to toss Yvette a silver necklace and devour half of her birthday cherry cheesecake.

As always, they gave themselves to each other, leaving Yvette with half a dessert, the pity of one friend on the block, and tapioca-colored sheets on which to replay her pre-birthday encounter with Vinny.

On the day before her thirteenth birthday, he had taken Yvette to the back of her building, lifting his dairy white loafers over tufts of emerging weeds. He took her hand in his; he lured her like a cat to a full dish of milk. Vinny whispered in her ear, and she felt his breath, thick from the rich DelGreco treat. He told her that thirteen was a special age, that she, Yvette, was a special girl.

Vinny toured her ear with his chocolate-soaked tongue, sending sweet shivers up her spine. Then he took another gulp of the milk, but in his haste DelGreco milk was delivered to her breasts—one, two, three, four, and more drops showered her blouse from the bottle Vinny held.

This was too much for twelve-year-old Yvette, and too much for nineteen-year-old Vinny, as well. Yvette stood straight, like a stick thrust in a Creamsicle. At any moment, her blouse, or what was left of her resolve, might melt. Vinny dropped his bottle, he dropped all pretense, he dropped to her breasts and began caressing them through her blouse. He wiped at the droplets, he licked them, still over her top, then over her bra, in an instant he had reached her bra, and Yvette knew he felt her incautious nipples, thickening like pudding on top of a stove.

Yvette might have gone further, but she saw both bottles, contents spilt on the weeds, and she felt spilt, or was it split? She pulled from Vinny, pulled on her blouse, pushed herself into her home.

Of course she thought about Vinny on her birthday. She hoped he didn't think her immature. After the Steins had left, Yvette could think of nothing else. She cried as she removed her vanilla linen blouse, a birthday gift from her friend on the block, she cried as she took off her plaid butterscotch shorts and butter-milk lace bra and panties, gifts from her to herself.

Yvette placed them all on the back of a chair and got into bed, this time without her parents' manual. This time, the manual wouldn't do.

Thirteen-year-old Yvette recalled the milkman's hands on her breasts, the first hands other than her own to take this journey. She thought of the milk on her mounds, such cool, sweet droplets, but now the drops became a drizzle, the drizzle a torrent, and in her mind Vinny was pouring one, then two, full bottles onto her breasts and stomach. The chilled liquid gave her goose bumps, made her back arch with delight. Rivulets of chocolate milk poured down her ample breasts, her sides, and onto the tapioca sheets. Vinny was lapping at her like a lactose-starved kitten, he was grab-bing her breasts, licking and sucking her dairy-drenched nipples.

Then Yvette imagined another hand, another strong hand. This was impossible: Vinny's hands and mouth were all too busy, causing her happy nipples to pucker and point. He was milking them for all they were worth.

These new hands were slightly rough. Yvette heard a rustling. Something fragile was being torn, something more solid removed. While Vinny DelGreco licked chocolate milk off Yvette's belly, Cabana Joe passed a melting toasted almond bar over her legs and thighs. Joe was spreading her thighs and licking off bits of almond coating where they fell.

Cabana Joe smeared what was left of the bar over her swollen pussy lips. He moved gooey fingers slowly over her clitoris. Yvette was shivering, yet molten. Vinny chocolate-milk-tongued her vir-ginal slit, Joe ice-cream-caressed her contracted clit. The two men's heads were so close they could have kissed.

Yvette's fingers circled her sex more rapidly now. Cabana and Vincent . . . Vinny and Joe, making her so…very happy. She *was* a special girl. On her bed, *in her mind,* she received many happy returns of the day.

That was half a lifetime ago, half a lifetime after which Yvette realized she had received more thrills in her own mind and by her own hand than she had ever been given by all the men in her life combined.

Yvette had always been reticent in person. Too reticent to grab the man who could give her what she wanted. Too reticent to ask for what she liked. Too reticent to travel as far in her cotton-covered bed as she did in her auburn-tressed head.

Yet she believed her best days were imminent. Everything, these days, was close to her surface—her dreams, her desires, practically sizzled on her skin, like milk splattered atop a range. Thirty-two-year-old Yvette was ready to receive. She had primed herself. And she knew in her now wide-open heart that her dairy king Maury would deliver.

And so Yvette whipped herself into readiness. Early in the week she called King Dairy, requesting that Maury King make her his last stop on Thursday, telling them she was having guests for the weekend and needed her items beforehand. King Dairy was happy to accommodate Yvette: she was a steady, longtime customer who tipped as readily as a contented country cow.

Thursday, Yvette reasoned, would be preferable to her usual Saturday. Yvette might appear desperate if she set this up for a weekend, plus she couldn't assume Maury had no Saturday night plans. Yvette would not miss this chance to celebrate the still sweet cream of her youth.

On Tuesday evening, Yvette purchased a velvet dress, deep V-necked and slit at both sides, soft and gold as the finest crème caramel. She intended to answer the door in this dress, new cocoa suede stilettos, cascading hair, and little else.

Come Thursday morning, after eyeing and caressing three sets of sheets, the fussy seductress opted for bittersweet-chocolate-hued silk, appreciating the advantageous contrast to her skin. Yvette changed the sheets before leaving for work. She knew she would make it home early enough to dress for Maury, but would have insufficient time to prepare anything else.

This fateful morning she bathed and shampooed with King

Dairy whole milk. Yvette dipped and re-dipped her washcloth until every inch and orifice had soaked up the life-giving liquid. Leaning back on a foam pillow, body bobbing in a contained milky sea, Yvette felt as if Maurice King himself, and maybe Vinny DelGreco and Cabana Joe, too, inhabited her every pore. Only a distaste for shriveled fingertips convinced her to emerge from the tub. Other than leaving refrigerator shelf space for her upcoming King Dairy delights, Yvette had nothing left to do that day but work at her marginally irritating job.

Yvette was Northeast headquarters office manager for a well-known, lactose-free coffee flavoring manufacturer. She had been working for this company seven years now, having started one year after her marriage. Yvette kept her private stash of milk, as well as butter and dairy desserts, in a tiny refrigerator in the south pantry. She kept this contraband in brown paper bags at all times. One never knew when guests or clients might walk in, and her company did not look kindly on the presence of competing brands, dairy or nondairy, in main or peripheral pantries.

These mounting ironies were not lost on Yvette. Some days she felt like crying, others she suppressed a smirk. Today she daydreamed of tossing all natural, dairy-laden foods onto her desk, rolling her suit-clad body in the glorious mess, and strutting in front of her boss like a queen—a lactose queen.

Yvette Stein evened her smile into a line and went about her work. Requisition forms and purchase orders teetered atop her desk. It was time to get her mind out of the dairy.

On the way home, Yvette fretted about whether she should take a second bath, whether she was pretty enough for Maury. Then it hit her—what if this didn't work? What if he wouldn't consort with customers? What if—oh, God—she didn't turn him on?

Yvette hastened to recall Maury's smile each time she came to the door, the way, every week, he'd hold her glance a little longer, the warmth of his hand when he'd shake hers goodbye. Suddenly Yvette tingled, thinking: He shook her hand so he could touch her! With her confidence bolstered, Yvette nearly danced through her apartment door. She would not lose her faith—or her nerve.

Yvette freshened up and slipped on her dress. She slid on her shoes. Velvet and suede against her skin made Yvette pause to appreciate lushness and warmth. Ah, this is what Maury's hands will feel like . . . only better.

It was almost 5:00 P.M., almost time for King Dairy. Yvette stopped pacing. It was time to breathe deeply and trust that the night would take the shape it was made for. With her efforts, this night could now develop—like a sumptuous homemade ice cream in her freezer.

At 5:05, Yvette wasn't so sure about "dessert." Maury's truck must have stalled. At 5:10, she worried he'd had a flat. 5:15, it had to be an accident. At 5:20, Yvette knew he'd figured out her plan. He hated her, her white-as-milk skin, soft-as-pudding thighs. Maury must have rearranged his route and sent someone else. Slipping into self-recrimination, Yvette almost yelped when she heard the buzzer. It was 5:30. Her doorman informed her that the King Dairy men were on their way up.

Men? With all her planning, how could this have happened? Before the bell rang, Yvette realized her mistake: She had ordered too much! Of course it would take two men—or two trips—to carry all the lactose-laced goodies Ms. Greedy had called in. Yvette had no contingency plan. All she could do was wait.

Vincent DelGreco was the last man Yvette expected to see standing alongside Maurice King. There Vinny was, strong hands holding a well-stocked crate, immoderate brown and gray chest hair erupting from a King Dairy shirt. And he had that grin on his face, that same grin he'd had before giving Yvette her thirteenth-birthday chocolate drink.

Oh. Oh, God. She wanted to shut the door. She wanted to open it wider. She wanted to kiss the grin off goddamned Vinny's face.

Maury's eyes darted between Vinny and Yvette. Sweat was

beading on Maury's high forehead, and one drop began a journey toward the tip of his substantial, masculine nose. Yvette yearned to extend her tongue and catch that bit of liquid Maury.

"Ahem!" Maury stroked the top of his crate's contents, then he stared at Yvette. She watched the perspiration droplet attach itself to Maury's generous lower lip. "Good afternoon, Yvette. Are you planning to let us in?"

He carried his crate to her kitchen table, the usual drop-off point. Vinny followed. Yvette was a distant, slow-moving third.

Maury wiped his olive brow with the back of a hand before continuing. "I was going to introduce you to my associate, but it seems you've already met."

Yvette was sinking, sinking fast, like an engorged raisin overcome by cream and rice. She would land in the bottom of a deep dessert dish, done in by richness and greed. Pudding, pudding, everywhere, too much, too soon, to eat.

Vincent turned toward Maurice. "Ms. Stein's family was one of DelGreco's customers in Brooklyn."

Now he turned toward Yvette. "I guess you don't know, but DelGreco Farms went out of business two years ago."

"I'm sorry." Yvette looked down at her dress and shoes, she looked at the two beautiful men, she looked at the overwhelming array of dairy before her, and she felt afraid and not a little foolish.

"Sit, Yvette, sit." Maury was talking now. Bless his take-charge self.

"I should be asking the two of you to sit. I'm sorry. After carrying those heavy crates . . . Please . . . please . . . join me." She was incapable of finishing her sentences. With this pitiful display, she'd never have a chance with Maury. Or with Vinny. Both would leave her like half-eaten sorbet after a gut-busting meal—they'd leave her to melt into a warm and widening pool.

Vinny pulled out a chair and sat down. Maury remained standing.

"What about these perishables?" Maury asked, waving a hand over her order. "Do you want us to refrigerate them?"

Vinny pawed lazily at his chest hair, then spoke up. "How about it, Yvette? Do you want help?"

"I . . . I . . ."

Maury looked carefully at Yvette. She saw his fudge-brown eyes travel from her thick auburn hair to her pale neck and arms, then to her cleavage, felt his eyes linger there as her breathing became shallow, saw those eyes follow the curve of her hips to the tops of her thighs, the very top of her dress slits. She watched Maury study her calves, ankles, and shoes.

Behind them, still seated at her kitchen table, Vinny was watching, too. He was widening his eyes and smirking. Maurice finally spoke. "Yvette, it looks like you've planned a special evening."

"You could say that."

"You look absolutely gorgeous."

"Thank you." Yvette heard her voice crack.

"You do, Yvette." Vinny stood up. "Always have."

Yvette thought she saw Maury's olive skin darken. "I shouldn't say this now," he whispered, his hands grazing his King Dairy whites, "but you always do."

"Thank you," she stupidly repeated.

Maury turned to Vinny. "Why don't you help me put away Yvette's order before something spoils?"

Bless Maury. Bless his chivalrous heart. Yvette plastered herself against her kitchen counter and watched the men work.

What to do? What to do? She'd have to go somewhere by herself to figure this out. "Excuse me." Yvette clutched the back of the counter while facing Vinny and Maury. The two men turned toward her. "Excuse me for a moment. If you finish before I get back, feel free to help yourself to juice or spring water. I shouldn't," she paused, then looked away from the two handsome milkmen, "be long."

Yvette escaped to her bathroom. She smoothed her dress, then sat on the toilet-seat lid. How would she ever get Maury alone? Why did Vinny look so good? In what way could she have foreseen this? And why were the very tops of her thighs becoming damp? She'd walk out of the bathroom smelling of sex, and God knows what the two of them would think.

Think. Think! Smart, take-charge divorcée unable right now to understand anything beyond swelling pussy lips and throbbing clit. I think, she almost said aloud, I think I finally understand men.

"Yvette?" Oh no, it was Maury. They must be ready to leave, and still she had no new plan.

"Yvette." Vinny this time. "Everything's packed away now."

Yvette stood up to wash her hands. She must have lost track of time. "I'll be right out." Panic rose in her like bubbles in boiling milk.

When Yvette returned to the kitchen Vinny was seated at her table, glass of apple cider in hand.

Maury walked up to her. "Yvette," he said, his voice as smooth as his Extra-Thick New York Original Chocolate Syrup, "we didn't mean to disturb you, but we parked near a meter, and if I don't feed it, I'm going to be very sorry." He smiled at her, lowered the lids over his brown eyes for a moment. "One has to pay attention to a hungry meter, don't you think?"

Oh, this is it. He's on to her. Mocking her.

Before Yvette could postulate further, Vinny spoke up. "Maury will put in some quarters while I settle up with you. I have the bill right here. Sorry to say we have one other delivery in the area. Then Maury will come back for me. Okay?" Vinny dabbed at errant cider on his lower lip with a determined index finger.

"Of course. I'm sorry I kept both of you so long." Her bubbles of panic and excitement were dissipating. Now she would never get a chance with Maury. Plus she was being left alone with Vinny. Nothing good could come of this.

"Not a problem." Vinny again.

"A pleasure to see you, as always," Maury spoke up, nearly out her door. He extended his hand. "I hope the evening is a success."

"What?"

"Your evening," said Maury. "You said you had special plans."

"Oh." Yvette toyed with one of the dress slits. "We'll see.

Sometimes you build up something in your head that doesn't come to pass."

"And sometimes what looks like skim milk can turn out to be as tasty as cream."

"Really?" Yvette responded. "Is that an adage from King Dairy?" She couldn't help smiling.

"Nah. I just invented it. You looked like you could use some cheering up."

Her bubbles were gone. The milk had stopped boiling. The pot handle was tepid. And the pilot light was out. Both Maury and Vinny felt sorry for her, she was sure. Why, why, why had she done this?

"Well, yes." Yvette patted down her pointless dress. She extended her hand. "Thank you again. See you at the next delivery."

"You bet." Maury shook her hand. He closed the door almost before she had retrieved her hand.

Before, however, the disappointed divorcée had time to bemoan her loss of Maurice King, Vincent DelGreco appeared in front of her. He tugged at his pants pocket. "I guess we should settle up, since you're going to be busy soon."

"I'll get my checkbook."

"Listen," Vinny took another step in her direction, "I can cheer you up as well as Maury. How about some chocolate milk for the two of us?" He idly caressed his biceps. "I know you have some. Unless you're in a hurry."

Yvette felt frozen, like the inner core of a strawberry shortcake bar, to her hardwood floor. She knew, however, that the likes of Vinny could rapidly melt her.

"Are you?"

"Am I what?"

"Are you in a rush?"

Vinny walked to her refrigerator. He returned with two uncapped pint bottles of King Dairy chocolate milk. "I don't believe you are."

Yvette looked away. "Vinny, I think . . ."

The macho milkman wiped his mouth of chocolate milk. "That's always been your trouble, Yvette. You think too much." He tipped the bottle slightly, inserted a finger into its neck, then traced a stream of sweet liquid onto Yvette's right hand. Vinny genuflected, then licked off the milk. He looked up. "Oh. You wear too much, too."

Maybe Vinny was right, even if what he said reflected the means to his own ends. Yvette thought too much, acted too little. Hell, if she couldn't have one dairyman tonight, she'd treat herself to another. Those chocolate silk sheets would serve a purpose after all. With that Yvette began walking toward the bedroom, gesturing with a waving hand for Vinny to follow. On the way, she lifted crème caramel velvet over her head.

The milkman of her pubescent reveries was unbuttoning his shirt, lying against her headboard, watching her walk over to him wearing nothing but three-inch-heeled cocoa suede shoes. She saw one pint of King Dairy chocolate milk on her night table, sure to leave a ring in the morning. She didn't care. She also saw a bulge in his nether region ready to burst through what appeared to be the flimsiest of barriers.

Now Yvette stared at the hairiest chest she had ever seen, gray and brown hair almost evenly distributed, hair threatening to climb up his neck, hair engaging in a mad primate sprawl as far as her eyes could follow, almost eclipsing the vulnerable-looking, tiny brick-red nipples no doubt desirous of attention, too. She watched this hair seemingly march down a path, down his flat abdomen, willing her to follow it down, down to what was now covered by the contrast of stunningly white and superfluous King Dairy pants.

Yvette grew bolder. She placed her still-shod foot against his trousers, pressing the toe against the buckle of his belt. He grinned at her, that Vinny grin, and grabbed the bottle of milk. Was she that sex-manual-obsessed girl all over again? Or, better yet, the Lactose Queen—with Vinny's help—come to life?

Just as she was enjoying a warm chocolate-milk-drenched tongue slithering up her calf, just as she was envisioning mixed syrups, clotted cream, molten fudge, and all other wondrous things dairy and sweet to go with the chocolate milk and her and Vinny, just then there was knocking *and* buzzing at her door. Why did someone—other than the two of them—have to come here?

She looked down at Vinny. He was still smiling. No doubt oblivious. Then: "I'll get it," he said, and jumped up.

"Why? What for?"

"Don't worry. I'll put something on and tell whoever it is to go away. You stay here."

This was chivalry worthy of Maury. Oh. Was she somehow being unfaithful?

Yvette was under the covers when she heard the front door shut and a series of whispers. Then her refrigerator door opened. And closed. And opened again. Was Vinny suddenly in need of a sandwich? Was he talking to himself? She should have known better than to succumb to his advances. Or to her quiescent desires.

Yvette closed her eyes and turned over onto her stomach. She threw off the covers, punched her pillow and began to cry. Only when she felt a warm thick substance being spread over her thighs and a cool thin trickle being poured on her buttocks did she twist her head and see the impish faces and delightfully employed hands of Maurice King and Vincent DelGreco.

Bowls of warm fudge, bottles of cool milk, melting bars of ice cream, all were on a tray balanced on her queen-sized bed. Was Yvette still alive, or had she died and drifted up to Lactose Heaven?

Maury touched the back of her knee, then licked fudge from one finely formed finger. "Yvette," he said, his voice thick and creamy as the fudge, "the Reign of Dairy has officially begun."

GLOSS

by Rachel Kramer Bussel

Standing in front of the mirror, I apply the gooey liquid over my lips until they shine like glass, not gooey but slick and hard, almost icy. I'm keeping in mind my friend Alice's advice that "lip gloss should look like you've just given someone a blowjob." Whether or not they approximate this maxim, I know my lips will draw attention tonight, which is precisely the idea. They are slick and shiny, like a red racecar, boldly drawing attention to itself, whether the viewer wants to look or not. The rest of my ensemble works too—tight black top and short tight black PVC skirt, but I want people's eyes firmly on my lips.

I head over to the bar, a plush new one that's just opened. I've been lucky enough to land a coveted invitation, and I know the crowd will be the cream of the crop. I could have brought a guest, but tonight is by necessity a solo excursion. I'm on a specific mission and need to conduct it in my own way. Finding the right man for a one-night stand, for an electric connection that burns and sizzles as fast and hot as a firecracker, and lasts about as long, requires a unique combination of savvy and intuition and I can't have any distractions.

Red is the theme of the night, with lush red curtains and a deep garnet shade painted on the walls. I order the watermelon martini, the night's featured cocktail, and perch on the barstool. My legs are tucked under the bar and I don't bother to showcase them, even though I know they're magnificent. I'm alone and know exactly what I want—a hot guy, a stud, someone to entertain me for tonight and tonight only. Someone with a cock that's hard and hot and needy, just for me. As I close my eyes and lean forward to sip the cold, sweet drink, I feel a presence behind me. After I swallow I slowly sit up in my chair, leaning back ever so slightly and brushing against the shirtfront of a very slick, well-dressed handsome man. Not a cute, shaggy hipster like I normally meet or a yuppie Wall Streeter straight out of college, but a real man—a little older, crisp and clean, sophisticated.

I slowly swivel my stool around to look at him, our gazes holding. My knees skim his thighs, and instead of smiling I reach for my glass and bring it to his lips. The ghost of a smile forms on his face as he lets me tilt the icy red liquid down his throat. I bring the glass back to my own lips and sip again, slowly and deliberately, still meeting his gaze. I'm vaguely aware of the crowd surging around us, the commotion at the bar, but this stranger is occupying the bulk of my attention. I have the urge to wrap my legs around his waist and draw him closer, but I stay composed. I open my mouth and am about to introduce myself, searching for a witty line, but the longer we stand there staring at each other, the more difficult words become.

Instead I take his left hand and bring it to my mouth, sliding his index finger inside and then carefully sliding it out, my tongue pressing against it the entire time. I push it back in again and repeat the process, this time lightly grazing my teeth along his slightly roughened skin. As I'm about to go for a third round, he moves his hand and trails his wet finger along my neck, ending at the neckline of my dress, his hand resting on my chest.

He reaches his hand out for mine and even though I have half a drink left, I let him lead me into the unisex single occupancy bathroom. As befits the rest of the decor, the bathroom is lush and lavish, with red tiles and smooth surfaces and a plush upholstered chair along with the sink and toilet.

I look up at him, my lips slightly pursed, poised to smile or laugh or smirk, not letting him know which one it will be yet. I keep my eyes locked on his as my hand goes to his crotch, feeling the heat and hardness beneath. I like that I'm in control here, that even though I just met him I know that he's at my mercy. He led me here but now I will be leading him. Even down on my knees I will be the one in control and that thought sends a shiver through my body. Ignoring the chair for a moment, I step closer and then drag myself down his body, my breasts sliding along his torso, my nipples hardening at the friction as I sink to the floor. It's hard to keep my commanding gaze as I look up at him from the floor, but somehow I manage even though inside I'm melting. I close my eyes for a second as my hand reaches up reverently to stroke his cock through his pants.

I glance briefly at the chair but then realize that I like it better down here on the cold floor, the tiles pressing into my knees as I fumble with his belt buckle. I'm soaking wet and will surely have to remove my panties later but for the moment all I care about is his cock and getting it into my mouth. He helps me undo his zipper and before his pants are even pushed down his thighs I'm leaning forward, my tongue darting forth to lick a slow, teasing line along the length of his cock. I move closer so my knees are pressed up against the sides of his shoes, my legs slightly spread as I try to taste all of him at once. He sighs and groans and I look up at him for a moment, no longer smirking at all, simply acknowledging how right it feels to be right here in front of him. His eyes are almost too intense and I close mine before guiding the length of his smooth warmth into my mouth, going slowly until I have all of him inside of me.

I try to push him deeper, to feel the tip of his cock at the back of my throat, to take him as far inside of me as I can. I would hold his cock and press the tip along my throat, ecstatic, until finally sliding it out and starting the whole process all over again. I tilt my head and run my pursed lips along his cock, up and down and around, my own slippery sexual harmonica that I can play any way I want. I love the way he feels against me, how hot his cock is and every time I move to try something else like licking his balls or kissing my way along his length, I suddenly need to have him inside me again. I devour his cock, slamming it down my throat, rocking my whole body back and forth in a special kind of dance. As I do, my thong presses tightly against my pussy and I let out a groan of my own that reverberates against his cock. I feel like I could stay right here forever, learn every curve and crevice and nuance of his cock, and still want more.

He is enjoying it too, I can tell, but as his hands flick agitatedly from my head to my hair to his sides, I know he's getting close and I don't want to deprive him. I slide him slowly out of my mouth, teasing him by sliding him back in slightly and then continuing. I rub my cheeks against his cock, press it against my neck, caress it and adore it. Then I spread my legs wider, into a split and look up at him before opening my mouth, sticking out my tongue and slapping his cock against it again and again. Now he really groans, louder and fiercer than before and I move faster, then shake my head back and forth, slapping my face against his cock and his cock against my face in a frenzy that makes me feel dizzy. I want to talk, to tell him to please come for me, to tell him how much I need his hot cum splattered all over me, to tell him how wet he's making me, but I don't want to ruin the mood. I think he knows how I feel though, as we thrash energetically and then he grabs my head with one hand and his cock with the other and forces his cum onto me, giving me exactly what I'd asked for as the warm whiteness spills all over my face, my lips, my hair. I lunge for his cock and suck the rest of it out of him, holding him there even after I know he's done.

Finally I stand up, too nervous to look at him. Instead I look in the mirror and try to rearrange my hair and clothes so that it's not quite so obvious what we've been doing. It feels like we've been here for an hour but I think it's only been about ten minutes, which is still long enough to annoy the bar patrons. I smooth my hair back into its barrettes, adjust my collar, splash water on my cheeks and wipe them clean. But my lips, well, my lips I leave, looking wet and moist and red and sexy. I don't need the lip gloss anymore to do the job for me; I've just done it myself. I wink at the stranger and then stroll out the door, a smile on my wet red lips.

LILITH BROKEN TO BRIDLE

by Molly Weatherfield

The two men trotted their horses down the path. It was early morning in April, not a fashionable hour for riding in London in 1890, and they encountered few other horsemen. But coming toward them, visible in the distance because her horse was galloping down over a rise, was a woman on a large chestnut, her own long mane of hair—chestnut as well—tumbling over her shoulders, loosed by the speed at which she was traveling.

"Unusually good seat for a woman," the older of the men commented. "Almost as though she were part of the animal. Damned unusual."

The younger man murmured something under his breath, which the older one took as agreement.

Damned unusual indeed, Lord Robert Arthur Ashleigh, 12th Earl of St. Bartlemas, murmured to himself again, his eyes flooding with a warmth he hoped his companion wouldn't discern.

❧ ❧ ❧

He'd begun to notice her the previous summer, galloping by with her hair tossed and her face flushed. Her horse was harnessed in the fashionable "bearing rein" style—head much too high for comfort, probably bridled with the knobbed "gag bit" as well.

Cruel to the animal, he'd thought, showy and unpleasant; she was clearly a shallow, fashionable, most irritating young woman. He'd forced his thoughts brusquely to other things—the statues he was casting in bronze in the barn of his country house at Overton. And the beautiful roan mare he was exercising.

But he'd had to admit she was striking. Slender, upright, a marvelous, fearless rider. It had taken him an additional month to observe—because he'd tried so hard not to—the odd symmetry between her self and her stallion. For she was as extremely and compactly corseted as the horse was tightly and smartly harnessed. Why?—he'd found himself wondering idly from time to time—why lace herself so tightly when she'd be slim with no corset at all? It couldn't be comfortable to ride in that condition.

But it had only been idle speculation, until a tedious rainy afternoon late in August. Trapped in his sister's back parlor and leafing through a copy of *The Englishwoman's Domestic Companion* (that's how hideously bored he'd been), he came upon a letter to the editor, describing the "delightful sensation of feeling the tightly borne up horse spring under you when you are equally tight-laced." Signed by a Lady Catherine Andrews.

The London humidity was oppressive. His breath came raggedly.

But there was some benefit to be gotten from a sister who knew all the town gossip and delighted in sharing it. He had no difficulty learning that the Lady Catharine was "of unimpeachable breeding, a little withdrawn since she was widowed in that horrid boating accident a few years ago. But utterly devoted to her little boy. He's really her only occupation, except for riding. I hear she's a terribly smart rider. Rather pretty, I suppose, if you like that very severe look.

"But why do you ask, Robert? Lady Catherine isn't the sort to interest herself in a lazy lord who sculpts in a barn. Actually she doesn't seem to care about men or marriage at all—not that she hasn't had offers. Well, she's rich enough, I suppose, not to have to . . ."

The weather was clearing. He needed to take the roan mare for a ride.

❧   ❧   ❧

Of course she wasn't out that day. Or the next. And then he had to go to Overton to attend to some repairs.

"And should I go ahead and tear down that small shed near the barn—where we used to keep the donkey cart when you and your sister were babies, sir?"

That had been the plan he and his steward had agreed upon. But no, he said. No, he'd changed his mind.

"Very good, sir. And if you don't mind my asking, what do you intend to do with that shed?"

"Remodel it, Wright. A personal project."

"Not into a new donkey shed?"

"Oh no. A folly, Wright. A folly was what I had in mind."

❧   ❧   ❧

He worked night and day on the folly, servants and tenants staying away at his instructions. He'd get back to the bronzes some other time. And now that it was finished—shiny and painted, the leather and gleaming metal hung just as he wanted—he had to face the possibility that he'd never use it.

❧   ❧   ❧

But there she was, on the paths. It was autumn now, the leaves ruddy in the crisp air. Wait, she was dismounting, her brow knit. She bent over her horse's leg, whispering, patting, and comforting him.

He walked his horse over to her and asked if he could help.

Her dark eyes were large and liquid above a straight nose, a pointed chin.

"Oh no, thank you," she said, "Lucifer just has a stone in his shoe that I can't get out. It will be a long walk back to the stables, though."

Sorry, Lucifer. And thanks.

"You can ride my horse and I'll lead him back," he offered. But she wouldn't dream of leaving Lucifer when he was in pain.

And so they led their horses back together.

"You haven't been out for a few weeks," she said. He wouldn't have minded if she'd said it flirtatiously, but she didn't.

"I noticed you," she explained, "because you ride well, and because you're handsome, and because you obviously disapprove of my riding style."

He nodded, not knowing how to answer.

"There's cruelty, you know," she added, "and there's . . . cruelty."

"But can a horse tell the difference?" he asked.

She paused before responding.

"I think," she said, "that Lucifer loves me. Or pities me, more likely. In any case, he indulges me."

He cleared his throat. *Say it, idiot. Before you lose your nerve entirely.*

His voice surprised him by sounding quite natural.

"Actually, I've been considering . . . your riding style. I've recently acquired a new mare. And I've been doing some research. But I need a bit of help."

"Help?" She smiled and met his eyes.

"She's a magnificent chestnut," he said, "slender and high-strung, and with extraordinary character, I believe. I've resolved to start training her tomorrow."

Her black lashes swept over her cheeks.

"And you want my assistance."

"If you had the time," he murmured. "And the inclination."

She looked up at him again, for a longer moment than either of them had expected.

"I do have the time, Lord Robert. And do you know, I believe I have the inclination as well."

❧ ❧ ❧

She'd been silent, but pleasantly so, on the way to Overton the next morning.

Ah, she said, stepping out of the chaise, it's good to move again.

She made polite compliments on the house and grounds. He thought the house had never looked so venerable, the grounds so lush, as with her striding through them in the austere black and white of her riding costume.

No, she didn't want any tea, thank you. Perhaps later, afterward.

They walked out past the barn, to the folly, which was a small trim stable hung with shiny tack. There was a little training ring next to it, its fence painted bright white. He'd enjoyed building the fence.

"And the mare?" she asked, smiling.

He didn't answer.

"What's her name?"

"I call her Lilith," he answered. "The first woman," he added before he could stop himself. "Well, *really* the first woman," he said.

The look she returned was calm, amused.

"How will you begin?" she asked.

"I need to make sure her tack fits," he answered. "I've never bridled her." Were her breasts swelling slightly over her corset? Her white stock front was so crisp it was hard to tell for sure.

"I don't know," he added, "if she'll submit willingly." And yes, a sigh escaped her, though her mouth retained its curve.

A moment of stillness. He turned to examine a riding crop hanging from a nail; slowly, he ran a black-gloved finger down its length.

And when he turned back, she'd begun to unbutton her coat.

She undressed quickly, pausing only to hang each garment on one of the brass hooks mounted in a row on the wall. The sky was changeable, shadows sweeping through the little stable's open doorway. The lights and darks of her body shifted balance and combination with each garment she removed.

The jacket of black wool faille shrugged off her white shoulders. The white stock unwound from her long white neck. She'd stepped quickly out of the narrow skirt and lace pantaloons, revealing white thighs above black boots laced to her knees, taut white belly over dark triangle. He'd taken the riding crop down from the nail and was balancing it in his right hand.

"Part your legs slightly," he said. "And then turn to show me your hindquarters."

"My *hindquarters?*"

One said *derrière* to a lady. Or perhaps, in certain situations, *arse*. Her voice was husky, savoring his inappropriate word. A small dimple deepened at the right corner of her mouth.

He flicked the riding crop at her left flank.

"You won't be able to speak," he said, "after I've bridled you. But even now, you must respond silently and immediately to my commands." He hit her again and she turned to display the white, curved rump thrust out by her corset. It looked wider than it was, in contrast to her constricted waist. His fingers tightened around the riding crop.

She'd wear a tail, of course. He'd exercised some ingenuity designing that apparatus, with the help of a very understanding lady in London who'd been under his protection for some time.

But he didn't want to get ahead of himself.

He slapped her rump with his gloved hand, to communicate that she was to turn again to face him. She'd lowered her eyes, thick black lashes casting shadows on her flushed cheeks.

He put the crop into his boot and wrapped his hands around the waist of her corset. He wouldn't need the measuring tape in his pocket; his hands would never forget her waist's span. Or the other distances: small of back to top of the corset's bust; curve of hips beneath. Next time she visited, there would be a leather corset, with many cunning rings and buckles, to be used for . . . well, for all sorts of things.

So much to do. He cautioned himself to take his time. But he couldn't help the next impatient gesture. He'd waited quite long enough to see her breasts, thank you; he cut away the chemise from over the top of the corset with a penknife. Champagne goblets, just as he'd hoped, the nipples pink, erect, obedient: they stood at attention, swelling proudly beneath his gaze. He'd mount silver bells on clips with little spring mechanisms. He'd adjust the clips with jeweler's tools; they shouldn't bite, just pinch a bit. Cling to her flesh to fill the air with clear, shivery jingling as she moved.

She breathed calmly, eyes still lowered. How must it feel, he wondered, to accede so completely to the gaze of another?

"Outside." He prodded her to the door. "Where the light is better."

The clouds had passed, the sun glared on the bridle in his hand, the knobbed, arched metal bit that could make a horse froth at the mouth.

He raised her chin with the riding crop until he saw the bit reflected in her eyes. Or perhaps the spark he saw was fear instead. Well, she'd be a damned fool not to be a little afraid. But she forced herself to be calm, to relax and even to part her lips.

And to send him a haughty glance.

Fear had made her imperious, as he'd rather hoped it would. Still, it wouldn't do. She gasped—and then softened—at his hard swipe against her thighs.

Oh yes, much better.

But how could he bridle her with all that hair coiled at her nape? He pulled out the pins, sending the hair tumbling almost to her waist. He brushed it with a wire currycomb into a tail at the top of her head, tying it clumsily with a leather thong. She'd need a groom, he thought; delightful and diverting as all this preparation seemed to him today, in time he'd find it tedious.

And her eyes? Calm, wary. If anything, they'd softened a little more as her mouth opened, moistened to receive the bit.

He adjusted the straps, pulled the buckles. He hadn't attached the blinders yet; he wanted to watch her eyes as the bit settled to the soft roof of her mouth, the panic as she realized that the pain wouldn't go away. That every tug of the reins would make its demands on her in the same harsh language.

He stroked her hindquarters gently—he'd taken off his glove and was using a bare hand—he stroked her arse and breasts as she stamped her feet in terror. He played with the reins, pulling to the left and right. And upward too, communicating that she'd be required to keep her head smartly erect, her chin eagerly raised.

She stamped and shuddered, dancing, careening, trying to pull away. She knew better, of course, than to create this unnecessary pain for herself, but her fear was genuine—fascinating for both of them. He slapped her arse and shuddered in momentary wonder as her whole body flushed, her pink nipples turning deep brown. Sensing his arousal even through the monstrous veil of pain, she made a valiant, clever, sidelong feint, pulling one of the reins out of his hand.

He grabbed it back, jerking her head up and then suddenly relaxing his hold. She lost her balance and tottered forward. He pulled straight downward, and she sank to her knees in front of him.

"Head down." His voice was soft: no anger, merely the slightest suggestion of disappointment. He nudged her forward, the sole of his boot pressing her upper back and shoulders toward the ground, "You will learn to obey my hands on the reins." Her hindquarters rose as her shoulders sank to the ground.

He prodded her with his boot until she reversed position, skittering on her knees to present herself for punishment. Hindquarters. White and vulnerable. Never chastised.

"You will walk" (a swat of the riding crop).

"And trot and canter" (another).

"Prance and bow" (a third).

"As I direct you" (two more).

"And you will *never*" (a particularly stinging one, for emphasis) "oppose your will to mine." He gave her the other four strokes in measured silence.

She gasped and sobbed behind her bit. But she remained still beneath the blows, receiving them, he felt, with pride and generosity, the dark ropy-looking welts rising on her buttocks.

He pulled her to her feet, holding the reins loosely now with one hand and prodding her lightly to turn toward him. Proud. Calm. Broken to bridle and needing only the lightest touch to indicate his will. She was his.

❧   ❧   ❧

Or was she? He trained her to pull carts, to preen in the dressage ring. She trotted all over the property, head high and proud, silver bells jingling, mouth exquisitely responsive to his hands' subtlest tug at the reins. He engaged a groom to wash and feed her, to brush her hair into a tail as elegant as the one that streamed from the cleft between the fresh stripes on her rear.

She liked his sculptures, too—often after she'd dressed herself they'd walk over to the barn and discuss how his work was progressing. And sometimes, when her son was on an overnight visit to cousins or grandparents, she'd stay the night in her little stable, sleeping soundly on straw and eagerly lapping oats and water from her trough. She had done so last week, in fact.

But no, Lord Robert, she'd said—and, to his shame, she'd had to say it more than once—she had no intention of marrying again. The boating accident, the loss of Edward (oh no, Edward hadn't been a horseman—his talents had lain . . . elsewhere) . . . she didn't think she'd ever recover from it.

Perhaps, she'd added, he shouldn't be spending so much time with Lilith. Well, a handsome, talented, charming, and awfully rich man like him should marry.

But she'd had a lovely, a delightful time this afternoon, no it hadn't hurt too much thank you, just enough, just the perfect amount. Her mouth had curved, its shy dimple flickering at the corner.

❧   ❧   ❧

As it did this morning, in accompaniment to her cheerful greeting that wasn't it a lovely day Sir Robert, before she spurred Lucifer away.

The older man gaped. "Didn't know you knew her, Robert."

To which the younger one smiled sadly. "I don't. Not really," and galloped up the hill as though his life depended upon it.

Author's Note: Lady Catherine's letter to *The Englishwoman's Domestic Companion* is patterned on one that really did appear in the July 26, 1890, edition of the *Family Doctor*, a household periodical of the late Victorian Era. The paradoxes of control of self and others, as well as the erotics of imminent rebellion under tight rein, were discussed with remarkable candor in these magazines, and are not my invention at all.

BAPTISM

by Jean Roberta

Vancouver lay trapped, as usual, between the mountains and the ocean. As our plane descended through the evening rain, the lights of the city looked as inviting as I remembered. I was coming home to the jewel of Lotusland or British California, the Canadian port that welcomes all seekers, from the domestic migrants from east of the Rockies to the buyers and sellers of legal and illegal stuff from the Asian countries beyond the Pacific. I hoped the city would welcome me and my man.

I reached for Lars's hand, and its warmth was contagious. His honest face, decorated with the new brown shrubbery of the beard he was trying to grow, lit up with a smile. His short stocky frame and the Scandinavian peasant features which looked like those of a troll when I first saw him had changed my standards of masculine beauty over the past three years. Just the thought of the strong, compact body under his clothes made me grow moist, and his generosity made me want to give as good as I got. He embodied my best notions of manhood, and I thought he knew it. Whether he could satisfy me for a lifetime seemed irrelevant, or so I told myself. *Who lasts that long anyway?*

As the plane approached the land, I could see the lights of distant ships in the vast blackness of ocean that kissed the violet-grey sky. I was bringing Lars here to my childhood home from the sharp and gritty cold of Toronto in winter. He had grown up in the eastern industrial heartland, hardly aware that Canada, like the United States, had a laid-back west coast where the rain has always nourished dreams as well as gardens.

"Maxine," rumbled a voice in my ear as I watched the approaching runway from the window. I turned to Lars, and he held my face to give me an unexpected kiss. My clit and my stomach jumped just as the plane touched solid ground, and I laughed breathlessly into his mouth. He withdrew first, gently reminding me that I couldn't afford to melt in his arms just yet; we had things to do, and someone to see. "We're here," he smiled.

In the chaos of disoriented passengers scrambling for their luggage, I resisted the impulse to kick all the strangers within my reach. I wanted to be alone with my man, but I had to focus on the tasks at hand.

Christmas music floated through the airport, urging the distracted swarm to be merry. Lights, shiny balls, and real evergreen trees of various sizes were everywhere. It was December 27, and we had rushed from a snow-filled Christmas with both sets of our parents in Old Canada to be with my friend Willow on New Year's Eve. We weren't sure when else we would get enough free time to travel.

I wanted Lars to consider the possibility of living on the coast, even if it was destined to fall into the ocean during the next big earthquake. On a deeper level, I felt I had to introduce my present to my past, even though I couldn't predict the results. Like a rainy day on the beach, I thought, life is fluid.

I wasn't sure I would recognize Willow after ten years apart, but I needn't have worried; she looked like an older version of the girl I remembered. Her long hair was now raven-black and shiny enough to hurt the eyes; she looked aggressively healthy in the style of those who work at it. Her brown eyes had more depth than I remembered, and her face looked more defined. Her Eurasian roots were clearly visible, even proudly displayed, and I was shocked at my own reaction: *she's not really white at all*. I blamed myself for living too long in the white and grey rigidity of the east.

"Maxine!" she yelled, beaming. She gathered me into a hug,

which felt like a jolt of electricity. She even rocked me a few times, humming under her breath, as Lars stood politely holding the cart with our suitcases.

"Willow," I caressed her name, almost pleading, "this is Lars."

"Lars!" she responded on cue, sounding forced. "I'm glad to meet you." After a moment of hesitation, she hugged him too. He responded awkwardly, not having lived in the coastal culture of acquaintance by touch.

Willow soon bundled us into a taxi where she sat beside the driver to give directions. We sped past miles of roadside greenery before we were slowed by city traffic. We reached the funkiness of Kitsilano, where Willow was subletting a house she could not have afforded otherwise. She was adept at making useful connections.

The two-story house had a balcony crowded with potted plants and rusting tools. The backyard was a jungle of tomato cages, weeds, grass, wild blackberry bushes, and a pear tree, which seemed to have been awaiting a partridge for many years. Indoors, the house was a collection of generous-sized rooms furnished in new wicker and old walnut. The kitchen featured a gas stove and three bicycles in an alcove. Vintage rock posters and paintings of whales hung on the walls of the front room, which were a womb-like shade of dull red. A small Yule tree, adorned with tiny metal ornaments in the shape of moons and stars, sat on a parlor table.

"I'll show you your room," offered our hostess, posing on the staircase. Our suitcases were soon parked in a bedroom with a four-poster bed covered by a red-and-blue quilt. One purple wall was dominated by a sepia-toned photo of two nude women in a full embrace. Willow's space, Willow's art. "What would you like first?" she demanded. "Wine, rum and coke, herb tea, some weed? That's all I've got for now."

"Rum and coke for me, Willow," Lars stated, as though setting his limits. "I'll help you." He followed her to the kitchen as though suspicious of her intentions. I trusted the two of them to pour me an honest glass of wine.

Alone in the front room, I tried to drink in the flavor of the house, which was owned by luppies: a lesbian couple currently living in Italy for reasons connected with the art business. Various dyke friends of the owners had occupied the house for various lengths of time. From what I had heard, bisexual women and very feminine men were also tolerated, as were intoxicating substances of all kinds. Meat-eating, weapons, and straightness in all forms were discouraged.

Lars and Willow were deep in conversation when they emerged with drinks. "It's such bullshit," she was explaining to him. My breath caught in my throat before I recognized the topic.

"But didn't they win?" asked my man with a respectful show of interest. I was tempted to point out to him that women had not actually taken over the world yet, despite anyone's best hopes or fears.

"The Supreme Court said they were victims of discrimination. Everyone knows that by now, so it's not a big victory. That's not the point. Little Sisters has been suing the government for YEARS for keeping obscenity laws on the books that are unconstitutional. They're right, of course. But do you think the government is going to admit that some of their laws contradict their other laws?"

The question was rhetorical, and no one answered. I accepted my drink from Willow, and took a large gulp. I knew that the brave legal fight of the Vancouver gay/lesbian bookstore against the federal government which had been seizing its shipments of American books and magazines at the border since the 1980s did not keep Lars awake at night, as it did Willow. She had a vested interest in the outcome.

"Your book was seized, wasn't it?" I asked politely. This was also a rhetorical question, since I already knew the story. I wanted to lead the conversation into a safer channel.

"A few years ago," she agreed, "but now it's selling again. You haven't seen it, have you?" she asked Lars point-blank.

"No," he told her, looking receptive.

In a flash, Willow had located her coffee-table book in a bookshelf. It was a collection of her erotic photos accompanied by poems; admirers of the three poets seemed to regard Willow's pictures as illustrations for the words, while Willow preferred to think of the poems as captions for her images. "I'll sit in the middle," offered Willow, squeezing her firm butt between me and Lars. "Cuddle up," she urged us, "so you can both see."

The first photo spread showed a young woman with chin-length reddish-blonde hair like mine, an angular jawline like mine, a plump figure like mine, and big red nipples which might have been enhanced by lipstick or by stimulation. She was lying in the lap of a darker-skinned woman with elaborately coiffed black hair, who dangled three cherries over the open mouth of the blonde: very symbolic. Lars turned as red as the various kinds of fruit in the picture. I resisted the impulse to explain: *It's not me. Or her.* He didn't seem to be looking at the poem, and I doubted whether he could focus on the metaphors in either composition.

The second photo featured two athletic-looking young men, both tan but European-looking; one was holding the other supine on a beach as they gazed into each other's eyes. *Thank the Goddess*, I thought, *there is nothing here to shake up Lars.* A glance at his face showed me I was wrong. The accompanying poem was about brotherhood through the ages, which almost made me snicker. I knew that Lars had an older brother whom he had fought with all through their childhood; as adults, they rarely spoke to each other.

The third photo was a parody of conventional porn imagery; a Mediterranean-looking woman with short bleached hair was looking over her shoulder at the camera like Betty Grable, aware that her round ass was the focal point of the picture. A muscular blue-eyed man with a toothpaste-commercial smile had one arm around her waist. The accompanying poem was named "Dangerous Curves."

"What is this for?" demanded Lars, looking Willow straight in the eyes.

"It's eye candy," she smirked, trying to maintain her cool.

"But what reaction are you hoping for? When people see these pictures or you show them? You must be expecting something."

He laid a hand deliberately on her thigh, something he would not do lightly. Whatever she was expecting, this didn't seem to be it.

"Lars," I muttered, embarrassed at being embarrassed. "It's art photography. That's what she does."

"Oh, it's art," he responded dryly. "But it's not hanging in an art gallery. You're showing it to us. I like your pictures, Willow. Is that what you want? Would you like us to pose for you? Do you want to pose for one of us? Did you think I'd be shocked, or Max would be embarrassed? Is that a turn-on for you? I'm not attacking you, angel. I just want to know."

I hesitated just long enough to catch a glimpse of Willow's face, which answered the man's blunt questions: she had not invited us here with the intention of discreetly ignoring our hopelessly retro male-female relationship, or of pulling sisterly confidences out of me behind Lars's back. Willow's plan had been to spark something, anything, a twosome or threesome as dramatic as crashing waves in the shadow of cloud-covered mountain peaks.

"Hey, man," she protested lamely. "I didn't want to raise any shit. I just thought, you know, you might like to—I'm Maxine's friend and you know I—" The steady look from Lars's steel-grey eyes seemed to be drying up the flow of her words. "Look," she pointed out. "I like Maxine and you know that, but I respect your relationship." I glanced at Lars's crotch and saw something which did not surprise me.

"Do you want a taste?" He was openly teasing her. "Would you like to know what Max gets?" To my amazement, he stood to his full height, approximately the same as Willow's, and unzipped his fly. In three years of fucking and sucking, I had not seen such a performance.

Willow glanced quickly at me, and she couldn't keep the fear completely out of her eyes. I had never realized before how intimidating I had always found her (*not her fault*, I told myself): how talented, how glamorous, how radically fearless. Now I couldn't suppress my exhilaration. "It's okay with me," I assured her. "I don't own him. We trust each other." We had discussed such things in the airy realm of theory, but an opportunity like this had never presented itself before, and we had both balked at the thought of fishing for playmates in bars or personal ads.

Willow unbuckled his belt, and I helped her to pull his pants down. I tugged at his sweater, and he held one of my hands between both of his for a moment. I pushed my breasts into his back and breathed in the warm smell of his neck and armpits. *He's mine*, I thought, *regardless*.

We soon had him naked, and I wanted to show him off to her: my imported pet man. "See this," I told her. "Hairy chest and balls. He likes to have them played with." I could see her shaking with silent laughter at our version of the Captain's Paradise.

Lars was running his hand experimentally over Willow's silk blouse, finding her small, tight breasts. "Will you show us your tits?" he asked crudely. She grinned, but made no move to undress.

"Willow," I asked, "do you suck cock?"

"No," she laughed. "I'll leave that to you."

I had Lars's stiffening rod in one hand, and I felt it jerk in answer. "Lie down," I told him. "I'll take care of him."

Lars seemed increasingly conscious of how he looked, naked and erect between two fully clothed women. He refused to budge from a standing position, and I could sense his frustration as Willow wriggled out of his reach. I knelt in front of him to stroke his hungry animal. "Suck him, baby," he growled, desperately trying to regain control of the festivities as our Lord of Misrule.

I licked his shaft, first soothing and then teasing his touchy male flesh. He responded to me as he always did, with pulsing insistence. I gently supported his balls, and accepted him as far into my mouth as I could. I could feel his trembling need for release. "That's it, Max," he sighed, stroking my hair. "You're so good, baby." Both of us were ignoring Willow, which was a mistake.

Lars's thick shaft began to spurt. "Aww!" he yelled. "What're you doing?" He gushed into my mouth, unable to stop. Willow was behind him, one hand holding him by a hip. She chuckled, slowly removing a gloved finger from his ass.

"It helps things along," she explained calmly. "I'm glad you liked it," she told him.

I could see that the smug look in her eyes enraged him, and that he was determined not to be taken by surprise again. He ran a hand down my back as though to reassure me that I was the good girl. "Come here," he barked at Willow. He reached for her blouse and barely avoided popping buttons as he unfastened it.

She shrugged out of her little sports bra and shimmied out of her tight pants, making a dance of it. "Unsafe sex," she commented.

"We've been tested," I told her.

Willow tossed her hair out of her face, rolling her eyes at me. "Men spread it, Maxine," she reminded me. "I hope you know what you want."

In answer, Lars wrapped his wiry arms around her and guided her to the chesterfield. "Like this," he instructed, showing her that he wanted her face down. She gracefully complied. "Maxine," he asked in a softer voice, "will you bring me a sock and some lube?"

I bounced up the stairs to the bedroom that contained all our traveling supplies. I dug a foil package, a pair of latex gloves, and a tube of lube from a suitcase, and ran back downstairs like a paramedic rushing to an accident scene.

Willow's smooth, glowing back was more alluring than I remembered. Her beautifully curved buttocks held my gaze like two half-moons. I watched with pleasure as Lars pulled a glove onto his square fingers, thoughtfully coated one with lube, and pushed it steadily into Willow's anus. I could feel myself growing wet as he reached under her with the other hand to harass her clit.

I found a cushion and slid it beneath her to make the next phase easier. Lars pushed his hard, latex-coated cock into Willow's eager cunt as she moaned loudly. He gained momentum, slowly and surely, as he fucked her toward a state of gasping delirium. "This—what—you—wanted?" he panted in her ear. Judging from her reactions, the answer was yes. I stroked her hair, watching the look of surrender on her face.

Willow came with a moan that rose almost to a scream. Lars's pumping butt showed his willingness to let go, to let a rainbow of feeling explode into the disposable bag that was meant to protect Willow from him, and him from her. Coming up for air, he looked transformed.

Willow sat and looked at me, a question in her eyes. "He's good, isn't he?" I asked, or stated.

"Quite a stud," she agreed. Her voice dripped amused sarcasm as her face shone with the pride of one who knows she can make things happen, a witch who can harness the tides. She reached for both my arms and pulled me down beside her. Her lips touched mine, and she held me close for a long, tender kiss.

I had undressed to the waist, and my breasts rolled against hers like friendly dogs, as we lay entwined from head to knees. Lars reached under my skirt, inserted a hand into my panties and found the heat he sought. Neither the man nor the woman was willing to let me go. As Willow held me close enough to feel my heartbeat, two of Lars's fingers found a home in me, and burrowed deeply past my cervix. In his steady, patient way, he worked me up to a level of flowing wetness that brought a smile back to his face. Not really knowing whether I squirmed in gratitude or uneasiness, I rocked between the two of them, smelling our combined sweat. My unbearably tickled twat erupted in spasm after spasm, as though screaming for peace on earth.

We sprawled together, breathing in harmony for an endless moment. Willow spoke first. "Are you hungry? There's a leftover Greek feast in the fridge." She brought us dolmathes and spano-kopita, and we all ate together in a warm silence.

When we had filled our stomachs, we remembered to exchange Christmas presents: candles, incense, liqueur-filled chocolates. At this point in the evening, thanking each other for such things seemed slightly ridiculous. Lars wrapped an arm around my shoulders to lead me upstairs, and Willow graciously bade us good night.

In the morning over Moroccan coffee, Willow invited me to see the new lesbian hangouts, which had not existed ten years before. We sighed together over the death of various small and cozy cafés. With an unreadable face, Lars said he wanted to check out several music stores. He offered to meet us for dinner.

Being alone with Willow for an afternoon in the holiday season made me feel giddy, partly from guilt. Her questions made it worse. "You say he's a computer geek?" she joked.

"Not a geek," I answered too defensively. "He plays stringed instruments. Guitar, mandolin, banjo, even a lute. He writes his own songs."

"Cool," she affirmed unconvincingly.

While pale winter sunlight still bathed the West End, Willow steered me possessively into a lesbian café-bar where the bored bartender stood on display, a metal chain dangling into the deep cleavage above her black leather vest. Willow and I drank complicated cocktails named Nectar of the Goddess and Dyke's Milk, which somehow made me realize where I really wanted to be. "Let's go to the beach," I suggested.

"It's cloudy," Willow reminded me.

"I don't care," I pointed out. I insisted on walking, since I wanted my feet to know that the city has always been married to the ocean.

When we reached the sand, I was glad to sit on a bench like an old woman, holding hands with an old friend. We watched the grey water under a grey sky, contemplating the boundless depths. "You have this all the time," I couldn't resist saying.

"So could you," answered Willow.

We rode back to the house on a swaying bus, and I comforted myself by thinking of it as a boat. "Do you still write?" she demanded over the sounds of traffic.

"Oh yes," I insisted. "Not only the textbooks at work." Nothing of mine seemed noteworthy enough to be seized at the border or anywhere else. Willow didn't ask whether I was planning to write anything about her and me, or Lars and me, or the three-way relationship I was already thinking of as the Vancouver Triangle. Neither did she suggest a photo shoot.

At Willow's house, as I thought of it, we found ourselves alone. She put on a CD from the 1980s so we could dance to the soundtrack of our past; I knew the melodies better than the titles. I caught the words "share you" or "won't share you" as she held me with arms so strong that I could forget I was with a woman.

After the song ended, she guided me upstairs to a room crowded with jade, porcelain, and wooden objects, where the goddess Kwan Yin smiled down at us from a print on the wall as Willow tied my wrists to the bed frame with cotton rope, spread my legs, and licked me until I wept along with my reflection in the mirror. She sucked, nibbled, pinched, and rolled my nipples until they looked as red and full as ripe fruit or open sores. One finger at a time, she showed me that my cunt would accept her whole fist.

"You're such a woman," she murmured, her head between my breasts. "You never really left, you know?" she goaded. "I still have you. You'll move back." She washed the various fluids off me in the shower, then carefully applied liquid foundation, mascara, eyeliner, and lipstick to my face before we went to meet Lars.

Days passed, and the games went on. Lars and Willow seemed to have reached some agreement about how to divide me up, as though I were a body of water claimed by rival nations. They treated each other with courtesy except when they fucked strenuously in my absence. I discovered this after I had returned from lunch with Sylvia, an old friend from high school who was now a born-again mother of five; I found Lars grunting on his back on the floor with Willow bouncing on him, her hair flying in his face. I watched unnoticed until their awareness of me disrupted their rhythm, and they finished awkwardly. Lars stood up, scooped me into his arms, then lay me on the chesterfield for a long, slow session of kissing, stroking, and sensual fucking.

On New Year's Eve, Willow took us to a loud party at the home of a male artist friend of hers. A diverse assortment of couples, singles, and clumps of friends danced and ate until midnight, when noisemakers were handed out and we all tried to deafen the strangers closest to us. I kissed Lars first, then Willow before I was snatched away by various women and men who all wanted to start my New Year with a kiss. I must have looked approachable.

In the early hours of the morning, several joints circulated through the crowd, and I became pleasantly high, then hungry enough to eat the remaining snacks until the real or imagined laughter of several onlookers made me stop. At four o'clock, I insisted on leaving with my two companions. I was planning to take part in a more important ritual in the morning, and I needed as much sleep as I could get. I knew from experience that lack of sleep makes it harder to withstand cold.

New Year's Day dawned bright and breezy. I woke up Lars, who grumbled and stayed in bed, open-eyed. I called to Willow: "We have to go!"

She called back, "I don't. Are you really going to take the dip?"

"Yes," I announced, wanting to make it clear that I could not be talked out of it. "Come and watch," I urged both of them.

I wished I had a flashier swimsuit for the occasion; I hoped my old black one at least had a slimming effect. I pulled a pair of jeans and a T-shirt on over it, then put on my jacket and paced the floor until Lars and Willow were dressed enough to accompany me to my destination.

The beach was crowded with dippers and observers. I recognized the logo of the Canadian Broadcasting Company on a camera. The Polar Bear Dip was a tradition I had missed whenever I spent New Year's Day away from the coast, although its appeal was hard to describe to skeptics.

A group of teenagers, approximately half a dozen of each gender, ran screaming and splashing into the icy water of English Bay with the camera trained on them. I could almost see the photographer shiver in sympathy, or with the sadistic pleasure of a voyeur. I assumed the parents of the dippers would be pleased to see their offspring on the six o'clock news for such an innocent reason.

"Ready?" grinned Lars, who had already told me with some admiration that I had more guts than brains.

"As ready as I'm gonna be," I answered jauntily, peeling off each item of outer clothing and handing it to him until my pale arms and legs, covered with goose bumps, were revealed to the world. "Here goes," I told my audience. I deliberately walked into the photographer's line of sight, took a deep gulp of air, then ran into the foam.

As the icy water struck my skin like a thousand tiny needles, I let out a shriek but kept moving. I was determined to immerse myself to the neck, if only for as long as it would take me to wade that far. A large collie splashed in beside me, providing a welcome distraction. I filled my mind with visions of tropical islands as the liquid cold rose up to my clenched nipples, to my collarbone, and past my shoulders. "Ahh!" I yelled, giving myself permission to turn around. I ran as fast as I could back to the sand and the crowd as the restless air struck my wet skin. The air was filled with hoots and applause, but I couldn't be sure which were for me. Willow threw a thick towel around me like a trainer caring for a champion boxer.

"You did it," approved Lars.

"She always did," Willow informed him, rubbing it in.

"I've been baptized," I gasped, trying not to shiver. "I've paid my respects to Mother Pacific."

"Silly girl," grinned Lars in patronizing mode. "You live in Ontario. And we're going back tomorrow."

"Lars," I objected, "I don't just live in one place. And we'll be coming back here too." I didn't voice my threat: *I'll come back to the coast, with or without you.* I was glad to have a good reason for wearing water on my face, and I remembered that human body fluids are chemically similar to ocean water: we carry the ocean within us. "Group hug," I begged Lars and Willow, and they obliged by throwing their arms around me. Their combined warmth was intoxicating.

The next day, Willow came into the room as I was packing my suitcase. "I'm sorry," I told her, reaching for her. She held me against her firm body.

"No need to be sorry, baby," she explained. "I'll be okay. You know me. Stay in touch by e-mail, let me know how you're doing." Lars entered. "You too," she told him, sounding strangely open and honest. "Let me know what's happening in the computer world. As much as I can understand."

"I might start something here," he remarked, as though talking to himself. "There's a market."

Too soon, we were on a plane flying eastward. Tears sprang to my eyes as I noticed how snugly Vancouver fit between the mountains and the ocean, as it always had. I wondered where the tides of my life would carry me in the following years. For the moment, I felt blessed just to be alive in such a large, bright, and stinging world.

EYEWASH

by Michèle Larue

The three of us sat on the back seat of an Ambassador, bumping along the road from Madras. Our reward was to be Mysore, where the Indian driver ultimately set us down. One of my friends, big-boned and Irish, led us into the first hotel that came along, the Sapphire, next to the bus station. Corrupted by Indian fatalism, we let her make all the decisions. At dawn, the bus drivers tested their engines beneath our windows before venturing out onto the streets. Kate, the Scot, lit her first *Beedee.* Our skin was oily, our hair lusterless, we were haggard and marked from the road. We needed to move upmarket.

Built for some British Vice-Consul, the Lalitha Maha Palace was the best in town. In a dining room done up in the manner of English pastries, Kate began finding fault with the waiters' baggy trousers. She came from a family of penniless aristocrats and had latched on to the Irish Laura, who didn't seem to mind paying her way. They both had the same scapegoat: the English. Kate was into females, but Laura paid no attention to her overtures, she was a man-eater who couldn't go three days without a fuck. Whenever sex was in short supply, she had a change of personality.

Then the bonze came in and our laughter froze on our lips. Athletic-looking, holding his shaved head high, he looked the diners over with mischievous eyes as he strode to a tableful of Americans. A childlike shoulder protruded from his saffron robe. Kate and Laura commented on his physique and asked my opinion.

With tears in their eyes from the spicy food, they went over the games they might play at his expense. Kate would lift the sacred robe with her teeth—"100% cotton, soaked in musk!"—Laura would tickle him with the feather tips of her earrings—"Only ten quid at Harrod's, darling"—and finish with his bare feet, so appetizing in those sandals, with their well-cared-for toes. Then together, they would lick his buttocks—"Butterscotch, dearie, but zero calories." The texture of his skin was anybody's guess.

The program included exploring his anus with a finger, and Laura held out the copper-green nails she stuck on with Crazy Glue. Kate would make comments on the boy's expressions while Laura burrowed into him with her ring finger. Would he keep that serene expression that they both envied so much? One thing would lead to another and the next vile act would be tasting his anus. They would suck their greedy fingers right under the bonze's nose, and soon a makeshift dildo would take their place, such as the penlight bulging through Laura's pants pocket.

They finally decided on a banana, Kate would stick it in, but which orifice? They argued. First the mouth, to get it wet. No, no, the asshole first, "It's so much more humiliating, dearie!"

My religious sensibility kept me from taking part in this deluge of pornography. Whenever one of them sought my approval, I would answer with a cowardly nod. To keep the fantasy alive, Kate kept ordering fresh pots of tea from the waiter. Beyond the range of their cocky voices, the living statue shone forth.

Later I learned that the monk lived in a nearby camp of Tibetans. He was a political messenger, pleading the refugees' cause to foreign benefactors. Kate led the way out of the restaurant and managed to touch the saffron robe. A flicker of amusement lit up the lama's pupils. Surely that dazzling sparkle was meant for me . . .

Out in the street, I put my hallucination down to collective hysteria. Kate resolved not to wash her hands for the rest of the day.

En route for Blue Valley, we passed an elephant with her baby, then a busload of Japanese. An Indian army colonel was waiting for us on a wildlife preserve, in the middle of the unspoiled savanna of my dreams. The camp included a few permanent bungalows. During dinner, an officer wearing a blazer jacket told us of the elephants' mating season and their sexual excitement, the *musth*, when they trampled everything in their path. Late that night, in spite of the fire in a ditch, a troop of them destroyed the lamps outside and beat on the walls of our bedrooms with their trunks.

The next part of my dream materialized the next day. Perched on the back of a tame elephant, I photographed wild animals in their natural state; on the other hand, the idea of wild beasts terrified my two friends and they kept to the camp day after day. There was a private courtyard, safe from prying eyes, where they could strip to sunbathe. In the end, they got an urge for colonial nostalgia, just like their English "enemies," and set off for Oloon, a tea-growing town in the hills. After a week of safari I'd had my fill of bears and buffaloes, and set out for Mysore, where we were to join up again.

The windows of my hotel looked out on a ruined palace in an unattended park. By noon, the heat was stifling and I went for a swim at the Lalitha Mahal Palace. Feeling relaxed from the pool, with my hair still wet, I glimpsed a saffron robe going round a hallway turning. I met my rickshaw driver at the entrance. As we drove slowly over the dry lawns, the bonze appeared and waved to us. He was taking an elderly monk to the bus station. Sitting in the middle of the seat, the young lama took advantage of the first turn we took to put his arm around my waist. At the bus stop, I loaded sweets into the old man's bag and we helped him to his seat.

Lobsung, for such was the bonze's name, came back to the hotel with me. No sooner had he come into the room behind me than he'd seized upon a pair of binoculars lying on the bed. Braced against the balcony railing, he was peering at the ruin across the way when he burst out laughing. I took my turn at the binoculars and saw across the lawn a tiny monkey hanging by his rear legs from a children's swing. He was holding a kitten coiled in his long tail and buggering it as he swung. We could even hear the feline mewing. The monk's laughing mouth blew cool air on the back of my neck. He pressed his chin into my flesh, began rummaging under my blouse with one hand while the other stroked my belly with juvenile awkwardness. I was dying to slip my fingers inside his robe, imagining the warm gap between his cool skin and the cloth.

I showed him how to kiss. After that, I had to slow him down. He'd have licked my tonsils, so hungry was he for a woman. He peered down my cleavage: the virgin wanted to see everything there was to see on a female.

He sniffed me and I did likewise. He had a sharp, woody smell, his skin tasted salty. He gave me the impression of someone who'd been told about sex and was busy checking out his second-hand anatomic knowledge. His breathing was slow and abdominal. "Working on his *chi,*" I said to myself while his girlish hands stroked my thighs.

The moment the idea of *chi* entered my mind, all my thoughts focused on Lobsung and his breathing honed in on me. His mauve lips chanted weirdly into my vulva. The buzzing of a fly. Or sometimes the throbbing of a trombone. He blew his breath into my sex and sucked it out, humming all the while. He drew muted sounds from my nether parts, cavernous echoes of his own melody. I had become a Tibetan bagpipe. Blasts of hot air, gusts of wind, a Buddhist hurricane, blew my dress away like a Montgolfier balloon.

Now his rangy body emerged in turn from the folds of orange. His legs grew thin at the ankles and his penis hung pointing at the floor. Without further ado, he sat down on top of me and began rubbing his perineum and buttocks against my belly. Then he came into me from above. Only our internal muscles moved, exchanging a series of voluntary contractions.

He was attentive to my sensations, and waited until the time was ripe to move his organ in the proper way. My pleasure peaked each time he stopped. Orgasm was not a goal in itself, but a point of no return, a killjoy both of us were determined not to reach.

To make the pleasure last, we drew apart. He lay on his back and worked on his energy, breathing slowly through his nose, not breathing at all for long stretches of time. Propped on my elbow beside him, I watched.

After our first "climax of delight," we began to explore further. With this man, pleasure involved different levels of intensity, stages to be negotiated. It was my turn to sit on top, with my legs wrapped around his hips. My belly shuddered electrically and I opened for him all the way. He lay with his eyes shut, motionless inside me, his firm hands resting on my shoulders. Then he withdrew. Wrapping a towel around himself, he went to the window, had a look at the monkey, and giggled.

He wanted me to sit on him again, but the other way round, facing his feet. This time there was a whole succession of tiny movements and muted vibrations rose to my skull: the Will to Pure Pleasure by osmosis. A Bengal light began to sizzle in my head. Nirvana lasted a long time, but in the end I couldn't keep up with his tantric apprenticeship and collapsed on top of him, worn-out before I could come. Lobsung muttered something in his language, more like onomatopoeia than words, and went to sleep with a smile on his lips.

In the cool of the morning, I went looking for my two friends near the bus station. By telepathy or bush telegraph, the desk clerk at the Sapphire predicted that "the English ladies" would be a day late.

Back at the hotel, I saw Lobsung in the ruins across the lawn, weightlessly leaping between the windows. He did a double somersault, landed on his feet in a martial stance, went on to do forms. Then he levitated on the veranda steps. I remembered Kate's horrified expression when a child stuck his fingerless hand through the car window for a cigarette and Laura's cynical remark: "Eyewash!"

I was on my way back to the hotel when I saw two silhouettes hobbling up the road with familiar-looking giant-sized suitcases rolling behind them. My friends were on the verge of exhaustion. From a distance, they'd taken me for a boy in my baseball cap.

The Oloon-Mysore "express" had broken down in the middle

of the wildlife sanctuary. Neither Laura nor Kate had left the bus for fear of elephants. They'd been terrified to see several passengers actually go off into the bushes to answer the call of nature. And when they opened their sponge bags, a horde of monkeys had swarmed into the bus through the open windows and made off with their cosmetics! At the Sapphire, they asked the desk clerk for their old room back.

The final blow fell later that evening when they came to see me in my hotel in a state of extreme nervous fatigue. The peace and quiet, the panoramic view from my window, made Kate hysterical. She took it out on Laura for having chosen the Sapphire, but Laura wasn't listening, she was gaping at the saffron robe on a chair.

My head bounced off the wall from the slap she gave me. She grabbed me by the hair and Kate pitched in with a kick to my kidneys that knocked me to the floor, then she kneeled on me and squeezed one of my breasts in the crook of her elbow. They dragged me over the linoleum and called me a hypocrite.

When they finally left me alone, I looked for the bonze's robe. It was gone. The bathroom door was banging in the evening breeze. On the windowsill, a tiny monkey with knowing eyes stood swaying on its paws. I thought to myself: "That wasn't fair: two men ganging up on a girl."

BODIES OF WATER

by Cecilia Tan

Her skin is more sensitive now, she's sure of it. As the water trickles over her back, she can feel every drop, each rivulet tracing a line down her back like a fingertip caress. Water never felt like this before, not even in the most luxurious shower.

She remembers the shower at Argyropoulos's palazzo. One of Steve's rich investors, taken in by the adventure of treasure-hunting, he had not only bought in to the expedition company but insisted the team stay at his palatial home while they were land-side. She barely remembers what the bathroom looked like, only that the shower was such a luxury—hot water, dry towels—after three weeks on the ship sifting through sand-covered artifacts and always being damp.

It was one morning when getting out of that shower she had seen the blue speck on her skin, just glimpsed it in the mirror on the underside of her arm. No, no it can't be . . . she thought to herself. It was blue like a spot of spilled ink, just like Jackie's, just like Karros'. She refused to believe it. In a few hours she would be back on the ship, and they would be that much closer to solving the mystery of the wreck. The fact that Karros was in a hospital in Athens and Jackie was on her way to the CDC in Georgia affected her only slightly. Not when we are this close!, she thought. She felt sure they were on the verge of a breakthrough.

The wreck was a mystery, and that was what mattered most to

Lydia. When she had gone into archaeology she had thought she would be sifting dust in an Egyptian desert or hacking through the Yucatan jungle. But there was pioneering work being done in undersea archaeology, and her fiancé Ambrose had hooked them up with Steve to do a few voyages. No matter how much he claimed he wasn't a treasure hunter, Steve still hoped for a large haul of gold to pay back his stockholders with. Ambrose hoped for prestige and fame. But Lydia just wanted the answers to questions history had left for them.

Her arms are crossed over her chest, but the water flowing down her back feels so good she wants to reach up into the stream. She lowers her hands, her fingers sliding over her skin, and she shivers in delight. She has never been comfortable in nakedness, but now she forgets modesty as she leans back to let the water spatter onto her breasts. She reaches up and spreads the water between her breasts, over her nipples, her neck and lips.

She had argued with Ambrose over the origin of the wreck. That morning at the palazzo, before they had set sail again, he had picked a fight with the other archaeologist, a young man named Tomson, Will Tomson, who had speculated that if they couldn't find evidence for a Mediterranean culture who whaled, who was to say the cargo came from the same place as the ship? Ambrose had practically bellowed at the man, "What sort of twisted logic is that? You'll never get anywhere with thinking like that, my boy. You'll spend your life on one wild goose chase after another. Simplify!"

Lydia had been pretending not to hear the exchange, putting sugar into her coffee with slow deliberate spoonfuls, and stirring so that the spoon did not clink against the side of the mug. But when it had come to that she had stood up, and approached their table.

Ambrose had put his hand around her hip as she came over, proprietary as always. But he took it away again when she said, "It very well may be that our explanation is going to be a complicated one. Where did the whale oil come from? Where did the ship come from? They may well be two different answers." As she walked away, she could feel Ambrose's usual daggers in her back. She would pay for defying him later, she was sure of it. But no matter the consequence, Lydia could not allow an incorrect or foolish statement to stand.

And they certainly had to consider every option. This wasn't like the Spanish galleon they had recovered off the continental shelf last year, doubloons and rare artifacts and a diary clearly revealing the date of her voyage. No, this wreck was older than any ever found, probably three thousand years or more, and nothing they had brought up yet had matched their body of knowledge. There were amphorae and other jars they expected to be full of olive oil. But some were found with their seals still intact, and when opened they were found to be whale oil. Some of them were strangely fragrant, as if perfumed to last over centuries, millennia. The scents of some civilization older than any they had previously encountered. Staggering.

Almost as staggering as the news that came to them after the ship had set out to sea once again. Lydia had been standing on the deck of the ship, her hands gripping the railing. The sun was hot but the spray was cold and damp as they headed back to the deep water where the wreck lay. She barely felt the pitching and yawing of the converted trawler as it sliced through the waves, her eyes fixed on a far spot on the horizon. The answer was out there, somewhere.

Tomson disturbed her reverie with a hand on her elbow. At first she was glad to see him. He was such an inquisitive fellow, so delighted by every puzzle, every discovery. But his face was closed, now. "Jackie just radioed in."

He sounded like he was choking as he said it. Lydia saw the distress on his face. "What is it? Is it the blue fever? What did they find?"

"Karros died in the hospital, some kind of pneumonia-like symptoms, but they weren't sure if it was related to the skin condition or not. But the CDC thinks it's some kind of infectious agent. They've got Jackie in a bubble."

For a moment, pure human emotion took over. "Oh, poor Karros . . ." She crumbled and he put his arm around her, held her for a moment. She coughed up a few tears, though she mostly held them back. But then she straightened up and looked into Tomson's eyes. Like the ocean, their blue was brighter in the sun. "What do they want us to do?"

"For now, stay out here, and tell them if we have any more cases of it. We shouldn't try to land anywhere, that's for sure."

She watched as his eyes roved the horizon like hers, and she felt their hips touch as they both leaned on the railing. "It's just lucky we were out here when the news came," she said.

"Why do you say that?"

"Because now we have no reason to stop operations," Lydia said. "We can keep digging."

Tomson nodded and a relieved almost-smile warmed his face. "I'm so glad you feel that way about it. Steve wants to keep going, too."

"Who doesn't?" Lydia asked, already suspecting the answer.

"Your partner," Tomson answered. "Ambrose thinks we should head straight for the mainland and all get ourselves into a hospital right away."

"A hospital didn't do Karros any good." Lydia stared back into the blue. "Do you feel it, Will? We've barely begun to investigate, but we're on the verge of something quite extraordinary."

"You sound quite sure of yourself."

"It's rare I find something so totally outside of my knowledge base." Lydia liked the way her voice sounded when she said that, at last finding that note that reminded her more of a professor than of a student. "Whatever we find, they'll be rewriting the history books, I'm sure of it."

Will Tomson nodded then, and they both watched the sea roll under the ship for long minutes.

She opens her mouth to let the water dribble in, letting it run down her chin and over her closed eyelids. Her lips tingle where it touches, and she lets the tip of her tongue emerge. She touches her wet cheeks with her hands and then brings them together in front of her mouth—she looks like she is praying. She has never felt anything quite like this before. It must be the fever. Her chest heaves as she breathes, the water falling faster now, over her face, her breasts, and down her belly. Water, who would have thought water would be the key to it all?

Ambrose had fought her bitterly that night in their cabin. "You'll get us all killed. Crazy woman . . ."

She had held her ground as much as she could. "They've ordered us to stay in quarantine. And no one else is sick. There's no reason to stop the expedition. For all we know, Karros' pneumonia wasn't even related."

Ambrose rumbled like gathering thunder. "It's still too dangerous. I'm not handling anything that comes up from the wreck and neither are you."

"What do you mean . . ."

"You're my wife-to-be and you're mine to protect. You're not going near it. Let little Willie do it."

She tried to deflect him by teasing, but it was a mistake. "You sound like those old Egyptologists, running from the curse of the mummy."

"I'll have to tell the others that you're not feeling well, that you have a headache." He left then, and she realized what he meant, as he bolted the door from the outside. The converted trawler was all steel—there wasn't even a porthole for her to shout through.

She beat futilely on the bulkhead door for a few moments and then sat back on the pallet bed, unable to believe that Ambrose would really keep her locked in there for long. He was touchy, she knew that. She had known it even when he had proposed, that he had a temper, fits of ego and irrationality. But he had courted her so earnestly, with flowers and dinners, and always on his best behavior, shaking hands with her father and asking his permission . . . how could she say no? All those years, college, graduate school, the Yucatan, she had never had time for a companion. Ambrose had seemed ideal in some ways. They could work together, live together, grow old together. He was what they called "old-fashioned" and she had liked that, at first. Before all this talk of protecting and property.

She licks the water from her lips. They had been chapped from sun and wind but now they feel like rose petals, the water droplets beading on her face like dew. She cranes her neck down to lick the water from her breasts, and leans back again to let the water rain down her midsection, pooling in the triangle of her crotch, her bush half-wet like a shore plant in a tide pool.

That night Ambrose had brought her dinner, canned stew heated in the galley with some crackers. He unbolted the door and swept in with the bowl in front of him, placing it on one corner of the bed with a flourish. So pleased with himself. The ship rocked slightly, but the seas were calm and there was little danger of spilling. "I thought you might be hungry," he said.

"Not really," she replied, just to annoy him. His face said he was expecting praise, as if he had forgotten she wasn't really ill, forgotten that was a lie he had invented.

But then, she thought, she really was ill. While he had been gone she had examined the underside of her arm—the spot had grown bigger. There was another spot in the small of her back, as well.

He shrugged off the annoyance and came over to sit next to her. He took her hand in his. "Lydia, my dove, please don't be angry. You have to realize how irrational you can be sometimes. It's better this way—you'll see how it will all work out. You'll be glad . . ." He was leaning toward her, to kiss her. She pulled back almost involuntarily, as if he were the one with the contagion. He pressed forward more, his eyes closing, until their lips met.

She allowed him to kiss her for long moments, until she broke away saying, "That stew smells good."

He straightened, remembering his pretense for being there. "Of course. Here you are." He stood up and she gathered the bowl to her. Then he left, and bolted the door behind him.

She ate the stew, but didn't taste it. She ate it because she supposed it was better to be fortified than not, but her mind was elsewhere. What was Tomson doing right now? He might be opening a basket brought up by a remote right this minute. The wreck was so deep human divers, even in submersibles, couldn't reach it. But machines, guided from the deck with video monitors, could go anywhere. She felt sometimes that it was her hands, not the robot's, picking through the wreckage, lifting an ancient astrolabe out of the silt, peeling apart the remnants of a wooden carton to find whatever lay inside.

She hesitates a moment, the rapture frightens her a bit, and she questions what is happening. But pleasure is a reassuring thing, it feels right rather than wrong, and she gradually separates her knees. Pooled water cascades between her legs, and her mouth quivers as the trickle touches a place she has only let Ambrose touch when he fumbles to insert himself in her. Unlike his hard knuckles, the caress of the water opens her, and she feels an outflow of her own juices come forth to meet the cascade of water.

Lydia had been locked in the cabin two days when someone came to the door while she was sleeping. The knock woke her, a muffled voice.

"Open the door!" she shouted, her voice hoarse from sleeping. That sounded like Tomson. She banged on her side of the door.

With a clank the door came open, and Will Tomson stepped in with a wrench in his hand and a puzzled look on his face.

She grabbed him by the hand and pulled him down the corridor to the dark, empty galley. The room was lit only with the orange emergency light above the door and they blinked at each other. "Will, you have to tell me, what have you found?"

"Lydia, wait a minute, were you trapped in there?"

"That's not important right now. Please Will, what's been going on?"

"That's why I came looking for you. I found something you're not going to believe." He shifted the sack on his back to the table, opened it carefully to reveal what looked to Lydia rather like a book. It looked to be some kind of leather, and Tomson folded it open once, then again like a road map, to reveal several sheaves of skin.

"How could something like this survive in the water all that time?" she asked, even as she began to take in the drawings and symbols.

"Have a look at this," he said, taking out his flashlight and flooding the table with white light. The pages were blue. "Tell me, please, Lydia, did Ambrose lock you away because you've been infected?"

She shook her head. "No, to keep me from being infected. But Ambrose be damned, do you realize this is a map?" In human measure of time, the coastline of Spain and Portugal looked essentially the same. But this showed some land one did not see in the modern era. The drawing detailed a tiny map-size city, and a route from the mainland to it. A route that they had followed to arrive at the site of the wreck.

He nodded and turned the sheaf over. "And it looks like an instruction manual, as well." On the other side were drawings of a man and a woman, the odd-shaped whale-oil jars, and more. Lydia was reminded of the safety instruction cards in airplanes. The final picture in the sequence, if they were reading the correct direction, was of the two humans swimming with two dolphins.

The other page also had a sequence of pictures on it. Lydia felt almost dizzy as she looked at them. "Can I be interpreting these correctly?" she thought. It appeared to tell a story of a city being engulfed by the sea, the same drawing of the city as on the facing sheaf, with the water level going up and up and up.

"It's not possible," she said, her voice so low Tomson was not sure she spoke. "A lost civilization? Who had the know-how to make a book that would not decay after thousands of years underwater?"

Tomson put his hand on hers. "That's not all. We got word from Georgia."

"Oh no, not Jackie."

"She's alive. They said she's almost completely blue now, though. Antibiotics, antivirals, they aren't effective. They are assuming now if it's an organism, it's something like a prion, something they haven't seen before. They say her cellular structure is changing. Not just on her skin. They are seeing changes in her brain."

"What sorts of changes?"

"Cognitively she still appears the same, but they are seeing increases in activity in some very unlikely areas . . ." Tomson was blushing red again. "I have some theories . . ." He shook himself a little. "But this is the important thing. They're keeping her alive by keeping her wet."

Lydia's hand went to the small of her back of its own accord. "Oh my."

Tomson grimaced as he saw it. "Lydia, there's something else you should know."

She heard the tremble in his voice and looked up from the diagrams. He was unbuttoning his shirt, his head down, his blond curls hanging over his eyes as he pulled the garment out of his pants and opened it.

Lydia could see the blue creeping up out of his waistband, climbing his stomach and up his chest.

"I won't be able to hide it from the others much longer," he said. "It's spreading upward and outward."

Almost without thinking, she reached a hand toward him and touched the skin of his stomach. It felt smooth, hairless, soft. He gasped and she pulled back. "Did that hurt?"

"No, no . . . it's just, very, very sensitive." He quivered then, as if her touch reverberated throughout his body.

She rubs the water on her thighs, splashing up handfuls of it from the puddle around her. The pleasure is unlike anything she has felt before. She rolls over now, letting the water run over her back, then rolls over again, letting it bounce off her stomach. She lets her knees fall apart and invites the droplets to fall there, as well. She is soaked now, wet over every inch of her skin, and she reaches for the jar.

We must keep away from Ambrose. That was her only thought as she and Tomson made their way to the hold where the recovered objects were prepped. If she was reading the diagrams correctly, then what Tomson needed to survive was there. She located one of the jars with the curlicue top as shown in the drawings, and opened it. The scent of some extinct flower filled the small room, and the slight motion of the ship made her grip the jar tighter.

Tomson pulled his shirt completely off and Lydia stood close to him. She dipped two fingers into the jar and came up with a dab of something with the consistency of honey. She smeared it into his back where the blue part of his flesh met the pink, and began slathering it upward. As she watched, she could see the blue edge beginning to spread. "It's working," she said to him. "The ointment is encouraging the blue to grow."

He trembled under her touch and when she tried to come around the front of him he shied away. "Let me do it," he said, holding his hand out for the jar.

She knitted her brows in puzzlement, but then saw the embarrassment on his face. She turned away as his trousers dropped, but she could still hear the sounds he made in his throat. He could not stop himself as he covered his legs and private parts, and then huddled away from her, hiding his crotch with his hands.

"Now we need to wet you down," Lydia said, her eyes still averted by studying the diagrams. There were hoses with small nozzles here, made for rinsing away sediment on artifacts. She turned the spigot on one and brought it over to where he was sitting in a ball.

He cried out as the water hit his back. "Not too hard!"

She reduced the flow to a dribble and let the droplets spatter softly over him. He moaned and then sighed, the tension seeming to go out of his body as she wet him. He let her run the water down his chest, and she saw that he had been hiding a rampant state of turgidity from her. His eyes were closed now, and she watched his penis curiously. It was thoroughly blue, standing up like a finger of coral, and he whimpered a bit when the water sprayed it.

"Will," she said in a hushed voice. "What do you know about dolphins?"

He lay back into the puddle and let out a long breath, his shyness gone. "A bit. Why?"

"Do you think it's possible that the transformation taking place here is to make us more like them?" Lydia began to untuck her own shirt. "To survive the day when our home is overrun by water?"

Will sat up and blinked water from his eyes. The blueness was creeping up toward his neck and she wondered if they would remain the same color when it reached them. "No one will ever believe it."

She shook her head. "I believe it." She turned to show him the spreading patch of blue on her back, her shirt hiked up. His wet fingers traced the edges of it and she knew then why he had moaned. His hands reached around her then, and she felt his cheek pressed against the small of her back.

"I'm sorry, Lydia, I just can't help it . . ."

"It's all right, Will." Dolphins, she thought. "Help me with it, now."

He helped her to shed her clothes and then handed her the jar, so she could slather herself. But then she came to her back, and he helped her with that as she had with his. And then she tilted her head back and waited for the water to come down.

❧   ❧   ❧

She opens her eyes to see him standing above her, the hose still in his hand. She reaches up and pulls him down to her, wanting the feeling of his water-slick skin against hers. Their still-red lips meet, and she feels like they are drinking each other. She laps at his mouth, her hands buried in his curls, as his hands run up and down her back. She licks him, licks at his cheeks, kisses his eyelids. His mouth answers, making its wet way down her neck, to the delicate nipples, standing erect from the water and from rubbing against his so-slick torso. He rubs them with oil, his thumbs brushing across the tips, and then he lowers his mouth to them, wetting them, his tongue lapping at the flower scent mingled with the taste of her skin.

His tongue follows the trail of water down her belly, down to the triangle between her legs. She is wet and slick there by more than just oil and droplets from the hose. As she reaches her hands down to spread her lips apart some part of her knows she has never blossomed this way for Ambrose. Will's fingers dig into the jar of oil and he slicks her from anus to clitoris with the fragrant stuff. Lydia writhes under the touch, her hips rising up until he sinks his fingers deep into her, the pleasure rippling outward from her center. She clings to his neck, wanting skin on skin, wanting wetness on wetness.

She wraps a leg around him and almost before either of them realizes it, he mounts her. Every part of her is slick, both inside and out, and she sucks in a breath. No, it was never like this with Ambrose. She reaches a hand between their pumping bodies, curious to feel if something else in her anatomy has changed. The breath keeps getting deeper, and her fingers slide over her clitoris, fundamentally unchanged and yet . . .

The intensity of it makes her want to cry out, and yet she does not want to exhale. Breathing has become a secondary thing to the urgent need between her legs, and she clings to him hard with three limbs, the fourth a moving blur between them even as he speeds up the rhythm of his own motion.

And then suddenly she feels him break loose, she feels the burst of hot salt liquid inside her, and her own pleasure cascades throughout her body, rippling from one end to the other. They cling together as the spasms quake through their muscles, and then, as one, they exhale.

They sit up slowly in the puddle on the floor, the hose still running, and look around them. Lydia looks down at her own body—the blue is everywhere their bodies touched, and spreading. She clasps Will's hand in her own. "Do you feel like you are coming down with pneumonia?"

"Actually, my lungs never felt better."

She nods. "Mine, too. In fact, all of me . . ."

Before she can finish, the door swings open to reveal Ambrose.

He flicks on the light. There is not even a moment for anger to register on his face before horror and fear set in. "Get me out of here!" he shouts, as he runs down the corridor. That sets Will and Lydia to laughing. A short time later, Steve calls on the intercom and they tell him about the oil, the water, and the change. "You're safe if you don't handle the jars," Lydia tells him. Her hands are touching Will as she speaks. His are exploring the hollows under the arms, under her breasts, anywhere he might have missed. Lydia's voice is breathy as she speaks. "We're safe so long as we stay wet. Are we still at anchor?" she asks. Steve's voice through the speaker says yes. "Good," she says, and takes Will's hand again. "We're going for a swim."

NEEDING A PUSH TO SWING

by Maria Isabel Pita

How to describe my first sight of Miami Velvet? The club is tucked away near an expressway in a dark lot subtly lit by a lovely lavender neon light that can only be seen if you're looking for it. There is something perversely enchanted about the realm of Swinging if you're truly in love. Obviously, there are utterly disenchanting reasons for belonging to a club like Velvet, but they don't concern me. I know how my Master and I feel about Swinging, and that's all that matters. Love is only cheated by lies, not by sexual contact with other people. If a relationship is truly sound, it can pull in and out of as many inviting harbors as it pleases and only be enriched by the experience. The bedsheet a man and a woman share has to be a sail alive with desire, which is what keeps the blood flowing even if it means going against the normal current. The mast of a marriage of souls can never be broken by the fickle winds of lust because its force is used to reach and revel in almost paradisiacal plateaus of intimacy . . .

That first night I was daringly dressed in a sleeveless low-cut black dress that clung gently to my curves and glimmered like the star-filled sky before light pollution. It flared gently out from my hips and barely reached the tops of my thighs. My Master had consented to my wearing a black lace thong panty beneath it, but I still felt wickedly sexy perched on six-inch heels with barely anything between my most private parts and the world. My Master,

Stinger, looked stunningly handsome in black shoes and slacks and a white long-sleeved button-down shirt, his long brown hair flowing freely down his back between his broad shoulders.

Admission was not cheap, but we could bring our own liquor, and my bottle of scotch along with my Master's bottle of gin received circular orange labels printed with our membership number in black ink. Carrying my vice openly in my hand, I walked into a Swing club. It was still early; there were only a handful of people in the main room surrounding the empty circular dance floor as we sat down at the bar. I wriggled self-consciously on the hard stool facing my Master, who immediately reached down and fingered my pussy through my panties, his smile telling me how much he loved having easy access to my intimate warmth in public. He was always telling me how beautiful I was and how much he loved me, and tonight was no exception. We sat as close as possible while we sipped our drinks, and I immediately appreciated a venue that essentially allowed us to behave as we would in private with the added stimulation of being watched. Both emotionally and physically, I clung to my Master's passionate assurance that Swinging was all about *us*; I couldn't stop touching him and caressing him and kissing him. I was more turned on by his physical presence than I ever had been, which is saying a lot, as fear and excitement sharpened all my feelings and sensations.

"Let's take a look around," he suggested, and drinks in hand, he proceeded to give me a tour of the club.

I liked the first floor, especially the little room my Master led me into. Leaving the door open, he shoved me back across the bed surrounded by mirrors. He unzipped his slacks, pulled my panty aside, and penetrated me as I raised my legs up around him. He took a few moments out of the tour to stroke his hard-on with my pussy, dipping his rigid cock into my welcoming wetness for a few delicious seconds. I was disappointed when he pulled out of me so soon, but he wanted to show me the second level of the club before the "robes only" rule was enforced.

My stomach clenched. "What do you mean, *robes* only? You mean I can't wear my clothes up there later?"

"No, just a robe."

"I can't even wear my *panties*?" I was outraged at the prospect of my individuality being stripped from me, and replaced with a generic white robe I imagined would feel like a shroud adorning the terrifying death of my sexual privacy. "And what about my shoes?" I added in despair.

"I think you can probably keep your shoes if you want to." He smiled. "I *hope* you can."

At the moment, no one was guarding the curtain over the narrow stairway leading upstairs. I ascended carefully, placing my treacherous shoes sideways on each step as my Master walked behind me to break my fall should it prove necessary. It did not, and yet I felt myself falling inside as my heart grew heavier and heavier beneath a weight of dread. I was afraid of what he might command me to do there . . .

Apparently, there were still hours of foreplay left to go downstairs, because for the moment we had the whole second floor to ourselves. My Master led me into a "hallway" the likes of which I had never seen before. One side was a wall with waist-high alcoves facing a row of elevated wall-to-wall beds framed by mirrors, which also covered the ceiling. It was clearly a space designed for people to stand and watch other people fucking as they watched themselves. And this carpeted corridor ended in a spacious room entirely filled with low mattresses allowing for no walking space between them. The sheets were black and red and artificial torches reflected in the mirrored ceiling gave the shadowy, slightly sinister atmosphere a disturbing cheapness.

It is impossible to describe what I felt in those moments as I gazed at this blatant "fuck room." I did *not* want to be there, in fact, I couldn't believe I *was* there, that the man I loved had brought me to such a tasteless den of iniquity. I wrenched my hand out of his, feeling my soul mysteriously arch inside my flesh like a cat's back as I was threatened by waves of undulating human flesh this man had the gall to think he could plunge me into so casually. Only how much I knew I loved him—not to mention my six-inch heels and the fact that he had driven us here in his jeep— kept me from bolting down the stairs and out of the building.

"Stinger, I'm not into orgies!" I gasped, my heart beating fast and furiously. "I told you how I felt about that. It's like being a worm in a box! I'm not going in there and letting just anybody fuck me! I'm not just another body, I—"

"Missa, *relax.*"

I don't remember exactly what he said to me. I think he assured me he was not into orgies either, and that he was not expecting anything from me I didn't want, too, even though as his slave it was my duty to obey him without question whether the prospect pleased me or not. This was a terrifying paradox to me at the time, because even though I was madly in love with him, I was still learning to trust him. I do remember, however, how firmly and inexorably he put a lid on my hysteria. Grasping my hand securely in his again, he showed me the rest of the second floor and I followed gingerly behind him feeling as though I was being given a tour of hell by a beautifully relentless angel. His long hair flowing down his back, he kept glancing back at me with a stern, determined expression, which at the same time was full of love and concern. I knew it was going to be a very long night, during which I had to accept the fact that sensual contact with other people was why we were here even if we only ended up playing with each other. My Master repeatedly assured me he would consider it a totally fulfilling evening if all we did was watch and be watched. He kept telling me how beautiful I was and how proud he was to be there with me.

I spent most of the rest of my first night at Miami Velvet with my head down, in my Master's lap. My hand clung to his as we walked slowly around the club, and my mouth clung to his dick when we came to rest on one of the black divans. I let the curtain of my hair fall around my face, but my Master caressed it away so the couples standing and lounging around us could watch me going down on him. He wanted them to see my beautiful features riding his erection. He wanted them to see my full red lips gliding up and down his slick shaft. I closed my eyes at first, as though the fact that I couldn't see them meant it didn't matter there were other people around, but then I opened them again and kept them open as shadowy forms rose in the corners of my eyes and my Master's cock rose in my hand and in my mouth. I was tense, and yet I could not help succumbing to the strangely dark thrill of sucking him down in public.

❧   ❧   ❧

I must admit, I reacted like an addict to my first taste of Velvet. Part of me dreaded it, yet I couldn't wait to go back. And the following Saturday night, for the first time in my life after fantasizing about it more often than there are stars in the galaxy, I had sex with two men at once. In order to protect the guilty, I will call this guy Ray, but he came later . . .

First my Master and I had a little superficial fun on the dance floor, where I enjoyed pleasing him by fondling a woman as she laughingly reciprocated. Then I found myself in a corner of the large playroom upstairs sucking my Master's cock before turning obediently around on the dark-red sheet so he could fuck my pussy from behind. There were no mirrors except on the ceiling so I couldn't see him, only feel how much it pleased him to be there, flanked by other naked undulating bodies as he thrust his almost painfully solid erection deep into my submissively crouched form. He was energized by the subliminal touch of people's eyes on us as he looked around him boldly, and I didn't need to witness it to know there was a soft smile on his lips above his rock-hard penis. Most of the time I hung my head, hiding shyly behind my long hair like a prima donna onstage ignoring her audience, because in my opinion no man could hold a candle to Stinger and I was the luckiest girl in the club to be on the receiving end of his beautiful cock. But occasionally there was a couple it pleased me to look at, and as I watched a girl being taken from behind by her handsome partner like a mirror reflection of us, my detached aesthetic appreciation warmed up into a melting excitement as the sight mysteriously doubled the pleasure I took in my Master's penetrations. She and I had not started out facing each other, but the passionately pumping hips of our partners swiftly positioned us directly across from each other on the public mattress. I was now face-to-face with an attractive woman whose figure was fuller and heavier than mine, and whose straight brown hair brushed against my more wildly curling black mane as we kissed, obeying the wordless desire being driven into us. I looked up, and saw her lover flash a secretly triumphant smile I had no problem imagining being returned by my Master, and it aroused me to know I was pleasing them both as I kissed her again.

A woman's mouth felt intriguingly different from a man's, softer and smaller, and yet while her tongue was more delicate it seemed even more demandingly playful. And included in the novel experience for me was the strangely sweet stimulation of moaning breathlessly together in response to the hard-ons stabbing us. It wasn't easy holding my body and head up as my Master banged me with increasing fervor, and when he suddenly pulled out of me, I collapsed beside her. It was wonderful feeling as though I momentarily had two bodies with which to please him; it doubled how sensual and beautiful I felt. Also exquisite was the contrast between his hard body pressing urgently up against me from behind, and her soft, yielding breasts and skin languidly merging with mine as we continued kissing. I didn't, however, like the sensation of her long nails as she fingered my pussy, so I was glad when a man's hand slipped between my thighs and took over for her. I couldn't tell who was finger-fucking my hot cunt, but I suspected it wasn't my Master and that he was busy experiencing another woman's slick depths as I lay sandwiched between them. Our four bodies had obeyed an inexorable sensual choreography that enabled my tongue to effortlessly dance with three others in turn. All I had to do was turn my head to the right and it was my

Master's beloved lips that opened over mine. Then when I turned my head to the left, I could kiss the girl again for a while, before she raised her face over mine and I watched her profile merging with Stinger's before closing my eyes and letting another man's tongue thrust into my mouth as his hard fingers dipped in and out of me even more hungrily, hurting me a little, yet the discomfort was also delicious. Glancing up at the mirrored ceiling in between kisses, I began feeling lost in an ideal dream of intertwined limbs crowned by beautiful faces wearing rapt expressions evocative of an erotic Renaissance painting come to life on the blood-red sheets of Velvet that night. The magical tableau ended when the girl asked me in a conspiratorial whisper if I wanted to help her go down on her lover, and I declined the offer, having no desire to suck a strange cock without protection.

As if in a dream, the next thing I knew we were in the "voyeur's hallway" with the blonde we had been playing with on the dance floor and her elfish spouse. My Master had made it clear to him that a full swap was out of the question, but apparently he was content to just watch his wife have fun. Meanwhile, a handsome man named Ray with black hair and a black goatee was standing as close to me as possible, and although I would normally have considered the gold chain around his neck cheap, in those highly intoxicated moments, framed by the folds of his white robe, it just made him look even more masculine. I realize now what his main charm was—the fact that I could indulge my superficial physical attraction to him without worrying about any other dimension to our relationship. I had already met the man of my dreams, the man I connected to on all levels of my being, the man I wanted to spend the rest of my life with, and he was standing approvingly beside me as Ray kissed me. Too late, I glanced at my Master to make sure I had his permission to kiss him back. He smiled and gave me a slight, almost invisible nod even as he leaned down to kiss the blonde. He is so tall and well built and she was so slight, I think I was turned on merely by the logistics.

Soon we were all in the middle of the big playroom. My senses swimming in red wine, I surrendered to the flow of events as to a current directed by my Master's words and expressions. I felt perfectly beautiful and natural following the lead of his desires. I also felt like the center of attention lying on my back as the blonde arched her slight body over mine and presented her pussy to my lips. I touched the tip of her clean-shaven little slit tentatively with my tongue, not so much seeking her clit as avoiding the juicier opening of her vulva. I was surprised and relieved by how clean and smooth and relatively dry her sex was, but apparently my Master did not want me beneath her, because a moment later I found myself sitting up facing Ray's cock. He was kneeling at the edge of our group, his body proud and straight as a statue's, his impressive erection clearly waiting for some oral devotion I had no intention of giving. I looked up into my Master's eyes again, and reached for the condom he handed me. I offered it to Ray, who promptly slipped it on as I watched my Master attempting to sheath his own flesh-weapon. Then I lost sight of everything when Ray pushed me back across the mattress and thrust into me as I lay soft and yielding as sand beneath his driving rhythm, oblivious to everything except the experience of a complete stranger ramming his rigid penis into my clinging pussy.

"Missa . . ."

My Master's deep, quiet voice reached me over the storm of Ray breathing in my ear with an almost divinely effortless authority my soul instantly heeded. The fact that my flesh was relishing Ray's energetic penetrations was irrelevant. I don't know how I got him off me, but almost the second after my Master said my name, I was on my hands and knees before him gazing worshipfully up at his face.

"I want you to suck me, Missa."

I didn't understand why he wasn't busy fucking the little blonde, who I had glimpsed eagerly awaiting his cock doggie-style while he struggled with a condom. I didn't know what had happened, but I was overjoyed by the turn of events. He was only partially erect and it thrilled me to think she hadn't turned him on like I did. I also dared to hope watching me with another man had made him jealous enough to affect his performance. It was with a blessed sense of triumph that I took my Master's beloved cock into my mouth, even as Ray gripped my hips from behind and thrust his erection into my grateful pussy again. I was finally living my favorite fantasy, and for a while I was aware only of how good the reality felt. But then I had to turn my face away from my Master, gasping as Ray banged me faster and harder, coming aggressively into the plastic pouch at the tip of his spurting cock buried deep inside me. He had stroked himself to an orgasm with my sex yet had never really felt it. Only my Master's erection is meant to experience the warmly loving caress of my innermost depths where other men are only superficial divers.

As though a cresting wave of sexual energy had just literally broken over the hedonistic beach of bedsheets, I knew this particular erotic scenario was washed up as Ray pulled out of me, discarding the latex tunnel heavy with his semen, and teasingly coated with my juices, which had not for a single second merged with his despite how hard he fucked me. I rolled over onto my back feeling wonderfully surfeited, given permission to relax for a moment by my Master's smile. As I lay there, Ray began licking one of my nipples, his tongue tasting the more delicate aspects of the lush feast he had just enjoyed deep between my thighs, which were spread shamelessly wide. And apparently the sight of my freshly fucked pussy proved an irresistible temptation to a muscular black man kneeling on another mattress, because he suddenly leaned over and gave my slick hot vulva a quick, hungry lick. I did nothing to stop him; I felt no reason to do so. For a delicious instant I had a handsome Latin man suckling my tit while a virile black man licked my slit. Then came my Master's softly resonant command again in the form of my name "Missa" snapping me out of my sensual reverie as he helped me up, and hand-in-hand we walked out of the room whose shadowy atmosphere was sinfully rich with the heady perfume of countless orgasms.

On our third Saturday night at Velvet, I remained relatively sober sensing my Master had an important lesson for me to learn. Last weekend he had proved he could get over the hurdle of watching me being physically possessed by another man. The fact that he had had to make some effort to do so afforded me a comforting degree of satisfaction, but also made me even more nervous wondering how *I* would react when forced to watch him fucking another woman . . .

My Master was fucking me from behind on one of the mattresses in the mirrored hallway. I was on my hands and knees looking at our reflections in the mirror before us while he took me from behind. I was literally flowing with admiration gazing at the intense cast of his features framed by his long hair, which he had flung behind his breathtakingly broad shoulders. I know that sounds like a romantic cliché, but to me it felt like anything but watching his magnificent physique thrust into my lucky cunt. Then suddenly a woman crawled up onto the mattress with us, very much like a cat rubbing up against my Master, who did not seem surprised by her appearance. He pulled out of me nonchalantly and I sat back, languidly watching as he fished a condom out of his robe, which he had spread across the sheet for me. He shoved it aside now as this smugly smiling woman with short black hair took my place before him. I watched as he grabbed her plump hips and penetrated her without further ceremony, swiftly wrapping her pussy around his erection. I watched as he began fucking her fast and hard from behind. She reacted to his violent strokes with an occasional soft moan as I tried to get in on the action by caressing his tight ass, but his hips were moving too furiously, so I gave up and sat back again to stare at my beautiful Master possessing another woman. Then I glanced at him in the mirror and realized she was seeing the same thing I had seen only moments ago. He looked just the same now fucking her as he had fucking me only a few heartbeats ago, *exactly* the same. The vision of his long hair and broad shoulders beneath the almost grim concentration of his features was as riveting now that his dick was buried inside another girl's body. And watching him, it seemed to me he was feeling the same thing he had felt with me, except of course that he was wearing a condom so she couldn't feel *quite* as good. I wondered if her pussy was as tight as mine, and it was as though my soul was bleeding out of me. I felt increasingly weak and indifferent to everything, vitally wounded by the realization that, physically, I was essentially the same as her or any other woman. A few minutes ago I had felt beautiful and special as my Master possessed me, but now it seemed there had been nothing truly special about it at all because here he was taking a girl who meant nothing to him in exactly the same way.

When she climbed onto the bed with us, she appeared to be alone, but apparently the slender man insinuating himself beside me now was her partner, and he was obviously willing to go for a "full swap." I thought this was what my Master wanted, and since all the life had gone out of me along with his attention and his erection, I succumbed to this soft-spoken man gently urging me back onto my hands and knees beside his companion, who had the great honor of being completely occupied by my Master's driving force at the moment. I glanced over my shoulder to watch the stranger wrestling with a condom, and was both surprised and infinitely relieved when my Master abruptly pulled out of the new hole he was enjoying, and stopped the man just as he was about to penetrate me. I was too dazed to understand what was happening; all I knew as my Master grabbed his robe and quickly put it on was that he was angry, and this was the most terrible thing of all. He barely allowed me enough time to get up and slip my own robe back on before he strode downstairs with me trailing behind him in despair.

Back down at the bar, my tearful intensity succeeded in diffusing his anger. He could see I was genuinely confused by his reaction upstairs, because I had believed our ultimate goal was to fuck another couple together, and yet when it was about to happen, he suddenly stopped the action. He agreed this *was* one of our goals, but tonight was supposed to have been about me watching him just as last weekend he had watched me with another

man. I assured him I had indeed been watching him, but all it had
made me want to do was cry, and it was all I still wanted to do;
I was having a hard time keeping up appearances so people
wouldn't stare at us where we sat at the bar wearing the incrimi-
nating robes. My emotions were in full flood and my Master,
blessedly his firmly understanding self again, calmly rode the passionate wave of my reaction to watching him fuck another woman
while leading me by the hand into the Jacuzzi room.

We didn't get into the water; we stepped up onto a raised platform of cushy black foam mattresses. He spread our robes out in
one corner, and our feelings and flesh became indistinguishable
from each other as we lay back across them and began making passionate love. I didn't need to be told that what we were doing now
was not *fucking* and bore no relation whatsoever to what I had
been watching him do with a stranger only a few minutes ago.
Our merging, undulating bodies on the black mats were the center of the universe and no one and nothing else existed. There was
only his presence inside me, which I couldn't live without, and his
face beneath me. He was saying things, but all I remember is the
moment he finally spoke the words I had been longing to hear.

"I'm falling in love with you . . ."

I was crying as the pleasure of his unique personality in the
form of his cock planted deep inside me merged with the pain of
still seeing in my mind's eye his beloved manhood sliding in and
out of another woman. "Well, I'm *already* in love with you!" I
sobbed, kissing him and riding him and clinging to him.

"It's true," he said. "Part of me keeps thinking it's too soon,
but it's true . . . I love you, Missa."

Only recently my Master explained to me that this was a necessary order for events to take in our relationship. He wanted to
make sure my love for him was not conditional upon anything. I
don't know exactly what he was thinking, but I understand what
he means. He needed to make sure I truly did love him and
desired to be his slave and that I wasn't just saying that in order to
tie him down. He also wanted to see to it I didn't make the mis-

take of confusing our profound feelings for each other with sex. If he had told me he loved me before I watched him fucking another woman, I would have seen it as a betrayal of our bond and not as an exciting part of it. He was also wise to let me be the first to prove with Ray that having sex with other people in no way affected our love for each other.

I was so happy now it was as though my soul was climaxing and not just my body. So when he turned me around and told me he was going to fuck my ass, I wanted him to more than anything. I don't think we had officially begun my anal training yet, but I was so open to him, so relieved and relaxed and aroused anticipating our future together—painfully challenging as it might occasionally prove to be—that when he thrust his hard-on through my sphincter's tight ring I felt truly and fully betrothed to him, my Master. Our passionately kinky engagement was witnessed by four black men, who my Master later told me watched him jealously, apparently amazed such a beautiful woman was not only letting her lover fuck her up the ass but loving it, too. He had to hold them back.

PERCEPTION

by Lisabet Sarai

He was late, of course. They always were. Undergraduates these days had no sense of responsibility. They didn't seem to understand that she had a schedule to keep. Her time was scarce and constantly overcommitted. Fortunately, he was her last subject of the day but she had a long night of work ahead of her nevertheless.

And the way they dressed. He'd probably arrive in a stretched-out T-shirt, jeans bagging around his ankles, and a baseball cap turned backward. Never mind that she was a member of the faculty. Respect? She snorted to herself. That went out with the twentieth century, or maybe the nineteenth.

Of course the girls were just as bad, with their universally blonde hair and bare midriffs, pierced navels, and painted-on jeans. Just like the one that Allen had screwed, blatant sexuality and no substance.

Dr. Knowles grimaced as the familiar pain lanced through her. Damn him! It shouldn't hurt so much, two years later, but she couldn't help it. Despite everything, she had loved him, loved him still, never mind that he was a totally different creature from her. Gregarious, easygoing, imperturbable, with that quick, crooked smile and those ever-so-blue eyes. Relaxed and comfortable in his lithe, lanky body, while the tension sang through her frame. His students loved him, and no wonder; the way he clowned and postured in his classes, he was more an actor than a teacher. He always appeared to be enjoying himself. Sometimes she envied him, even though she knew that she was more intelligent and a better scientist.

His bitter laughter echoed in her memory, from that awful night when she had finally confronted him with his infidelity. "What do you expect, Jessie, when you're so frigid? I swear, your work turns you on more than I do!"

It wasn't true. She ached at the sight of him, his taut muscles and fluid movements. She adored the heat of him, breathing against her neck, coaxing her legs apart with his own. There was just something in her that couldn't quite let go, perhaps some remnant of the iron control she had needed to exercise in order to get where she was in her career. Whatever it was, he sensed it. At the deepest level, he never touched her.

Perhaps, after all, she had never really trusted him. Of course, in the final analysis, he had hardly proved himself trustworthy.

Maybe she was lucky to be rid of him. Since the divorce, she had no conflicting demands on her time, but could focus entirely on her research. She should be grateful. It was just a question of adjusting her perceptions.

A soft knock on the door of the lab interrupted her musings. Finally! "Come in," she called, steeling herself for the ordeal of the next half hour. Sometimes she wished that she had specialized in animal behavior instead of human cognition.

"Good afternoon, Dr. Knowles. Sorry that I'm late."

He was not what she had expected. He appeared more mature than the typical student subject, in his mid-twenties at least, with angular features and frizzy ginger hair pulled into a ponytail. He wore well-fitting jeans that were faded but clean, an elaborately embroidered shirt, a leather vest, and cowboy boots. Nobody dressed like that these days. His flamboyance reminded her of someone she might have known back when she was a student. She gave him a half-smile.

"Good afternoon, Mr."—she consulted the sign-up sheet— "Murphy. Thank you for volunteering to participate in my study. If you will please read and sign this release, we can get started."

Her subject fixed her with startling eyes the color of jade. "Whatever you say, Dr. Knowles. But please, call me Ian."

His stare made her feel extremely odd. The room wavered for a moment, like air shimmering above hot pavement. She was relieved when he sat down in the chair to her left and bent over the clipboard to read the legalese of the document. She turned to her computer and typed in the pass code to begin the experiment.

The lab control program generated a number for him, and then randomly assigned him to one of the three experimental treatments. Group S. Her stomach knotted. If only he had been in Group A, for athletics, or even Group V. He seemed very relaxed, not at all the violent type; she wondered if the aggression materials would have affected him at all. But the S group . . . Dr. Knowles swallowed hard, opened her desk drawer, and pulled out a copy of a girlie magazine.

"Now, Mr. Murphy—Ian. The purpose of this study is to investigate how emotion influences perception. For the next ten minutes, I'd like you to read this publication. Then we'll perform some tests using the tachistoscope."

"The what?" Ian grinned at her, jeweled eyes flashing. She felt a flush climbing into her cheeks. Something told her that he was teasing her. "'Tackystascope'? Is that for measuring how tacky something is?"

"Of course not. A tachistoscope is a device that exposes visual stimuli for very brief periods of time. Fractions of a second."

Embarrassment made her tone frosty. But why should she be embarrassed? "It allows us to evaluate perception without the influence of conscious thought."

"Really?" Now she was sure that he was mocking her. "Fascinating!"

"Please read the magazine, Mr. Murphy. I'll let you know when it's time to move on to the next phase of the experiment."

Ian just smiled, and began leafing through the images of smooth, abundant flesh. Dr. Knowles set the timer and tried to ignore him, reviewing some notes from a previous study. But her eyes were repeatedly drawn to the pictures that he was so eagerly perusing.

Here was a woman bent over so that the globes of her derriere filled most of the page. She was looking back over her shoulder, an inviting half-smile pouting on her lips. Despite herself, Dr. Knowles felt a stirring between her thighs. The woman in the picture seemed so—accessible. Dr. Knowles forced her attention back to the computer screen, but the whisper of a page turning pulled her eyes back to the tabloid.

Now the image was of a slender black beauty, her skin shining as though oiled. She cupped her breasts in her palms, offering them to the photographer. Her thumbs strummed over her nipples, which were the size and color of roasted almonds. Against the slick chocolate of her face, the woman's teeth were shockingly white.

Dr. Knowles's own nipples tightened in sympathy, pressing uncomfortably against the starched cotton of her blouse. Her panty hose were suddenly hot and constraining, and outrageously damp in the crotch. What was going on here? She had looked at these images a hundred times without any kind of reaction. She had chosen these stimuli. Why were they suddenly having this effect?

Ian glanced up and she hastily turned back to her monitor, but she knew that he had caught her surreptitiously examining the photos. Her cheeks flamed, and the ache grew in her sex. She was careful not to look up again until the timer rang, marking the end of the conditioning phase.

"Now then, Mr. Murphy, we'll move on to the next stage of the experiment. Sit here, please." She indicated the high, backless stool in front of the tachistoscope eyepiece, which stood on a table against the right wall. "I want you to look through here. Everything will be dark. Then I'll show you some pictures, very briefly, and I want you to describe what you see. Don't be concerned if you cannot grasp the entire scene; these pictures are deliberately designed to be complex. I just want you to tell me what first catches your attention."

"I'd rather continue looking at the *Playboy*," her subject said with another of those disturbing grins. "But I suppose that I need to follow your instructions. For the sake of science."

"If you please." She stepped aside so that he could reach the equipment, feeling the familiar frustration that the university had given her such a cramped laboratory space. She deserved better.

Despite the close quarters, there should have been plenty of room for Ian Murphy to pass her. Nevertheless, as he did, he deliberately brushed against her, hip to hip. Startled, she pulled away, and slammed her backside into the computer desk. "Damn!" she hissed under her breath. It hurt. She'd have a bruise tomorrow. Meanwhile, she still felt the ghost of his touch, a kind of warm pressure that didn't abate even though he was now sitting tamely in front of the apparatus.

Murphy was looking at her, clearly amused. Her cheeks burned. "Sorry," she apologized lamely. "This room is a bit tight."

"No problem. So, I just look through these goggles?"

"That's right."

"It's all black."

"The pictures will start in a moment." She turned and clicked the button on the screen that initiated the experimental sequence. After a second, the light in the tachistoscope flashed, briefly.

"Wow!"

"What did you see?"

"It's a street scene, someplace picturesque. Paris, maybe. There's a couple, a man and a woman."

"Yes?"

"It was hard to see, but I think they were in an alley off to the side. Her back was against the wall. I think that her skirt was raised."

A thrill of satisfaction coursed through Dr. Knowles's upright frame. The apparatus flashed again.

"Hmmm . . ."

"What did you see this time?"

"A naked woman."

"Anything else?"

"She's on a balcony. One foot is on the railing, and she has one hand between her legs. She's jacking off."

Jessica Knowles blushed deeply. There *was* a woman in the picture, along with cars, buses, a hot air balloon, a crowd gathered around a unicyclist, an armed holdup taking place off in a corner, two dogs sparring in the foreground. But the woman was clothed, and definitely was not touching herself.

"Are you sure?" She shouldn't be questioning his perceptions; it might ruin the experiment. But she couldn't help herself. She'd never had a subject respond so strongly to the pre-exposure sensitization.

"Well, it went by pretty fast, but I could swear that her mouth was open and she was coming. I could almost hear her."

She gave him a sharp glance, but he was still peering into the scope, waiting for the next image. His right hand was in his lap, though, and she was horrified to realize that he was languidly stroking a substantial erection through the worn denim of his trousers.

Jessica was sweating now. This man played havoc with her objectivity. Perhaps she should terminate the experiment right now.

The computer sent another image to the 'scope. Murphy sucked in his breath.

"Whew! That's hot!"

"What is?"

"It's a threesome. Two guys and a woman, mounted between them. She's, like, suspended from their cocks. One in her pussy and one in her ass. Her feet aren't even touching the ground!"

"Mr. Murphy!" Jessica felt panic, but her voice was ice. "Don't play games with me! Tell me what you really see."

"I swear, Dr. Knowles, that *is* what I see. Come and look for yourself."

Flustered and annoyed, Jessica clicked to pause the sequence, then again to loop the last stimulus. Murphy relinquished the stool; she had to hike up her skirt to get onto the high seat. She felt his eyes on her legs as she got settled.

She took a deep breath and lowered her eyes to the viewing port. For a moment that seemed to stretch for hours, she stared into the blackness, her heart pounding in her ears. A faint trace of a scent reached her nostrils—sweat and man-musk. It reminded her vividly, painfully, of Allen. Then the fluorescent bulbs flashed, illuminating the scene for an instant.

She wasn't prepared, wasn't paying attention. The scene was a jumble of lines and curves; she couldn't make any sense of it at all. Releasing the breath she was holding, Dr. Knowles tried to relax and concentrate.

"What did you see?" Ian asked, alarmingly close. "Did you see them?"

"No . . ." There was a disturbing quaver in her own voice. "No, I didn't see anything. I wasn't ready."

"Pay attention, Jessie," he whispered. Then two events occurred simultaneously. The tachistoscope flashed again, repeating the image in question. At the same moment, Ian reached his arms around her and cupped her breasts in both palms.

"Oh!" she cried out in surprise and dismay. Because she caught a glimpse, just a hint, a tangle of naked bodies, left of center in the scene. Her field of vision went dark, but the afterimage burned in her brain. She didn't know which she found more shocking, the unexpectedly lurid perception, or the fact that her subject was now unbuttoning her blouse and sliding his fingers across her bare bosom. She had always thought that it was ridiculous for her to wear a bra, considering how flat-chested she was, but in his grasp, her breasts felt fleshy, full, and exquisitely sensitive.

"You must pay attention, now. Don't ruin the experiment." His voice in her ear was honey, warm, sticky, dangerously sweet. The tachistoscope lit up again, and now the image was clear, the rutting threesome drawn in obscene detail. The woman's back was arched, her head thrown back, her mouth wide with a scream of ecstasy. The view went dark just as her subject grasped both her nipples and twisted them hard.

"Oh, please . . ." she moaned. She had no idea what she was

pleading for. Her sex was damp and heavy. The throbbing that his fingers induced in her nipples echoed between her legs. She continued to gaze into the eyepiece, not daring to look at the man who was teasing, was tormenting her.

The instrument lit up again. It should have been the same image, but now Jessie could swear that the man whose penis had been buried in the woman's pussy now had removed it, and was forcing its rampant length down her throat. Then again, darkness. "No, no, it can't be . . ." The fingers on her body began to wander downward, across her belly, but were foiled by the waistband of her skirt.

"Put your feet on the rungs and lift yourself off the seat, Jessie. You can put your hands on the table for support. But don't stop looking into the machine."

Why was she obeying him? Her confusion was complete. He loomed behind her; heat radiated from his body, so close, too close. She squirmed nervously as she felt him raising her skirt from behind, hitching down her hose and panties, baring her buttocks. She should scream, should resist somehow. Instead, she stared into the tachistoscope, surrendering to the lascivious scene that was playing itself out before her eyes.

"Arch your back so that I can reach your butt," he murmured. "Yes, that's right, that's perfect."

His hands were cool on her rear cheeks, and gentle at first. Then he pulled the globes apart, roughly. Fear shot through her, as another picture filled her field of vision, the woman's bum held open and exposed by one of her companions, her recently reamed anus gaping. She tried to speak, to protest, but somehow the words died in her throat. Her breath left her completely when he bent over and fastened his mouth on her sex.

He was brusque and forceful, stabbing into her folds with his hot tongue. She felt him nip painfully at her clit, then the pain dissolved into radiating waves of pleasure. She didn't realize that she was pushing backward, grinding herself into his face, riding his tongue like a jockey riding a mount. Her attention was momentarily distracted by the picture that flashed before her, the woman now dangling by her wrists from above, her legs held open by the two men while someone she could not quite make out plunged an enormous dildo into the woman's vagina.

"Ah . . ." The vision burned into her retina and the rasp of his tongue against her swollen clit set up a reverberating circuit. With each wet stroke, her mind elaborated the picture, noticing the juices streaming from the woman's crotch, the veins on the artificial cock, sticky as it was pulled out of her, the woman's taut muscles as she strained toward her climax. With each new lascivious detail that Jessie noticed or imagined, her own cunt gushed and grew more sensitive.

The 'scope flashed again and now Jessie could see that the person wielding the dildo was a second woman, raven-haired with pendulous breasts and meaty thighs. The scientist melted into an animal as simultaneously the 'scope went dark and Ian thrust three fingers into her lubricious depths. Grinding herself against his hand, she felt the first shimmers of an orgasm, flickering in the distance. It had been so long, too long . . .

She shut her eyes, unable to bear the intensity. The lights flashed again, and even through closed lids, she could swear she saw the dark woman burying her fist in the other's cunt. Her moan sounded obscenely loud in the small room.

"Tell me, Jessie," Ian said softly, the hint of mockery still there even as his fingers danced inside her. "Tell me what you want."

"No . . . don't call me that. He used to call me that."

"Your husband? He was a fool to let you go, Jessie. So what should I call you then? Jessica seems too formal, don't you agree?" He flicked his thumb across her engorged clit, making her squirm. "Jess? Jezebel? How about that, my scarlet woman? You seem quite inclined toward fornication this evening."

"Oh . . ." Jessie could not speak. The orgasm crept closer, teasing her.

"Tell me what you want, Jezebel, and I'll give it to you." He suddenly slipped a finger into her anus, and she screamed at the deliciously rude invasion.

She couldn't see him, behind her, but she could imagine his grin. She was mortified and at the same time eager, eager to have him use her, to open her body to him. The tachistoscope flashed another image, but now she was fully occupied by the sensations he was generating in her sex, and the tantalizing, distant vision of her climax on her body's horizon.

"What do you want?" he whispered in her ear, wriggling a slick digit deep into her bottom. "Say it."

She could barely choke out the words. "Please . . . please, make love to me."

"Make love?" he laughed. "No, that's not quite right, is it? Say it. You can say it, Jezebel. You won't shock me."

"Fuck me," she whimpered, finally, undone by his mouth and hands. "I want you to fuck me."

"All you had to do was ask," he said softly. He turned her around to face him. His cock protruded from his jeans, jutting proudly toward the ceiling. She blushed, then moaned as he lifted her from the stool and settled her on that thick stalk of flesh. The sensation of him sliding into her was both strange and wonderfully familiar. With thighs and cunt muscles, she gripped him hard as he carried her over to the narrow bench on the opposite side of the room.

Holding her up by her naked buttocks, he hooked the bench with his foot and pulled it away from the wall. Then he set her with her back against the polished wood, momentarily pulling out of her. She could not help grimacing at the obscene slurping sound her cunt made, reluctantly releasing his penis. Ian grinned, straddled her, and drove his cock back into her, pinning her to the bench.

For a moment, the force took her breath away. Then the pleasure welled up inside her, wave after wave, synchronized with his fierce thrusts. She tilted her pelvis, twisted against him, trying to force him deeper. His penis grazed her womb, and the twinge of pain only brought the pleasure into higher relief. Teasing her still, he nearly withdrew, lightly rubbing the bulb of his cock against her engorged and aching clit. Electricity shot through her. She closed her eyes, overwhelmed.

"Pay attention, Jessie," he reminded her. "Look at me." She fixed her gaze on his eyes, which were bottomless green pools. She felt transparent, light, suddenly free of her past, her present, herself. As he sank back into her depths, she clutched his shoulders and relaxed her cunt, opening to his probing. He went deeper than anyone ever had before. Her climax hovered nearby, just out of reach.

"You don't recognize me, do you?" he gasped between thrusts. She arched toward him in silent answer. "Two years ago. I was in your Psych 202 class. Sat in the very front." He slammed his cock into her, suddenly angry. "You never noticed me, though, did you? You weren't paying attention . . ."

He eased his attack, became gentler. "God, I loved to watch you. You seemed so cool and competent, a creature of intellect, not passion. But I knew. I could feel your frustration. I always knew that I could give you what you wanted, what you needed . . . When I heard your husband had left you, I thought, good riddance."

"When I saw you on campus, though, you always seemed to be deep in thought; I didn't want to interrupt. I sensed that you weren't ready. Not yet . . ."

His thrusts accelerated suddenly. He pistoned in and out of her, faster than she could have imagined, fractions of a second, instantaneous, driving himself, driving her to the peak. Then all at once she was there, at the top and tumbling over the edge into blissful oblivion, laughing and crying at once as she felt him pumping his own release into her.

It was dark when she regained control of her thoughts. She lay there still, in disarray upon the hard bench, her back and buttocks deliciously bruised.

Her cunt was empty, but still vibrating with recollections of pleasure. Semen had dribbled out all over her skirt, which was bunched beneath her.

The room was empty, she could feel it. He was gone. Her mind whirled. She would have to throw out his data. Maybe the whole experiment had been rendered invalid . . . What had happened, anyway? Had he somehow tampered with the lab control software? But that wasn't possible, the lab was secure, she was sure of it . . . Did she have his phone number, his e-mail address? She'd have to get back in touch, to apologize, to make amends for her totally unprofessional behavior . . .

Without her realizing it, her hand drifted to her pussy and casually grazed her still-sensitive clit. A bolt of excitement shot through her, leaving delicious echoes in its wake. The tachistoscope, still cycling in its loop, flashed in the dark room. She remembered the images of concupiscence it had revealed and smiled to herself, stroking one finger slowly between her slippery labia.

Never mind working tonight. She needed a long, hot bath. She'd think about the experimental implications tomorrow. And she was nearly certain, yes, quite sure, that she had included a field for e-mail address on the volunteer sign-up sheet. It wouldn't have been like her to omit an important detail like that.

BETTER THAN SEX

by Susannah Indigo

It's the hottest summer on record—way too hot to be on a boat without diving in the water every ten minutes. This sunburn I'm getting will kill me later, but I'm *almost* sure Terry is worth it.

He seems oblivious to the heat. I don't think I've ever even seen him sweat. I struggle with the French phrase he's trying to teach me. "I guess I'm only French in my kisses," I say. "The only thing you've taught me that stays in my head is *baise moi*."

"That's good enough for me, Mags," Terry says, laughing. I can see in his eyes that he's considering anchoring somewhere and taking me below.

The 32-foot Contessa glides through the sapphire blue water. I kiss Terry once, deeply enough to make him forget about educating me for a while. Lying back to continue my peaceful contemplation of life and love and my future, I'm dazzled as always by the possibilities that appear out on the ocean.

Shortly after we left the harbor in Newport Beach, Terry asked me to remove my top.

"Here? You're kidding."

"No, Mags, you're not in the Midwest anymore. It's okay." He reached to help me. "Do it for me."

I did. I always do everything he asks. I removed my red bikini top and blushed to match its color. The man makes me feel sexual all the time, no matter what we're doing, even if we're absorbed in our usual conversation about our work. Sex floats just below the surface. Some days I wonder if it's all we have in common, but, no, there's always the office.

"Hey, Terry, do you suppose any kid ever says 'I want to be an Account Representative when I grow up'?" I ask him.

Terry laughs. "No, probably not."

"Yeah, it's my theory that adults are always asking kids what they want to be just to get ideas for themselves. Kids have all the good dreams."

"Oh, it's a good job, Mags, and I'm proud of you for getting promoted after only a year there." Terry deftly adjusts the sails.

"Yeah, I know. 'Maggie Russ, Account Representative'—it's on my new business cards. Thanks for your help with some of that computer stuff I had to learn. At least I'm out of the clerical ghetto."

Sailing is as foreign to me as French, no matter how much he's shown me. He's introduced me to so many things—sailing, fine wine, vibrators, classical music, the juxtaposition of sadness and joy. He's an expert at everything he does, or he doesn't do it. How did I ever get involved with this man who's now twirling my bare nipples softly between his fingers?

"You're smarter than most people we work with, Mags."

I can't help but laugh. "Gee, thanks. They certainly don't pay me like I'm very smart—I think they figure the title is reward enough. It's such a crazy place. I don't know how you can work there—don't you miss being in music?"

Terry is silent for a while. So many subjects are off-limits for him. "Not really."

I pretend not to notice. "Boy, not me. If I could figure out how to support myself writing, I'd be out of Comstar in a minute. I'm scared of losing track of my dreams."

He's silent again, for a long time. I watch him and wonder why I can never crack that inner layer of secrets. Why he never opens up to me completely, even though he gives me more than I ever dreamed was possible from a man.

"You're so young, Mags. I can't even remember being twenty-one. Sometimes dreams just collide and fade away."

"Not mine." I know his dreams, at least his old ones. He knows mine too, but tends to ignore them. "You always make me dream, Terry. I dream up poetry while I watch you sail."

"Your poetry is almost as cute as you are."

I let it go by. Sometimes his compliments can be like a slap in the face, reminding me of my father's art of insulting with a smile. Sometimes I think his comments about my writing are a kind of envy—envy for his lost artistic side, from the man who was once a child prodigy and set to play for the L.A. Philharmonic before it all fell apart and he ended up working in middle management.

"In fact, you're almost perfect, Mags."

"Almost?" I'm fascinated by the sudden honesty. "Besides making almost no money."

"Let's see. Sometimes your optimism is just too much."

I have the urge to smile, but don't.

"And you spend too much time writing and taking those arty courses when you could be finishing your business degree."

He thinks that, and he doesn't even know the things I've been writing on all those late nights without him. I stop at the store on my nights alone sometimes and buy a bag of Oreos, a bottle of cheap white wine, and the *National Enquirer* to spark my imagination. I know if I ever tell Terry about this, he'll lecture me about buying the wrong kind of wine to go with chocolate.

And then I'd have to explain that the wine goes perfectly with the Oreo filling, especially when you're drinking straight from the bottle. So I just don't mention it. I don't own a television, mostly because the old one I had broke and I can't afford to fix it, or maybe I don't want to. Actually only the picture is broken—the sound works fine. On real lonely nights in my little walk-up apartment when music won't quite get me through 'til morning, I'll flip on the sound of the television and listen to laugh tracks of sitcom reruns and pretend I lead a normal life.

"And," Terry continues on my list of flaws, "you will never quite tan."

"All the better excuse for you to help put some of this lotion on me."

He pours the lotion on my breasts, rubbing them over and over again.

"But you do like whipped cream in strange places late at night, Maggie darling, and you're certainly the only woman who ever gave me an X-rated stocking for Christmas." His hands travel down over my belly and over my hips and I think I could live right here on this boat forever. "And the skirts, Maggie. You wear those short skirts so beautifully that I have to leave the room sometimes at work. The skirts make up for any flaw you could possibly have."

How nice. But his kisses melt me. His lips are following his fingers down over my belly.

"Go ahead, Mags, how about me?" he asks, pausing and looking up, knowing exactly what he's doing to me.

I'm hardly going to touch his main flaw on this beautiful day—I only think seriously about it at midnight under the influence of cookies and wine. "No, now that you've grown this great beard, you're perfect." My fingers caress his face. He *is* perfect in so many ways. How many people take the time to believe in you and push you forward in life? I have a wise quote taped on my refrigerator that says, "Our chief want in life is someone who will make us do exactly what we can."

He pulls the bottom of my bikini off over my legs and I sit naked on the boat, leaning back into the sun, leaning forward into his mouth. I didn't even know this existed a year ago. Another first in my life. He's kneeling between my legs and spreading me wide and I think I could die from this. *Can you die from this?*

He holds my hips tight and makes me come once, and then again. Everything he does he does like a pro. A year ago I was slogging through the snow to a part-time job at a drive-in movie theater in Michigan, and now here I am sitting naked on a boat in the Pacific Ocean with a handsome and smart man kneeling between my thighs trying to make me happy. *Yes, I'm sure you can die from this.*

❧ ❧ ❧

I get bolder as the day goes on. I flip off his incessant classical music and put on a tape I brought of Joni Mitchell singing about dancing up a river in the dark. I know he hates it, but maybe he'll learn.

The silence between us is wonderful sometimes. I think that if I could stay out here for a month or two I could write an entire novel in my head. I write a lot about sex. I never show it to Terry. He likes to talk about sex, and so do I. He's even taught me to say the word "fuck" out loud.

"You know, Terry, I used to think coming in my jeans was the height of sexuality. It was a high school experience, and everything since then, until you, has just been ordinary. You've redefined my whole idea about what's worthwhile in life." I know he loves this and that I'm feeding his insatiable ego, but it's true.

"Am I the best lover you've ever had?" he asks. Vanity rules in men—they say it's a woman's trait, but men outdo us every time.

"Of course. But I'm always looking for things worth living for, Terry. I think of it as things 'better than sex.' I even have a list."

"What's on it?"

"So far, only five things." I hold up an imaginary list. "Let's see . . ."

"First, music under the stars. Remember that night at the Hollywood Bowl? Then, the full body massages we gave each other out on my deck in the drizzling rain that day, and the rainbow that followed. Third would be the whole experience of the Renaissance Faire, playing at being a wench and living in the sensuality of it all."

"Yeah, I remember. You're right."

"Then the list gets practical." I turn the imaginary list over to continue. "Fourth is creating. Just creating, thinking, ideas, writing—that moment when it all clicks and you realize that there's a whole layer to your own mind that you rarely get to."

He doesn't say anything, just watches me.

"Last is getting promoted at work without having to ask for it."

"But," I continue quickly, "there is no 'Better Than Sex with Terry' list." Yet.

The wind has died completely. I have no idea where we're at, but Terry always pretends to know, like all men do. We've been sitting for almost an hour like this waiting for the wind. I don't know much about sailing, but I know there's a motor and that it can get us back safely. Terry's always pushed for time on our days out, but he's also a purist and says he has never used anything but sail power.

Instead, he decides to concentrate on me. He sits back and watches me, making me feel self-conscious. I put the bikini bottom back on a long time ago, with the excuse of feeling sunburn on my ass.

"Take it off again, Maggie, and let me watch you dive."

I'm sweltering in the sun and nothing sounds more appealing, being watched or not. He takes my suit from me and tucks it away under a seat, telling me to stay this way until we're back in civilization with people nearby.

Some days I think my life exists just to turn on men with my body. "God I want to fuck you," he says when I stand on the rail preparing to dive. I've heard that so many times in my young life I don't even know what it means some days. I dive and laugh to myself at the same time, because the opening of a poem flashes through my mind when he says it—

> I've heard the words so many times
> I don't know what to think
> "God I want to fuck you"
> said with passion and lies and heat;
> muttered by men who are only friends,
> murmured by bosses and neighbors,
> promised by lovers old and new,
> threatened by men on the street. . . .

The ocean is warm, so I dive down deeper to find colder water. I wish I could put on a tank and just stay down here forever, only surfacing now and again when the sky is clear and everything seems possible.

I play and swim around the boat for a while, getting used to being in the water without a suit. Terry watches and never says a word. When I finally climb back up, he pulls me in all my wetness onto his lap and begins to kiss me, that same kiss that got me involved with him in the first place in spite of my better judgment, the kiss that reaches from the tip of my tongue down to my toes and travels straight back to my heart.

He lowers his suit and wraps my legs around his waist and I think I will die of pleasure. "Baise moi," I whisper fiercely, and he smiles through the passion at what a good girl I am.

When a man's hands are on your hips and his mouth on your nipples and he is driving up as high as your heart and the water is sapphire blue and the sun is bright is the moment when everything in life is possible. All the dreams any person in this world has ever had are out there for the taking, if only you can see them clearly. God is watching from behind the clouds and saying, *yes*, and *yes, this is how it is supposed to be, this is why I made it all in the first place.*

The wind appears from the east and begins to rock the boat, and I can't tell the rocking of the breeze from the rocking of my hips and I begin to move into the man I want so much with all the love and abandon and innocence that has ever existed in the world.

❦   ❦   ❦

The sun is setting as we head back toward the marina. "I have a surprise for you this evening, Maggie. But first, you have that look in your eye—give me poetry."

"Oh, it's just something short." I don't think he'll appreciate the "God I want to fuck you" poem. "Close your eyes—ready?" I stroke his cheek and begin in a hesitant voice:

> chasing the colors
> of love
> down through the

lonely night
like a rainbow of desire
my heart leaps at the promise
of you
your magic
your passion
your might . . .

He opens his eyes and kisses me. "Wait," I whisper, "there's more . . ."

the full spectrum of hope
appears
before my trusting eyes
and I ask only that you
hold me tight
as we dance down through
our perfect night.

"Maggie, that's beautiful. I will always hold you tight."

I break away from the kiss. "So, what's my surprise?"

"I thought we could stay in the marina and sleep on the boat tonight. We'll be able to watch the dawn together."

"Really? You can do that?" I'm helping him out, I can hear it. I used to expect more. "Our first dawn after a year together?"

"Yes," is all he offers.

My optimism takes over. I've been waiting a long time for an announcement—maybe this is it, or at least a start.

"Where are Cindy and the kids?" I ask bravely about the subject I never bring up.

"They've gone to her folks for the weekend. I'm free."

It's enough for now. No more questions, only hope. "That's wonderful. I love you, Terry."

Terry just smiles, closing the subject again. The water glistens off the port side in the setting sun, and we begin to drop anchor.

MAIA'S PERFECT HANDS

by Jamie Joy Gatto

Maia works the *masa*, kneading and patting the corn mixture between delicate fingers, allowing the weight of the dough to fall into her palms. She plays with the gritty texture, which will soon encase her mama's painstaking recipe of homemade tamales. She relaxes; her breathing slows. Maia is finally succumbing to the rhythm of her careful work.

Maia's dainty hands belie her statuesque figure. She is a sturdy woman of goddess proportions held up on long stalks of legs. Maia's torso holds all her weight: her rounded belly, her strong back, the pair of pendulous breasts that arrived too early as a young girl. Her breasts sway in time to the patting and vigilant attention to her task. She does not notice them, even as a strap of her tank top strays, slipping down a brown shoulder, and comes to rest in the fringes of her dark hair.

Secretly, Maia hates her breasts. She thinks they make her look fat. She won't go braless in public. She hides them beneath extra-large T-shirts in warm weather, and conceals her womanhood in bulky sweaters in winter. Her breasts were once a childhood source of shame, and now Maia tries to erase the fact that they even exist. She does this subconsciously, a habit perpetuated on autopilot. Somewhere deep, buried in her psyche, are the taunts of boys, the memories of undressing in gym, the shame of being the only girl to have to wear a bra in fourth grade. Maia does not see the eyes of men, and sometimes women, following her voluptuous body wherever she goes. At the market, in the park, when she takes her evening walks to the coffee shop on Maple. Maia is beautiful. Maia doesn't know.

Herman serves Maia coffee several nights a week, carefully foaming her mochaccino, adding just the right touch of cinnamon to the blend. He wants it to be perfect for her. Just right. He wants her to remember him, wishes she'd say something hopeful, do something, anything to indicate an interest in him. He waits each night for her. Sometimes she comes in. Sometimes she doesn't. She tips well.

Whenever she arrives, Herman smiles at Maia with all the strength and puppy-dog might of a young man, making firm, present eye contact, then shyly, quickly he averts his eyes. He tries not to let his gaze linger on her breasts, but he cannot help the stolen glance. He wants to taste them. He wants to bury his face in her body, and lose himself there. He wants to nurse upon her while she pats his head knowingly, and as she offers him a nourishing refuge from the world, he would hope to drown in her love. He wants this most of all— the drowning, the consumption, the obliteration of the ego, of the man. In her arms he'd be skirted away from the humdrum of daily classes, from writing papers, from his too-easy but not-so-crummy job. He'd leave the tedium of day-to-day life and wallow in a sensual ecstasy of warmth and nurturing. He'd be alive, authentic. He'd be a real man, yes. Herman would finally be whole.

Maia takes the tender banana leaves between two perfectly manicured fingers and pats the *masa* into a sweet little cake, tucking it inside each leaf. Her hands carefully push the meal into soft mounds, then she pats, pats, pats, pressing the dough almost to the edges. This is an art she acquired from home.

The chili on the stove has left the house in fragrant glory. The smells of browning beef, pork, onions, and garlic still linger in the air, remnants from their sizzling fury in her great, cast-iron skillet. Delicately, deviously, the essences of cumin, black pepper, and the tiniest touch of cinnamon waft their way into nooks in her home, and find a place to nestle in Maia's hair and clothing. She is perfumed by her own work of culinary art, crowned by her heritage and her longing for this homemade meal. The work is ample, but it is worth it. When Maia misses home, she needs this meal, regardless of cost or effort. Nostalgia drives a hard bargain.

Maia licks the last bit of chili from a well-seasoned wooden spoon, dribbling a bit on her chin. She has stuffed each bundle and has made a row of fat, prize tamales. She finishes her work by carefully tying each bundle wrapped in leaves with cotton string, making each one look like a little present, the perfect gourmet gift. Now they are ready to be steamed.

As the house fills with warmth and the homey scents of her work, Maia finds a comfortable cotton shirt to wear outside. Fall is here, but it's still warm, and she is craving the addictive chocolate-caffeine combo that waits for her at P.J.'s. The sugar is calling to her, as well.

Maia always sits at the table near the window. She never carries a book or a paper. She comes to watch people. To sit. To be. She looks at her hands, wrapped around the steaming mug and admires them. She thinks they are the only beautiful part of her body. She pampers them, applying lotions and creams. She trims her cuticles neatly, shapes and files her nails, usually painting them an aubergine or a rich bronze to complement her skin. She prizes these hands, the smallest, most delicate part of her whole. She decorates them tastefully, sparingly, with rings and jewels. The rest of her body doesn't exist to her. According to Maia the rest of her body is too big, too tall, too much.

In between customer requests, Herman watches Maia at her table mentally recording her every movement for later reference. He notices her brown eyes, how they dance from person to person, so sage, so savvy, taking in the street life as if she was recording it all, too. His cock swells, plumping in his khakis as his eyes wander down her ample body. Drawing her with his imagination, he peels off each thick layer of cotton and denim, laying her bare. He pictures her lying draped across a huge burgundy armchair, legs open for him, her dark labia glistening with want for him, clit erect, her solid arms outstretched. Those perfect breasts are swaying with a welcoming gesture, outfitted with large purple nipples surrounded by oval aureoles, perfect for Herman to bite, to suckle, to knead.

Herman immediately has to adjust himself in his pants behind the counter. He can't allow too much more playtime, time spent with Maia in his mind's eye. He wishes he wasn't working. He wishes he had the nerve to go to her table and ask her to be with him, to love him, to take care of him, to fuck him, to date him. Somehow, he thinks it would never work. He knows he'll never try, but it makes him feel alive to think about it, to play with those thoughts. Herman sighs aloud, competing with the hiss and steam of the kettles and coffee machines. It's not enough to make Maia look his way, but at least he mentally tried.

Maia savors the last chocolaty sip from her mug, tosses her hair, then pulls her practical handbag over a shoulder. She approaches Herman's counter shopping for a pastry, a cake of some sort, hoping for dessert later. Usually Herman smiles with all his might at his coffee-shop goddess, but tonight he is feeling the weight of imagined defeat. He cannot help but offer a genuine smile, but there is something different about tonight's encounter; a small feeling of hopelessness flops around inside him.

Herman leans over the glass pastry case as Maia points to a plump blueberry Danish, stuffed and oozing with berries and lacquered in sugary shine. Even over the strong smell of coffee, Herman still catches a faint whiff of cumin, of black pepper, of barely there cinnamon as Maia waves her arms in delight at finding the perfect pastry. His cock plumps again, not with renewed hope, but from the nearness of her, and from her smell.

At the kitchen table, Maia sits before an earthen platter heaped with steamed tamales. As she carefully unwraps her bundles, she feels they are each one a gift, each perfect in their flavor, texture, and aroma. She cannot be home with her family tonight, but she can still taste the flavors of home. Maia is sated.

Maia, feeling somewhat regretful that she doesn't have a boyfriend to share with her this hard-won birthday feast, is still happy to be alive. She lifts the Danish, which is now transformed into a makeshift birthday cake by sheer imagination and by her simple declaration; there is no candle to blow out, no icing to lick, but it is exactly what Maia wants. She draws it tenderly to her lips with perfect, delicate hands and hums a traditional tune of happy blessings in her head as blueberries burst sour-sweet in her mouth. Maia smiles feeling hopeful for next year, knowing she won't—she can't—always be alone. She closes her eyes and prays, pursing her lips to blow out her imaginary candle. It goes out with a flicker, then curls of smoke. Maia's wish will certainly come true.

ST. LUCY'S DAY

by Helena Settimana

Gunnar Torvaldson rode in his cutter, his horse pulling with its head down against the combined weight of sleigh and occupant. Lamps swung on its sides. He watched the horse's haunches rise and fall, the crystalline air blowing from its nostrils. It was mid-December, in fact approaching Lucia's Day, where candles would be lit to celebrate the return of the fugitive sun. Today, it made a brief appearance, then sank again into darkness short hours later. The naked trees by the track crowded in and creaked, snapping in the cold. He had been driving all day. In this near darkness, lit in part by the brilliance of stars and wavering curtains of aurora, Gunnar fled to Oslo.

He had his reasons.

In the twelve weeks which preceded his exile, Gunnar worked as village clerk and bookkeeper to Peder Olavson, the dour pastor of St. Luke's—an ancient stave church nestled in hemlocks and birch of a small farm community on the outskirts of Frederikstad. He dutifully maintained the records of the parish—financial and otherwise—a job ordinarily performed by a rural pastor, who in this instance announced to the congregation that he had no mind for money and wisely sought the help of a man who did.

Gunnar was forty and nice-looking in an ordinary way. Neither tall nor short, he had dark hair, which fell in his eyes, a middling build running toward the thickness of middle-life. His hands were the soft hands of a man unaccustomed to labor. He was quiet, retiring, a little melancholic, distant. He was a widower. His wife, Anja Nilsdatter, died in Kristiansand, a victim of the consumption, which plagued the cities. They had no children. For this, he felt guilty—and grateful.

He did have an air about him—something that sat uncomfortably with the inhabitants of the village. None could entirely say what it was about the man that made them uneasy. Men who were good with numbers were not always good with people, they reasoned. But rumors persisted that he had led a different sort of life in Kristiansand—one that did not involve his late wife. All taken into account, he considered himself lucky to have found work. His move to Frederikstad allowed him a fresh start—he was young enough to begin again and he did have a head for numbers. Thus he dedicated himself to the betterment of the parish. Slowly its people opened to him, and hopeful mothers began to introduce their daughters. He was polite, nothing more. There was indeed *something* about him.

Olavson, his employer, was wiry and short, with sinewy arms, a deeply lined face and short, kinky, dirty-blond hair. A Lutheran with a peculiar love of the Old Testament and the Pentecost, he thundered from his pulpit, warning of hellfire and damnation for all gathered should they not heed his admonitions—sloth, greed, pride, gluttony, envy, wrath, lust . . . all awaited the unwary parishioner and all were sure to lead directly to perdition. Gunnar, so new to the village, and so much apart, twisted uncomfortably in his pew, troubled by conscience.

At the root of this was his experience of Christian, the grown son of his landlord, Per Jansson. He had spotted the young man in the barn some time after his arrival in the town, on the bitter, trailing edge of autumn. The man was tall—of heroic stature— with straw-blond hair and an open face, clear grey eyes, a full, ruddy mouth. Gunnar stood stock-still at the sight of him. Their gaze had locked for too long and the man had waved to Gunnar— a beckoning rather than a greeting—a lazy "come on over here" gesture that made Gunnar redden and hurry away to his room where he latched the door. He stood panting and desperate, until he tore at his clothing, rent his trouser buttons to beat and pull at his cock until he shot over the quilt-laden spindle bed with a bark. He imagined himself consumed by the generous mouth of this man. He heated some water on the kettle in the fire. He cleaned himself and the quilt, then sat on the edge of the bed and held his head in his hands.

His horse and cutter were in the barn. Eventually he had to see to them. When at last he ventured forth, the landlord's son acted as if he did not recognize Gunnar at all. He fetched the shaggy brown gelding without word or a glance at him. For this, Gunnar felt a mixed sense of relief.

Christian shrugged and stood back while the accountant inspected his animal, running his hands down its hard legs, passing his hand over its rump. He bent over and picked up a hoof; inspected the sole of its foot. He whistled softly to himself. That's when the young man had the impertinence to run his hand over Gunnar's haunch and down the back of his very own leg. He froze as a statue, his breath caught in his throat, his heart hammering a frantic tattoo in his chest, his cock a sudden, painful burning spike in his trousers. Christian Person stood close and pressed into his cheeks so that he could be felt hard, as well. He stepped back and walked without looking back, to the ladder leading to the loft and mounted until his hobnailed boots disappeared into the gloom over head.

Gunnar's head spun in helpless, mindless, arousal. He followed, an automaton. The loft was fragrant with the sweet vanilla scent of hay and there was little light except for that which rose through the floorboards and the mow hatch, cast from the lamps lit in the stable below. He blinked in an attempt to adjust to the light. A voice said "Here," and Gunnar reached out into the dark to find his hand clasped firmly and guided to the man's burning cock. He pulled the flesh back and breathed in its earthy stink— sweat and something richer, riper. He fumbled with the buttons of his trousers, felt them tumble to his ankles, felt the cool air assail his burning balls, felt the groom's calloused fingers pressed into his head, heard the rustle of hay underfoot, the soft voices of the horses calling below, the rasping prickle of the straw on his belly, under his knees, the burning tear of the big man's cock against his asshole, a rending and clasping, indescribable pleasure-pain, the clean linen smell of come, and the faint rotten fruit scent of shit rising on waves of light and warmth. He cried with the release of it, puddling his load in the dusty dried broken grass.

But Gunnar's guilt flooded back and he moved house the following week, finding refuge at Arne Stevenson's place. Gunnar tried to put the Viking out of his mind, but failed miserably. Compelled to return, he wandered the icy tracks back toward Jansson's, his path lit by the red glow of the guttering sun. His prints in the snow led again and again to the barn, to that savage tryst. After, filled with dread, he would promise himself he would never return. For two weeks he tried, running into the snow in the dead of the night, flinging himself naked and burning into the deep drifts in an attempt to cool his ardor. He scourged himself with a broom by the fire. He wept. Then on the thirteenth day, the young man tapped at his window, slid through its thrown-up sash, wound himself through Gunnar's nightclothes and suckled him until he was spent and shaking. All seemed lost.

And so he sat in the whitewashed interior of the church, on a stiff oak-hewn pew and reviewed his multifarious sins in the face of the all-seeing eye of God. He retreated to the office later to count the offerings and write to the parish seat for more funds to build a small school nearby. In his mind he composed desperate letters to the late Anja and lewder letters to Christian Person. He'd sit, looking vacant, staring at his ledger, or worse, would choke his turgid cock to a shuddering death beneath the desktop.

The door to the office creaked open and Peder Olavson hovered in the gap, a worried expression further tightening his hard-edged features. He stood in his severe, high-collared black robes and hat. "Are you unwell, Gunnar? You don't seem to focus so well on your duties as you did when you first came here. What is it? Are you still in mourning? Are you troubled?"

Gunnar considered for a long time. "I am well in body, pastor, but I'm troubled."

"How troubled?"

"By unclean thoughts, I'm ashamed to say."

"Of what nature?"

"Of Sodom."

Shock registered on the face of the preacher.

"Have you had these thoughts for long?"

"For all my life. Through my marriage. Forever."

"Have you acted on these thoughts, Gunnar Torvaldson?"

Gunnar looked away and wept, his hand shading his eyes.

"What have you done to rid your self of such thoughts? Such . . . deeds?"

"Prayer, pastor. Prayer and scourges and baths in the snow."

"And it has not worked." A statement—not a question.

"No."

"I will help you pray to drive this demon from your soul. Get on your knees."

Olavson returned with a birch switch and an ardent, fiery gleam in his eye.

Gunnar rose from the chair, its feet scraping noisily on the boards of the old pine floor. His knees buckled and he sank slowly over the chair's cane seat.

"Repeat after me: *'Oh Lord'* "

"Oh Lord"

"*Deliver me from this disease of sin which infects my soul.*"

"Deliver me . . .'"

The cane rose and fell on Gunnar's buttocks and back as Olavson's face reddened. The veins stood out on his bulging forehead, on his scrawny neck. Gunnar burned with mortification. When it was done, Olavson stalked from the room, ashen, casting a savage look at his wife, who stood by the door, an inquisitive look on her face.

"Go home," he said.

Gunnar was certain that his punishment would not end there. Olavson would certainly consult his bishop. They were almost surely to recommend he leave. The next day, Gunnar answered a newspaper advertisement calling for a bookkeeper at a mill in Oslo. Two agonizing weeks later, he received an invitation to be seen by the managers.

And so it came to pass, that on the eve of the eve of St Lucia's day, Gunnar Torvaldson, late of a small village near Frederikstad, loaded his cutter with his few possessions wrapped in heavy rugs, his lanterns ready to light against the mid-afternoon twilight, set off for Oslo. The bells attached to his harnesses jingled in time with the brown gelding's ambling gait.

❧ ❧ ❧

His hotel—a modest one—nonetheless had a view of the Royal Palace and the bustling street below. It was lined with shops and cafés. Gunnar, eager to unwind, ventured forth into a drinking establishment. He sat quietly in a corner, his hat still on his head, his muffler pulled around his neck. Looking up from his third ale, he noted a woman across the room. She bore a passing resemblance to Anja—thin and dark-haired, with the angular body of a boy. She laughed a bit too loudly, and wore too much rouge to be called pretty or to look respectable. Her hair had come undone under her bonnet. He returned to his drink and to his alarm, when he looked up again, found her walking toward him, a glass of cloudy liquor in her hand. The men whose company she had been keeping watched her, laughing and pointing, as she crossed the tavern floor, her dark silk skirts and crinolines rustling.

Her name was Lucia—Lucy—like the saint whose honor it was to return the sun to the sky. She made him drink more and try the foul-tasting stuff she herself swilled. Gunnar's head swam.

She held her head high as she walked ahead of him across the lobby of his hotel, past the concierge at the desk, who leaned out further to watch her as she passed. Gunnar watched as Lucy held the sodden hem of her skirts above her ankles and mounted the stairs in front of him, showing her buttoned shoes and the thick cotton hose that clad her legs and creased, sagging slightly at her ankle. She paused and pulled up a stocking, and resumed her climb, her heels clattering too noisily on the spiraling marble staircase.

In the room, she stood in front of the window watching the white-clad street with its glowing gas lamps and the hustle of holiday shoppers.

"Ten kroner," she said to him and unbuttoned the cape clasped at her throat. It fell to the floor in a puddle around her feet. "Twenty for a 'special.'"

"What's a special?" asked Gunnar, feeling oddly aroused and queasy all at once.

"Ten is for straight, twenty is for my bottom, or for games, or for my mouth," said Lucy.

"Twenty then," said Gunnar, reminded of how Anja would once upon a time beg him to press his cock into her backside, and how he was both reluctant and inflamed about pleasing her this way.

Like Lucy, Anja was boyish and slight. In a woman, Gunnar found this appealing. She stepped away from the window. He placed his fare on the nightstand and turned to kiss her, still wearing his dark topcoat damp with melted snow. There was so much hope in that kiss—hope for redemption, hope for communion with Anja, hope, hope.

Lucy smelled of violets and fennel. The scent shouted at him from her scrawny bosom. Awkwardly he began to explore, his right hand fumbling down her bodice to the gap between her legs, groping through the crepe and her crinolines, half hoping to find more than empty space there. He did not. His penis rose and fell with each fumbling feel. She undid her bodice, turning her back to him to unlash the corset which forced such womanly shape as she had onto her narrow frame. Her body was covered with red marks from the stays, like the excoriated marks which still, yellow and fading, crossed his ass. She undid her skirts, threw them over a chair. For a moment she looked like a holy woman, scoured and defiant. Her hair fell down around her shoulders; her face was pale, her lips and cheeks, livid.

Gunnar pushed her onto the bed. Its mattress, slung on ropes tied to its rails, swung and creaked. A mass of wild black hair bristled between her legs, strong-scented, feral. Gunnar wavered.

"If only . . ." he began.

"If only what, duckie?"

"God, forgive me . . . if only you were a—a boy . . ."

She was on her knees, her ass in the air. She peered at him over her shoulder.

"You like that? I can be a boy. I can be whatever you want . . . my bag—pass it here."

She rummaged in the bag, and eventually drew out a wooden replica of a penis. It looked like it might be of oak—it had a light color, almost like flesh, and a strong spiral grain. It was attached to a double belt.

Kneeling on the edge of the bed she buckled the contraption around her hips and thrust it at him, making it bob.

"See?"

Gunnar smiled, and stiffened perceptibly.

She looked at him with approval. "Do you like to give or receive?"

"Both . . . both . . . anything."

"I bet you've never had one this hard," she mocked. "Come here, let me see if you can take it."

Gunnar undressed and knelt beside her. She ran her hands over the swell of his ass, noting the fading marks. "You've been a bad boy, I see." She laughed.

Gunnar colored and groaned in agony.

She kissed the bruises, ran her tongue through the cleft of his ass, over the point of his tailbone and into the hard knot of flesh begging beneath it. She spat and pressed her finger into the pucker, which gave way easily. She spat again and again, noting with some satisfaction that he was quivering hard and when she finally pressed the tip of her tool into the gaping hole loosened by her fingers, he moaned as if in great pain.

"Do it," he said and knelt near the headboard, leaning over. She pressed into him again—four, maybe five strokes were all it took as she pinched his nipples to galvanize his pleasure and ribbons of jism shot against the board's polished walnut face.

She dressed perfunctorily.

"Stay."

"No."

"I love you."

"Don't be stupid: you don't."

"If only you could stay with me," he began. "If only you would stay with me—maybe I'd be different—maybe I could change. Maybe it would be alright." He sat on a straight-backed chair, naked, his shock of black hair in his eyes.

"No," she said simply. "That would not work." She dressed hastily and left, her head held as high as before.

He watched her leave, listening to the click of her shoes on the broad stone stairs.

Minutes later, a knock was heard at his door. It was the concierge. He stepped into the room, fidgeting, looking about nervously as if expecting a monster to fling itself from behind the heavy drapes. Gunnar was to leave immediately. The hotel was modest, but it was not a brothel. The woman who had accompanied him to his room was recognized by a chambermaid as one of the neighborhood's prostitutes. Gunnar remembered how the man had stared, leered, even, as Lucy crossed the lobby. He doubted the story of the chambermaid, but it was for nothing. The management could not tolerate damage to their reputation, said the concierge. Gunnar would find the bulk of his belongings in the lobby. His horse and cutter would be fetched from the mews. He was to go. *Now.*

In a daze, his blood thundering in his ears, Gunnar dressed and began to pack. Whatever would he do? Where would he go? What would become of his job prospects? In her haste Lucy had left her false penis behind. For a crazy moment Gunnar wondered if he should find her and return it. She was sure to miss it. It had been kicked under the bed. He wound it in a pillowslip, thrust it into the pocket of his coat, and stalked wordlessly to the lobby where he paid for his trouble with trembling hands.

He drove toward Nordstrand where great shards of ice heaved themselves into a jagged, blue-white mosaic. The Oslofjord blazed with red light cast by the sun's faint embers. He tethered the horse, and walked along the snowy pavement, looking desperately out across the water toward Holmenkollen. Couples walked alongside him, passed him, laughing in the swirling snow: women in fur, their hands held in muffs, men in greatcoats and beaver hats.

A tall boy walked toward him. They knocked shoulders and Gunnar caught the arched eyebrow and pursed pink lips of the youth, and knew the collision had been no accident. He spun around and walked on. The youth stood and watched as Gunnar leaned against the railing on the walkway by the edge of the shore. He drew the wooden phallus from his pocket and flung it over the floes into the fjord, flung it as hard as his shaking arms would allow. Turning toward the young man, he clutched his head and screamed back at the city, but his voice was lost in the frigid wind.

THE FRIEND

by Claire Thompson

Be careful what you ask for.

Dianne's grandmother used to say that to her. Now it was her turn to mull this over in her mind. She had just finished a pleasant meal with two men. One was her husband, Tom. The other was Andy, a friend of Tom's who had expressed his interest in exploring Dianne's and Tom's open relationship. The relationship was not open in the traditional sense of "swinging." Rather, the two were open in their exploration of their love for each other. This exploration sometimes included others.

Dianne is "owned" you see, but of her own free will. One need merely look at her to see she is loved. There is a calmness in her demeanor, a contentment in her bearing that is rarely seen in other women. And the one who has claimed her for his own was sitting now at her side, his hand casually around her shoulders. She leaned further into him as he continued speaking with Andy. They were speaking of Dianne, but she was not participating in the conversation.

"Does she *like* to be whipped?" she heard Andy ask, though she was too embarrassed by this question to look up. He leaned forward toward the couple. They were sitting close together on the love seat perpendicular to the couch where he sprawled back, full of Dianne's deliciously prepared meal.

"Answer the gentleman, Dianne. Do you like to be whipped, darling?"

She felt herself blushing but she knew she was expected to answer, and answer truthfully. "Yes," she whispered.

"Whoa. I've heard of this stuff, you know. I have always been curious, too. But I've never actually seen someone whipped," Andy said, with almost little-boy wistfulness in his voice. Both men seemed unaware, or unconcerned, with Dianne's discomfiture. Andy continued, "I don't really get it, though. I mean, it looks sexy, to see a naked, or leather-clad woman, with her breasts bared, being whipped as she writhes and moans. But it's like a fantasy. In real life it seems rather violent, brutal even."

"People who have never explored this sort of lovemaking are often confused. Perhaps it's something you have to be born loving. I'm not sure. But it is definitely not violence. It is certainly not pain for pain's sake. It is pain for pleasure's sake. Our passion is not always gentle, but it is always tender." With that Tom looked over at Dianne, with a smile on his face. She was looking at him with an intent expression; the love in her eyes making her radiant.

Andy was at once moved and excited by Tom's words. He had often had fantasies involving bound women submitting to his every whim, however outrageous. But to date he had not yet dared to act on any of his desires. Indeed, he was only just coming to realize that his impulses were natural, if not common. He was only beginning to explore that secret need in himself to dominate, to claim a woman with a passion so fierce he was still afraid of it.

Finally Andy said aloud, "Well, I'm curious. I would like to see you whip her. I mean, if that were okay. I would like to experience this passion you speak of." Andy said this last sentence in almost a whisper.

"I think that can be arranged," Tom grinned. He relished each opportunity to display his darling slave girl. Dianne tensed as he said this. She loved what she was; she yearned always to submit to her lover. This wouldn't be the first time he had whipped her or somehow displayed her in front of others. But up until now it had always been "scene" friends. People who understood what was being offered; people who did it themselves.

Her mouth felt dry; she licked her lips and looked down at her lap. Yet even as she squirmed nervously, she felt her own body responding to their words. She wanted to be used; she craved it.

Tom hugged her to him. Then he released her and stood up. "Dianne, our guest would like to see you whipped. And I like to please my guests. Stand up and present yourself, please. There at the side table will be fine." Dianne stood, unconsciously clenching her fists at her sides. She was stifling her impulse to shout, "No!" She knew she wanted this as much as he did, if not more. But she felt terribly shy. What if Andy found her unappealing? What if she disgraced herself in front of them both? These thoughts whirled through her head and left her paralyzed there before them.

"Dianne! What are you doing? Do as you are told, at once!"

Oh God. She knew she had to obey. On one level, she was glad it was not her decision. Her own perverse need to be whipped and used was taken out of her hands. He was commanding it; she had no choice in the matter. Slowly she began to unbutton her blouse. Andy was watching her intently; she felt his eyes boring into her. He saw that her hands were shaking ever so slightly. He found her shyness captivating.

Tom was also watching her carefully. Would she make him proud; would she prove her love and submission to him tonight? He was aware of her nervousness but he also knew she was ready for this. He knew that she yearned for this as much as he did.

At last her blouse was open. She allowed it to fall from her shoulders. Next she reached behind her back and unzipped her skirt. With a slight wriggle of her hips, the skirt dropped to her ankles. She stepped out of it and stood for a moment, clad in her demi-bra and matching silk panties. She had no stockings this evening; it had been an informal dinner at home. While she stood there, hesitating, trying to gather her courage to remove her undergarments, both men stared at her.

Dianne herself was still unaware of her own beauty. She knew Tom found her lovely; he proved this to her endlessly. But she still did not know that her voluptuous figure and her sweet face were admired by many. In a way Tom was glad of this; her modesty and demure behavior were becoming to her.

Tom shifted in his chair slightly, and cleared his throat. Dianne jumped, startled, and quickly fumbled at her bra clasps. As her round, perfect breasts were released Andy sighed in spite of himself.

Dianne was aware of his intent gaze and she felt the heat rise into her face as she blushed. She moved toward the table, fighting her impulse to cover her form with her arms. The table was level with her hips. Tom had used her there many times before; it was the perfect height for him to take her from behind. Now bending forward, she placed her hands flat, palms down, presenting her long shapely legs to the gentlemen. Andy's eyes followed the lithe curves up to her small but nicely rounded ass. His hand slipped down to the front of his jeans. He was becoming uncomfortable as his cock stiffened in response to her beauty and the situation before him. She was now bent at the waist, with her forehead touching the table. Her eyes were closed and she was trying desperately to relax and maintain her position with some grace.

Tom said, "Dianne, aren't you forgetting something?" She didn't respond at first and then she realized what she had failed to do. With a hand that seemed to move against its own will, she slowly dragged her black silken panties past the little round globes of her ass, and on down past her thighs, to her knees. They could see her pussy petulantly peeking out from between her legs.

She was quiet but Tom knew how she must be feeling—bending over, her ass and pussy exposed and open for the use and pleasure of these men sitting behind her. He stood then. He was holding a heavy black-leather whip. It was braided in about twelve tresses that hung down menacingly at his side.

Tom came around behind Dianne and whispered in her ear, "Prepare for a beating."

She felt her sex tighten as if he had actually grabbed it. Her whole body tingled as she readied herself for the first strike. The slap echoed in the air a fraction of a second after the lash met her eager flesh.

Andy moved suddenly, startled at the sound. He felt an almost physical sympathy with Dianne's tender flesh. And yet he was also keenly aware of his own hardening desire.

Tom continued to whip Dianne's bottom and thighs. She jerked a bit, and emitted a few moans and sighs, but other than that, she was still. Tom came up close behind her, and with an expert flick with his foot against her inner ankle, he spread her legs far apart. She was breathing hard now; it was audible even to Andy sitting on the couch across the room.

Tom put the heavy flogger down and picked up the long riding crop. As if testing it out, he swatted it a few times against Dianne's tender inner thighs. Still she kept her position, though her yelping cries showed she was not immune to his torture. Tom reached in between her legs and grabbed her nether lips between his fingers. Her wetness glistened on his fingers. His little slut girl was on fire. He pressed a finger into her. She moaned and moved her hips slightly.

"Be still," he told her. Then he withdrew the finger and swirled it around her now-sopping cunt. He found her little sweet spot and massaged and teased it until she moaned low and long. Again her hips were swaying as she felt herself nearing the edge of her own ecstasy.

All of a sudden, his sweet hard fingers were gone. She sighed and slumped slightly, trying to be still even as her body yearned for his touch.

"Didn't you hear me, Dianne? Didn't I say to be still?"

"Tom!" she whined, "you know I can't help it when you do that!"

"Then I'll have to help you, won't I? Since you lack the discipline even to stay still when your pussy is being handled, we need to toughen up that little pussy. Wouldn't you agree, little slave girl?"

Not waiting for her reply, Tom picked up the riding crop, and dragged it across her ass and thighs. Dianne shivered and tried to speak. But before she could answer, he smacked her delicate pussy. The wet slapping sound as leather met well-lubricated lips was lost to the sound of Dianne's cries.

He hadn't hit her hard.

"Well? Can't you even answer a direct question? Is this a sample of how well you are trained?"

She knew he was teasing her, but she also knew he wanted her to answer him.

"Yes, sir," she said, hoping that would suffice.

"Yes sir, what?" he said, smiling broadly. She could not see his smile. "Do you agree we must do something to teach your naughty little sex to control itself?"

"Yes," she hissed, now thoroughly embarrassed in front of Andy.

He was enjoying the show immensely. "Maybe you could whip her a bit more," he volunteered, perversely eager to see what would happen.

"Excellent idea, old friend," Tom replied. And he used the crop again, this time less gently. The stinging blows were reddening Dianne's tender flesh. She was trying very hard to stay still and open for him. But after one particularly sharp smack she gave up.

Forgetting herself and her position, she instinctively drew her legs in close to ward off any further attacks on her tender sex. Though he expected and indeed intended to elicit just such a response, Tom feigned disappointment in her.

"Oh, Dianne! You came out of position in front of my friend. You have shamed me! What do you have to say for yourself?"

"Tom," she breathed, "I'm sorry! I wasn't ready. You hurt me!"

"Of course I did, silly girl. I intended to. That has nothing to do with it. You have behaved in an untrained fashion. We both know you are capable of withstanding much more than that. On your knees, now!" With that, he pressed her down by her shoulders.

Dianne sank at once and pressed her head low into the carpet. She was ashamed of her lack of discipline. She tried to still her ragged breathing and await his bidding.

Andy was silent, his mouth open and his hand covering what must have been a huge erection.

Tom looked over to him. Then they both looked at Dianne, crouched there naked and trembling before them. "You're my guest, Andy. What would you have me do to help her remember her place? Shall I whip her with a single lash? It would raise some lovely welts that would help her remember for several days to come. Or shall we go easy on the girl? Perhaps you would like her to show you how sorry she is by helping ease your, er, evident discomfort." Tom looked pointedly at Andy's jeans.

Andy crossed his legs quickly, looking somewhat sheepish. But he realized what Tom was offering. And he wanted it—badly.

"I—I would like that, Tom. I would like that very much. Thank you. Um. What should I do?" Andy was like a nervous schoolboy but he desperately wanted Dianne to touch him. He was longing to feel her hot mouth and soft hands on his body.

"Just sit back and relax. Dianne will take care of you. This will be her chance to redeem herself. And because she was so naughty, I will not allow her the use of her hands just yet." Prodding her gently with his foot, he said, "Get up, little slave girl. Go service our friend here. No hands. And see that you please him."

Dianne scrambled up and hurried over to Andy. He sat back and spread his legs, allowing her to crawl between his knees. Not needing any prodding himself, he had already pulled his jeans and underwear down. Andy felt rather embarrassed to expose himself like this in front of another man, but his need outweighed his modesty. His erect cock bounced gently at the naked woman on her knees before him.

Dianne put her hands behind her back to remind herself not to use them. Nervously she glanced back at her Master. He came close to her and put his hand on her head. She leaned back into it and closed her eyes. He allowed her this for a moment. Then he gently guided her back to Andy's erection. He pressed her head forward until her mouth was level with the head of Andy's cock.

Then he pressed down, not quite as gently.

Dianne opened her lips and closed her eyes.

"Oh. God. Yes,"" Andy moaned, as he moved to allow her better access.

"Use her mouth as you like, my friend," Tom smiled. "I would just ask that you don't come in her mouth. On the face and breasts would be better this first time."

Dianne silently thanked Tom for this small reprieve; she still sometimes had trouble swallowing. Andy nodded as he grabbed her head. He pulled her down until his erection was all the way back in her throat. She tried to move back; she couldn't breathe. He held her there a moment longer.

At last he let her go and she fell back on her haunches and gasped for breath. Tears had formed in her eyes from the onslaught. But before she could recover, he reached out again and used her the same way. Over and over he plunged into her throat, gagging her with his penis. He was using her roughly, but his own desire was so fierce that he didn't use her long. After a few minutes he let her go.

"I'm coming! Give me your face; give me those tits!" There was no trace of modesty now as he spurt over and over across her face, in her hair, on her chest and breasts and belly. At last he fell back, spent and panting.

Dianne sat between his legs, covered in another man's ejaculate. She yearned to lose herself in her lover's arms. But she sat and waited, determined to behave as her Master wished.

Tom came up behind her and murmured, "Go clean yourself up, my love, and rejoin us in a camisole and panties." Dianne jumped up then and impulsively kissed him right on the mouth. Before he could respond she turned and fled the room. He gazed after her, wiping Andy's semen from his cheek.

As Tom looked over at Andy, he was zipping up his pants and tucking in his shirt. "How ya' doing, Andy?"

"Wow. I'm doing great. That was very intense. Very hot. You are one lucky guy."

After a few minutes, Dianne reappeared, wearing a white satin camisole and matching lace panties. Tom gestured to her and she came and sat on his lap on the couch. Casually he put his hand over her hot and very needy sex. Andy looked longingly at her nipples pressing against the silky fabric. But it was late and he had a lot to process.

"I think I'd better get to bed," Andy said. "I hope I wasn't too rough, Dianne."

Tom smiled and answered for her, "If you are pleased, then Dianne is pleased." Dianne sighed happily and snuggled back into Tom's firm body.

Tom continued, "Get some rest then; we'll see you in the morning. We still have the rest of the weekend to play and explore."

As Andy went off to bed, Tom turned to Dianne. "You were wonderful, darling. How do you feel?"

"Very happy, my love." She kissed him then, as her hands roamed his body. They made love there on the couch until the rosy fingers of the dawn spread over the sky. And that is how Andy found them the next morning, entwined in each other's arms, with sleep's sweet net still over them.

CONTRIBUTORS

Tara Alton's erotica has appeared in *Best Women's Erotica, Guilty Pleasures, Clean Sheets*, and *Scarlet Letters*. Check out her web site www.taraalton.com.

Rachel Kramer Bussel (www.rachelkramerbussel.com) is the reviser of *The Lesbian Sex Book*, coauthor of *The Erotic Writer's Market Guide*, and coeditor of *Up All Night: Adventures in Lesbian Sex*. She is also a contributing editor at *Cleansheets.com* and a nightlife columnist for *The New York Blade*. Her writing has been published in numerous publications including *AVN, Bust, Curve, Diva, Oxygen.com, Playgirl*, and *The San Francisco Chronicle*, as well as in more than twenty erotic anthologies, including *Best Lesbian Erotica 2001* and *2004, Best Women's Erotica 2003* and *2004*, and *Best American Erotica 2004*.

Kate Dominic is the author of the new erotic short-story collection, *Any 2 People, Kissing* (Down There Press, 2003). Her stories have appeared under various pen names in many dozens of magazines and anthologies, including *Best American Erotica, Best Women's Erotica, Best Lesbian Erotica, Best Gay Erotica, Best Bisexual Erotica, Best Transgender Erotica, Herotica*, and the *Mammoth Book of Best New Erotica*.

Novelist, short story writer, and essayist **Janice Eidus** has twice won the O. Henry Prize for her short stories, as well as a Redbook Prize and a Pushcart Prize. She is the author of the story collections *The Celibacy Club* and *Vito Loves Geraldine*, and the novels *Urban Bliss* and *Faithful Rebecca*, and is coeditor of *It's Only Rock and Roll: An Anthology of Rock and Roll Short Stories*.

Holly Farris is an Appalachian who has worked as an autopsy assistant, restaurant baker, and beekeeper. Her fifty published short stories, poems, and nonfiction have appeared in journals with content both fiery and tame. A retired biologist, she is now a housing advocate.

Jamie Joy Gatto is a New Orleans sex activist and author/editor whose work has been included in dozens of projects, such as *Best Bisexual Erotica 1* and *2, Best SM Erotica, Of the Flesh, Guilty Pleasures*, and more. She is the founder and editor-in-chief of *www.MindCaviar.com* and its sister sites, *www.OpheliasMuse.com*

and *A Bi-Friendly Place*. She has authored three collections: *Unveiling Venus*, a poetry chapbook; *Suddenly Sexy*, an e-book available at www.renebooks.com; and *Sex Noir* (Circlet 2002). She has edited, with M. Christian, *Villains & Vixens* (Black Books 2003).

Debra Hyde's erotic fiction has appeared in other Venus anthologies, including *Desires*, N. T. Morley's *Master* and *slave* anthologies, and *Leather, Lace and Lust*. She is the coeditor of *Strange Bedfellows*. Visit her website, *Pursed Lips*, one of the web's earliest "sexblogs." She also writes for the web sites *Scarlet Letters* and *Yesportal*.

Susannah Indigo (www.susannahindigo.com) is the editor-in-chief of *Clean Sheets Magazine* (www.cleansheets.com), and also the editor and founder of *Slow Trains Literary Journal* (www.slowtrains.com). Her books include *Oysters Among Us, Many Kisses: Stories of Dominant Love*, the *From Porn to Poetry* series, and the new anthology, *Sex & Laughter*.

Michèle Larue, a Sorbonne-educated journalist, has used her six languages freelancing around the world. As a director, she made two documentaries in Cuba, another on the European SM scene, as well as BDSM shorts. Les Editions Blanche (Paris) has published her erotic short stories since 1995. Editore Mondadori (Milano) picked up two of her stories for their collection of erotica, *Spicy*, in 2002. Her short stories have appeared in English translation in *Erotic Travel Tales* and the *Mammoth Book of New Erotica 2003*. She has also published her Cuban erotic tales, *Cuba Satissima*, with Descartes & Cie (Paris). Her twin BDSM novels, *Memoirs of a Left-Bank Dominatrix*, will spring out in English at Blue Moon Books in 2004. She lives in Paris.

Marilyn Jaye Lewis's erotic fiction has been widely published in the United States and Europe. She is the founder of the Erotic Authors Association, and is the award-winning author of such titles as *Neptune & Surf, When Hearts Collide*, and *In the Secret Hours*. Her upcoming novel, *When the Night Stood Still*, will be published by Magic Carpet Books in January 2004, and the collected works of her erotic short fiction, *Night on Twelfth Street*, will be published by Alyson Books in 2004.

Catherine Lundoff lives in Minneapolis with her terrific girlfriend and a small herd of cats. She's a computer geek by day and writer by night. Her writings have appeared in a number of anthologies, including the *Harrington Lesbian Fiction Quarterly, Erotic Travel Tales II, Shameless, Below the Belt, Zaftig, Best*

Lesbian Erotica 1999 and *2001*, *Electric* and *Electric 2,* and *Looking Queer: GLBT Body Image and Identity.*

Maria Isabel Pita is the author of five erotic novels, *Thorsday Night, Eternal Bondage, To Her Master Born, Dreams of Anubis,* and *Rite of Way.* She is also the author of a nonfiction book, *The Story of M—A Memoir,* a vividly detailed account of her first year of training as a sex slave. Maria lives with her beloved Master, Stinger, and their dog, Merlin. You can visit her at www.mariaisabelpi ta.com.

Jean Roberta teaches first-year English at a Canadian prairie university and writes in various modes. Her reviews and articles appear regularly in diverse print journals and web sites. Her erotic stories have appeared in the *Best Lesbian Erotica* and *Best Women's Erotica* series, as well as the *Wicked Words* series from Black Lace in England. Her novel, *Prairie Gothic,* is in the catalog of Amatory Ink (www.amatory-ink.co.uk).

Kiini Ibura Salaam has had essays published in *Colonize This, When Race Becomes Real, Roll Call, Men We Cherish, Utne Reader, Essence,* and *Ms.* magazine. Her fiction has been published in *Mojo: Conjure Stories, Black Silk, Black Women's Best Erotica, Dark Matter,* and *Dark Eros.* KIS.list is her monthly e-report on life as a writer. Visit her web site at: www.kiiniibura.com.

Lisabet Sarai is the author of three erotic novels, *Raw Silk, Incognito,* and *Ruby's Rules,* and the coeditor, with S. F. Mayfair, of the anthology *Sacred Exchange,* which explores the spiritual aspects of BDSM relationships. Her stories have appeared in a variety of collections including *Erotic Travel Tales II* (Cleis) and *Wicked Words 8* (Black Lace). Lisabet reviews erotic books and films for the Erotica Readers and Writers Association (www.erotica-readers.com) and *Sliptongue.com.* Visit her website, *Lisabet Sarai's Fantasy Factory* (www.lisabet sarai.com) for more information and samples of her writing.

Iris N. Schwartz is a Manhattan-based fiction writer and poet whose work has appeared in numerous print and online publications. Her erotic fiction has been anthologized in *Down and Dirty* and *Best Bondage Erotica 2003.* Her poetry has been anthologized in *An Eye for an Eye Makes the Whole World Blind: Poets on 9/11* and is forthcoming in *Listening to the Birth of Crystals.* She is currently at work on a novel, *Sirena Wailing.*

Helena Settimana lives in Toronto, Canada, where the northern climate perhaps influences her dark vision. Her short fiction, poetry, and essays have appeared on the web and in print in numerous erotic anthologies. She is Features Editor at the Erotica Readers and Writers Association, www.erotica readers.com.

Cecilia Tan is the author of many erotic books and short stories, including *Black Feathers, The Velderet*, and *Telepaths Don't Need Safewords*. Her work has appeared in *Ms.* magazine, *Penthouse, Best American Erotica*, and tons of other places. She is also editor and founder of Circlet Press, publishers of erotic science fiction and fantasy. Find out more at www.ceciliatan.com.

Claire Thompson has written numerous novels and short stories, all exploring aspects of Dominance & submission. Novels include *Sarah's Awakening, Hard Corps, The Stalker, Journey into Submission, The Toy, Slave Girl, Julie's Submission, Frog: A Tale of Sexual Torture and Degradation*, and, soon to be released, *Tracy in Chains*.

Alison Tyler's short stories have appeared in anthologies including *Erotic Travel Tales 1* and *2, Best Women's Erotica 2002* and *2003*, and *Sweet Life 1* and *2* (all published by Cleis), *Wicked Words 4, 5, 6* and *8* (Black Lace), and *Sex Toy Tales* (Down There Press). With Thomas S. Roche, she is the coauthor of two sexy anthologies, *His* and *Hers* (Pretty Things Press). She is also the editor of the *Naughty Stories from A to Z* series (Pretty Things Press) and *Best Bondage Erotica* (Cleis).

Molly Weatherfield is the author of *Carrie's Story* and *Safe Word* (both from Cleis), and likes to think of herself as a classic author in the very small field of Comic SM. As Pam Rosenthal, she's written the erotic romance novels *Almost a Gentleman* (Kensington Brava) and *The Bookseller's Daughter* (Kensington Brava, forthcoming 1/2004). And as Pam and Molly, she's written reviews and features for Salon.com.

Lisa Wolfe lives and writes in the San Francisco Bay Area. Her stories have been published in www.cleansheets.com, www.scarletletters.com, *Best Women's Erotica 2002*, and *Best American Erotica 2003*.

The Memoirs of Josephine
Anonymous

19th Century Vienna was a wellspring of culture, society and decadence and home to Josephine Mutzenbacher. One of the most beautiful and sought after libertines of the age, she rose from the streets to become a celebrated courtesan. As a young girl, she learned the secrets of her profession. As mistress to wealthy, powerful men, she used her talents to transform from a slattern to the most wanted woman of the age. This candid, long suppressed memoir is her story.

The Pearl
Anonymous

Lewd, bawdy, and sensual, this cult classic is a collection of Victorian erotica that circulated in an underground magazine known as *The Pearl* from July 1879 to December 1880. Now dusted off and totally uncensored, the journal of voluptuous reading that titillated the eminent Victorians is reprinted in its entirety. The eighteen issues of *The Pearl* are packed with short stories, naughty poems, ballads of sexual adventure, letters, limericks, jokes, gossip, and six serialized novels.

Mistress of Instruction
Christine Kerr

Mistress of Instruction is a delightfully erotic romp through merry old Victorian England. Gillian, precocious and promiscuous, travels to London where she discovers Crawford House, an exclusive gentlemen's club where young ladies are trained to excel in service. A true prodigy of sensual talents, she is retained to supervise the other girls' initiation into "the life." Her title: Mistress of Instruction.

Neptune and Surf
Marilyn Jaye Lewis

A trio of lyrical yet explicit novellas sure to challenge stereotypes about the stylistic range of women's erotica. *Neptune and Surf* is the fruit of the author's conversations with a group of women about their deepest fantasies. What arises is a tantalizing look at women's libidinous desires, exploring their deepest fantasies with a mesmerizing delicacy and frankness. With *Neptune and Surf* Lewis shows why she is one of the premier female voices in erotica.

Order These Selected Blue Moon Titles

My Secret Life $15.95

The Altar of Venus.....................$7.95

Caning Able $7.95

The Blue Moon Erotic Reader IV $15.95

The Best of the Erotic Reader..........$15.95

Confessions D'Amour $14.95

A Maid for All Seasons I, II $15.95

Color of Pain, Shade of Pleasure $14.95

The Governess $7.95

Claire's Uptown Girls $7.95

The Intimate Memoirs of an

Edwardian Dandy I, II, III............. $15.95

Jennifer and Nikki $7.95

Burn $7.95

Don Winslow's Victorian Erotica $14.95

The Garden of Love $14.95

The ABZ of Pain and Pleasure $7.95

"Frank" and I.........................$7.95

Hot Sheets $7.95

Tea and Spices $7.95

Naughty Message $7.95

The Sleeping Palace.....................$7.95

Venus in Paris $7.95

The Lawyer $7.95

Tropic of Lust $7.95

Folies D'Amour $7.95

The Best of Ironwood $14.95

The Uninhibited $7.95

Disciplining Jane $7.95

66 Chapters About 33 Women $7.95

The Man of Her Dream $7.95

S-M: The Last Taboo....................$14.95

Cybersex $14.95

Depravicus $7.95

Sacred Exchange $14.95

The Rooms..........................$7.95

The Memoirs of Josephine $7.95

The Pearl $14.95

Mistress of Instruction $7.95

Neptune and Surf $7.95

House of Dreams: Aurochs & Angels ...$7.95

Dark Star.............................$7.95

The Intimate Memoir of Dame Jenny Everleigh:

Erotic Adventures $7.95

Shadow Lane VI $7.95

Shadow Lane VII $7.95

Shadow Lane VIII $7.95

Best of Shadow Lane $14.95

The Captive I, II $14.95

The Captive III, IV, V $15.95

The Captive's Journey $7.95

Road Babe $7.95

The Story of O $7.95

The New Story of O $7.95

Visit our website at www.bluemoonbooks.com